Sam Lipsyte was born in 1968 and lives in New York City. His work has appeared in *Open City*, the *New York Times Book Review*, *Slate*, *Fence*, *The Believer*, *Bookforum* and the *Quarterly*, and he has worked as an editor of the online magazine *Feed*. He is the author of the much acclaimed novel *The Subject Steve*, and *Venus Drive*, a collection of short stories.

For automatic updates on Sam Lipsyte visit harperperennial.co.uk and register for AuthorTracker.

From the reviews of *Home Land*:

'Sam Lipsyte can really write. Sentence after sentence is clever, agile, amused; they torque away, at the last moment, from what you might expect. One-liners abound, often freighted with darkness and insight; Lipsyte is playful and lewd, bleak and farcical, walking a fine line between near-glib humour and a genuine existential fear'   *Guardian*

'Executed with an ear for the deadpan cadence of absurdism, which reminds one of the best contemporary American satire. Lipsyte's writing is inventive and playful . . . An absurdist picaresque that takes the same delight in bathos as the early written work of Woody Allen'

Literary Review

Sam Lipsyte

Home Land

HARPER PERENNIAL

Harper Perennial
An imprint of HarperCollins*Publishers*
77–85 Fulham Palace Road
Hammersmith
London W6 8JB

www.HarperPerennial.co.uk

This edition published by Harper Perennial 2005
1

First published by Flamingo 2004

Copyright © Sam Lipsyte 2004
PS section copyright © Travis Elborough 2005

PS™ is a trademark of HarperCollins*Publishers* Ltd

A catalogue record for this book is available
from the British Library

ISBN 0 00 717037 8

Set in Swift

Printed and bound in Great Britain by Clays Ltd, St Ives plc

To my father

Home Land

'The dream of life is dreamed on a bed that is too hard.'
JEAN PAUL FRIEDRICH RICHTER

That Taste on my Tongue

It's Sunday morning, fellow alumni, only a week removed from that fateful evening at the Moonbeam Catering Hall.

Sunday, for some, is the Lord's day. For others, it's a day of simple rest, replenishment. For others still it's an occasion for panic attacks and football, or getting a jump on the rain gutters, or eating an entire carton of take-out jambalaya and calling old lovers to tell them how well you're doing, except for the panic attacks.

Sunday is a good day to read the Sunday paper, chuggy-jam as it is with fascinating takes on current movie trends and measured screeds against foreign powers that cannot be trusted because their propaganda lacks the production values of ours.

Sunday is a day to soak your underwear in bleach, cook meat stew for the week.

It's a day to quit drinking for a day.

This Sunday is different, though. We have lost our innocence, if innocence can be likened to a shiny toy a child might fondle and chew until a larger brutish child appears to yank it away by threat of blows. Of course, maybe innocence is something else, and my analogy is what our beloved English teacher Ms. Tabor used to call forced, but I still have that taste on my tongue, the plasticky tang of our pilfered toy.

4   I write now with a sorrow unbounded. I write with a mighty fissure in my heart. My heart once bounded the sorrow, but since the fissure, Christ, it's a goddamn flood around here.

I write to maybe also smear the first goops of soothing balm on the wounds of the Eastern Valley High School alumni community, and maybe, in this hour of our stunned agony, to make sense of the horror which the Togethering, our doomed class reunion, somehow became.

Maybe these are too many reasons to write, and I realize, too, that what you read here is but one man's version of events. Perhaps my updates, written over these many months and presented here in their entirety for whomever dares to read them in defiance of alumni bulletin censors, have been skewed, muddied, even, issuing as they have from skewed and muddied me, but that's to be expected. I'm a human being, with human-like emotions. I'm not some robot. I could never even do that dance, as those who caught sight of me on the lit-up floor of the Moonbeam would doubtless attest.

But let's not get ahead of ourselves.

That's no way to begin.

Let's return to Sunday, another Sunday a long time ago, that foggy hung-over Sunday when I, Lewis Miner, class of '89, finally found the nerve to come clean.

Feeling Is Not Quite the Word

It's confession time, Catamounts.

It's time you knew the cold soft facts of me. Ever since Principal Fontana found me and commenced to bless my mail slot, monthly, with the Eastern Valley High School Alumni Newsletter, I've been meaning to write my update. Sad to say, vanity slowed my hand. Let a fever for the truth speed it now. Let me stand on the rooftop of my reckoning and shout naught but the indisputable: I did not pan out.

We've got Catamount doctors, after all, Catamount lawyers, brokers, bankers well versed in the Eastern Valley purr. (Okay, maybe it was never quite a purr. Maybe more a surly mewl. But answer me this: why did we fail so miserably to name this noise with which we spurred our sporting types to conquest? Moreover, why was the mascot of Eastern Valley an animal that prefers elevation? A catamount is a mountain cat,

Catamounts!) We've got a state senator, a government chemist, a gold-glove ballplayer, not to mention, according to the latest issue of *Catamount Notes*, a major label recording artist in our midst.

Yes, fellow alums, we're boasting bright lights aplenty these days, serious comers, future leaders in their fields. Hell, we've even got a fellow who double-majored in Philosophy and Aquatic Life Management in college and still found time for a national squash title. Think about it, Catamounts. We didn't have squash at Eastern Valley. We didn't have tennis, either, unless you count that trick with the steel hair-brush and the catgut racquet whereby the butt skin of the weak was flayed: Point being, this boy, Will Paulsen (may he rest in peace), left our New Jersey burg without the faintest notion of squash, yet mastered it enough to beat the pants off every prep school Biff in the land, and still carry a four point zero in the question of Why Does the Universe Exist Underwater?

Is this what Principal Fontana meant by the phrase 'well-rounded'?

It's fucking spherical, Catamounts.

Alas, my meager accomplishments seem somehow pale, if not downright pasty, in comparison. I shudder at the notion of Doctor Stacy Ryson and State Senator

Glen Menninger remarking this update at some fundraising soirée – oh, the snickers, the chortles, the wine-flushed glances, and later, perhaps, the puppyish sucking of body parts at a nearby motor lodge. Shudder, in fact, is not quite the word for the feeling. Feeling is not quite the word for the feeling. How's bathing at knifepoint in the phlegm of the dead? Is that a feeling?

This is just to explain why I haven't written in before, and to acknowledge the question you may now consider officially begged: why in God's name is the loser doing it now?

Good query, Stacy!

What happened was that Principal Fontana got me on the telephone, a rare feat in itself these days, and informed me I was one of the few from our class (minus the dead) who had yet to file an update. I'm sure you all remember Principal Fontana fondly, as do I, and have forgiven him the peccadilloes which cost him a good deal of his pension. (Those girls, whatever their biological age, were lucky to be in America in the first place, never mind the exorbitant sums the man laid down for their services.) These days poor old Principal Fontana's 'reduced administrative capacity' doesn't leave him with much on his plate save whatever bones the school board sees fit to throw him, *Catamount Notes* being a primary bone on the order of, say, a femur.

Perhaps I even feel some solidarity with Principal Fontana, both of us once rather promising in our way, now reassigned for reasons beyond our immediate understanding (fate, after all, is a need-to-know operation) to the category of also-rans. Men like Fontana and me, we come hard out of the blocks, maybe even lead into the first turn, but then, whammo, something happens, we pop a hammy, pull up lame, or just plain fade. Either way we have exposed our true natures, and this while wearing the appallingly skimpy outfits of the track-and-field metaphor.

Nonetheless, I submit this update not as plaint or wail at the lusterless course my life has taken, nor as a tale of cautionary note. I'm quite happy in my unhappy way. I'm more than satisfied to remain unsatisfied. You see, fellow Catamounts, I've been to the edge of the abyss on more than one unsavory occasion. The view down is darkly steep and scary, a chilling reminder that there is, in fact, an abyss. The wise turn tail, fly home, buy nachos, lime-infused. I count myself among the wise. My misadventures have taught me to covet the little things, to cherish, in short, the short straw.

Herein now I mean merely to sketch the contours of a life lived in the shadow of more celebrated Catamounts, an existence eked out in the margins of post-Eastern Valley High School America. This ain't no pity party, folks, so save your cocktail gossip for the rich and wretched of us. They want to be talked about, crave it, even. As for me, Lewis Miner, AKA Teabag, I just thought you all might relish some recent tidbits from my continuing story, AKA The Big Charade.

Here's the latest by me, Valley Kitties: I rent some rooms in a house near the depot. I rarely leave them, too. When you work at home, fellow alums, discipline is the supreme virtue. Suicidal self-loathing lurks behind every coffee break. Activities must be expertly scheduled, from shopping to showers to momentary episodes of hysterical catatonia. Meanwhile I must make time to pine for Gwendolyn, decamped three years this June, the month we were to wed. So much for scheduling. Valley Cats who maintained vague contact with me in the mid-Nineties may recall Gwendolyn, that doe-eyed, elk-like beauty I met at an aphorism slam in Toronto. What you may not realize is how much I truly loved her, if that's the word for wanting so much to bury your head and weep upon the coppery tufts of a woman's sex while reciting 'An Irish Airman Foresees His Death,' you can hardly sit on the sofa with her.

Gwendolyn's gone now. The sofa's still here. It's deep and velveteen, a goodly nook for napping, or reading in magazines about Gwendolyn and Lenny, her movie star brother, love and unacknowledged legislator of her life. They take lazy walks along the shoreline, buy antique paper lanterns for their patio. I don't begrudge them their bliss, if it's bliss. Bliss has my blessing. A patio, though, let a quake crack it open. Let the black earth eat them.

Gwendolyn always said I expected too much from the world.

'You wake up every morning like you should get a parade.'

I told her I deserved one with the dreams I endure, the kind that find me sobbing myself awake, groping for last night's roach, or else standing at the fridge until dawn sucking on a frozen bagel. I mean dreams where tremendous dragons rear their spiny heads, sink tall teeth in my neck, muss my hair, sign my report card, call me 'Darling,' 'Shmoo-Shmoo.' Survive that, you should absolutely get a parade, a lavish procession, a town car motorcade through the Canyon of Heroes with our very own Catamount legend Mikey Saladin, who, if you've been following his career, has really blossomed into a fiercesome example of the hulking contemporary shortstop. (Sorry you had to sit out the World Series, Mikey! Good luck in arbitration!)

But I digress from our topic: discipline. You see, good graduates of Eastern Valley, I'm my own boss. I'm also my own sex slave. I'll squander the hours I should be working trolling the internet for pictures of women whose legwarmers have been spattered with semen. You could call this my kink, Catamounts, and there are more specimens floating about in the ether than you may care to imagine, though not nearly enough for me. Lately I've stumbled across the same photos again and again. I'm beginning to know names, or else bestow them: Jasmine, Loretta, Brie. I'm sure those names will sound familiar to most of you, and as for Jasmine, Loretta and Brie themselves, immortal lovelies of the Jazz Dancing Club, what can I say but, 'Sorry, Ladies.' I've been beating off to you for half my lifetime, why should I stop now?

But fret not your frittered looks, ex-Eastern Valley girls, your time-slung slack and crinkle. When I exercise my right to self-love I run a sort of projected aging program in my mind, picture you vixens in your necessary twilight, your bodies dinged up by babies, gravity, regret. I figure it's only fair. I'm no young buck myself, though, of course, just turn to my 'Intimate Portraits' page in the yearbook and you'll see that I was never anything approaching buck-like. Not unless there's such a thing in nature as a buck turtle.

But enough about boring old me. Let me update you on Gary, my best friend Gary, a guy you might remember, though judging from back editions of *Catamount Notes*, most don't. Gary was the one-thumbed unsung genius of our age. Perhaps you recall him from his many nicknames: Goony, Guano, Dirtfuck, Captain Thorazine. But don't let the monikers fool you. Gary, as Gary once boasted, has never stopped being Gary. He still smokes weed on the sly from his twelve-step buddies, boozes it up, too, but I'm happy to report he's off the powders. This is good news, believe me. I've seen this boy with a needle in his neck, and it wasn't like he'd burned out his arm veins, either. He just wanted to stick it in his neck.

Gary never works, needn't. He's a retractor by trade. Some of you may remember the newspaper articles, how Gary got quasi-rich suing Doc Felix, that shrink who recovered Gary's so-called memories. These were old buried traumas Guano hadn't even known were in his brain. I guess his folks had kept their ritual sex abuse pretty quiet. But after Doc Felix got in there with some hypnosis and regression therapy all the gropes and probes by candelabra light were gruesomely recalled. Gary also came to remember a twin, named either Barry or Octavian, slaughtered with goats in the backyard.

Gary sent notarized divorce papers to his parents, passed out informational flyers at the River Mall, some of which included stick-figure diagrams of him being entered by his father. One day, though, the pills Doc Felix had been feeding him wore off. Gary had an anti-revelation. He was watching television and something he saw tripped a memory of something he'd once seen on television – a magazine show about Satanic cults. The boy'd been had! Gary joined a retractors' support group, sued the pants off Doc Felix, begged his folks to forgive him, even offered up his settlement money for their pain. They suggested he burn in his imaginary hell. His real brother Todd, with no recollection of goats, concurred. Now all Gary has is me and a few sober buddies who don't know about his bong, plus enough money to just hang out for the rest of his natural life, as long as it doesn't get too natural.

But it gets me thinking, this memory game. There was a story in the paper about a child of three, or four, the son of a cop, who snatched his old man's pistol up from the kitchen table, squeezed off a round. His father was home from the night tour, kissing his wife at the stove. The bullet killed him where he stood. What kind of life will this boy live now? Those tender years are difficult enough, but how do you go about them daddyless by your own whimsical hand? Christ, the terror, the shame. Tell me how it won't all end with some wee-hour schnapps and weeping, the grown boy's own service revolver, a groveling, snot-moist suicide note.

I've got a better solution. Why not bury it? You could hire a specialist, some cowboy of the mind. He'd jam that moment so deep in the boy's noodle no amount of free association or dream therapy could ever jimmy it loose. Or better yet, just bend the truth, blow it up and twist for a new animal memory balloon.

Make Daddy hit Mommy.

Make the bullet miss.

I should go back to school and learn the brain. I know, I know, I couldn't even get through Mrs.

Strobe's Bio II, but still, I bet they have new machines now, stud-finders for the walls of that gooey maze. As a brain man I'd ride from town to town, bury all the bad stuff. The atrocity gazettes could be my guide. Kid blows up the homestead with his blind mother inside. Little girl by the lake lets her toddler sister drown. I'd do the incest survivors, too, the verifieds, the real molested McCoys. Live not with the injustice, my little ones. The Erasing Angel is here.

'It's called denial,' said Gary.

The Retractor comes over sometimes to eat my corn chips, tell me what things are called.

'That's hit or miss,' I said. 'I'm talking about precision repression. Laser-carving of the actual.'

'Nobody knows how the mind works, man.'

'Don't you have a meeting to go to?'

Well, Catamounts, Gary didn't have a meeting, so we sat around my kitchen for a while. He told me a rather sickening joke about a fellating giraffe, then devoted the next hour to his crush on Liquid Smoke, which is what he calls the counter girl at the Bean Counter, that new gourmet coffee shop next to Dino's Shoe Repair.

'Hilarious,' he'd said the morning we spotted her. Whether he meant it was hilarious such beauty existed or just somewhat amusing that he'd never possess it, I didn't ask, though I figured it was both. You see too much in this world you can't have, you do start to laugh. Maybe it's a bitter laugh, but it's still a laugh. It's like what they say about bad pizza, how it's still pizza, but bad, or something.

Gary also confessed he'd been having his drug dreams again. The dream junk was blaze orange, the texture of saltwater taffy. God taught him how to cook it down.

Crazy Dirtfuck! What a doltish dreamer! But I love his Goony ass, I do.

Well, Catamounts, it's been a certifiable pleasure, but I suppose I should leave off here. Stay tuned for future installments now that this buck turtle has finally popped out of his shell. Before I sign off, however, I'd like to share a heartwarming anecdote involving a man we all know and adore. That's right, his municipal highness himself, Principal Fontana!

Last week Gary and I decided to check out this new titty bar in town. It's a decent joint called Brenda Bruno's near the River Mall. The dancers are all educated so there's no exploitation and the DJ is a connoisseur of the moody tunes I favor in the company of nude women who despise me. There we were, Gary and I, having a grand old time sipping our greyhounds, when in walked Principal Fontana. He seemed to stagger a bit, which we took for too much whisky, par for the Fontana course, until we noticed an unbelievable amount of blood pouring off the poor guy's head. His shirt collar couldn't soak it up fast enough and it was hard to believe he was still on his feet. He walked around the bar like that for a while, looking for all the world like a butchered zombie, or a man born old, full-sized, womb slime still on him. Nobody moved to help him and I could see the barback going for the telephone. Gary and I, we made an executive decision to seize Fontana by the elbows, guide him out to the parking lot.

'Get your filthy hands off me!' said Fontana.

'Principal Fontana,' I said. 'It's us, it's us!'

'I don't know you fucks,' he said. 'Your faces. Where's Loretta?'

'Jazz Loretta?' I said.

'Let him go,' said Gary.

Fontana loped across the parking lot and over the guardrails of Route Nine. We watched him weave off into darkness towards the boat basin. We stood and watched the darkness where he'd been.

'You should write this up for that newsletter,' said Gary.

'Are you nuts? Fontana's the editor. He'll never print it.'

'He has to print it. It happened.'

'So, it's an update?' I said.

'Damn right it's an update. An update is an update. The things that happen are the things that happen.'

Forgive me, Principal Fontana, but Gary has a point. Updates are updates, and it is in this spirit, assuming you survived your evening of massive blood loss on the trash slopes of the boat basin, that I know you'll publish mine.

The Awful Percussion of Shoes

Catamounts, here I come.

Perhaps a patient man would wait until his first update found its way into the *Notes* before submitting another, but patience has never been a virtue I could call 'Pal,' or 'Royko,' or 'Homes.' Hey, I'm an impulsive guy, a gun-jumper, a faith-leaper. I cannot, will not, hold my horses. My horses are gorgeous things, sweat-carved, sun-snorting beasts. Look at them go! See them gallop at some equine destiny I am ill equipped to comprehend.

It's been ever so.

It's been ever so since the candy bar incident.

Pardon? Candy bar?

Witness me briefly through the bent lens of history. See boy me: homely, surly, nipples afire with hormonal surge. This boy's mother buys him a candy bar. Big doings, a candy bar, in a household loyal to fruit, to kale, to sprouts and curd, to something called, apparently, bulgar. The boy guards the candy bar the whole ride home from the mall. He hides it in his sleeve from the sun. There beside his mother in their boatish beige sedan, he awestares up at her, her beautiful nose. It's a big, slanting, sacred thing, this nose of the woman who has given him life, sheltered him from Nor' Easters, asteroids, the death rays and Stukka dives of his mind, the nose of the woman who has now bestowed, against all nutritional creed, the only thing he truly craves.

'Don't eat it right away,' she says. 'Save it. I know a little trick to make it even better.'

A trick to make a candy bar better? She's a sorceress, his mother, a good witch. She takes perfection and perfects it.

'We'll put it in the freezer. Wait L., wait, and it will be worth it.'

He loves it when she calls him L.

Home, he bolts from the car with his candy bar under his shirt. He must shield it from the elements. It's a fine spring day but he knows full well there are elements about, eager to drench, to blight, to melt. He runs to the kitchen and eases the candy bar into the freezer, slides it between some cellophaned soy burgers and a foil-wrapped package he knows from past reconnaissance to be a half-loaf of zucchini bread. His mother trails in after him with the grocery sacks, sees him standing sentry at the freezer door.

'It's going to take a while, L. Go play.'

Go play? A mighty and delicious molecular transformation is taking place!

'I mean it, L. Go play in the basement.'

Go play in the basement? How far from the locus of his happiness must he trek? Okay, the basement. He treks down to the basement. Play commences with some British commando, his usual wade-in-the-river-scale-the-pylon-stab-the-Kraut commando, but when he gets the rubber knife in his mouth and starts up his father's stepladder, the blade, he swears, tastes of nougat.

He does Gettysburg instead, dons his Union cap, wipes out the Army of Northern Virginia with his plastic musket from the hobby shop. Those dead racist bastards pile up in some dry valley of his mind. The slaves make songs for him, a vaporish version of his father beams. Still, he notes, his musket is much the color of milk chocolate. Is Witch-Mommy's alchemy working? Go play, goddamnit. He wills himself back to slaughter, Omaha Beach, Khe Sanh, spits clips at

Victor Charlie until his musket, now by dint of an alternate grip an M-16, jams. Just fucking typical. The Cong burst out of the broom closet, AKs blazing. He hurls himself at the wood-paneled wall. Drool for blood slides down his chin.

'I'm hit, I'm hit,' he says. 'Medic!'

It's a bitch, but it's not Charlie's fault. He had no right to be in Charlie's basement.

The last thing he sees before he dies – and for a while afterward – is a spider on the new smoke alarm.

Spooky.

Enough is enough.

He finds his mother at the kitchen table. She's doing crossword puzzles with a fountain pen. There's a faint dark smear on the tip of her nose. The candy bar wrapper is bunched in a coffee cup. What's a five-letter word for traitor?

'Mommy,' he says.

'I was just . . .' she says. 'I had to test it, L. To see if it was okay. It was bad, baby. It was a bad candy bar. I'll get you a good one.'

God, the guilt, hers, his. She gets him cupcakes, candy corn, gooey-sweet tarts. They never speak of freezing things again. Years later, when he kisses her cold calves in a hospital room, he sees what the trick had been. The trick was to give unto others that which you mean to seize. He'd be a sorcerer, too.

'A sorcerer?' said Gwendolyn, one of the few times I told her this tale. 'Just because she ate your candy bar? My mom guzzled rye and beat us. My uncle put his dick in my armpit while I slept. My cousin hid my college acceptance letter until it was too late to reply. Your mother ate your candy bar?'

'It's symbolic.'

'That's what people say when they know they've come with the weak shit.'

'Fuck you,' I said.

'Excuse me?'

'I said fuck you,' I said. 'I've been meaning to say it for a long time. I just couldn't find the right words.'

Yes, this exchange occurred during a particularly frenzied juncture in our unraveling, but I always thought Gwendolyn missed the point of my story. The candy bar incident, aside from its obvious revelations regarding my character, or the deformation thereof, imparts a tremendous lesson about life's treats in general: Munch immediately! Maybe that could be a chapter of the self-help book I've been meaning to write, *The Seven Habits of Highly Disappointed People*, which I could probably bang out in an afternoon if I weren't so busy updating you fine people on the latest in the life of me.

Perhaps now you understand why I haven't waited for confirmation from that titan of secondary education, Principal Fontana, a man last seen bleeding profusely from one or more head wounds whose origins remain a delectable mystery. Doubtless he received my first installment, though it's no shock he failed to include it in the latest edition of *Catamount Notes*. I'm sure he's quite busy with whatever whirlwind he was in the midst of reaping that night we led him out of Brenda Bruno's. Maybe his stitches got infected. Maybe the lovely Loretta is smearing antibiotic ointment on them even as I write. Oh, Loretta, daub some on your leg wool while you're at it, hey?

Yesterday, Catamounts, it suddenly struck me that the vestibule of my house no longer reeks of human urine. It was some kind of olfactory epiphany, this absence of stench, and I traced it to the absence of my landlady, Mrs. Hildebrandt. This brittle gal lived below me for years and I'd help her with her groceries and such, though I must confess I wasn't what would fall under the rubric of devastated when she sold the building and moved to Green Bay. She liked to run on about her surgeon sons, how dexterous and charitable they were, though apparently neither nimble nor generous enough to visit their only mother.

'My Tommy would eat you for lunch,' she'd often say, even as I was fixing hers.

I'd just chuckle, nod. I've always been an easy mark for the decrepit, the infirm. Do you by chance remember the secretary at Eastern Valley, Edna O'Grady? Old Lady O'Grady, you called her, and proffered remarks vis-à-vis the probable aridity of her birth canal, as did I, admittedly, but did you ever notice all that caramel on her desk come Valentine's day? Who do you figure shelled out the cash for all those heart-shaped goodies? Like I said, I'm a sucker for the crones. Maybe they remind me of my mother, had the chemo worked.

Mrs. Hildebrandt, though, she kindly cured me of my sentimentalist streak. The lady was needy, belligerent. She did not believe in boiler repair, denied both the Holocaust and the very idea that I'd ever paid her a security deposit. Plus, she was wont to call the cops for a noise complaint if I did so much as quietly moan at my computer screen after dinnertime. It's a wonder I stayed so long. When dementia crept up on her like one of those ancient guild ninjas, I began to enjoy corroborating her suspicions that her visiting nurse was stealing bits of hair and skin from the divan. 'People will pay a fortune for a white woman's slough,' I told her. Mrs. Hildebrandt's probably dead by now, buried deep in cold Wisconsin dirt, and I'd guess that Tommy and the rest of her hand-eye Gandhi brood don't kneel at her tomb too often, either.

32   My new landlord Pete is a sweetheart. He's a kid, really, barely out of Eastern Valley High himself, where now, in fact, he teaches Phys. Ed. You can tell he's not born to landlordship, but he'll learn. (Remember Vinnie Lazlo? Pete looks like Vinnie with muscles, hands.) The kid hails from a family of landlords, and someday, doubtless, he'll be exhorting county marshals to spray buckshot at evicted spinsters, but for now he treats my tenancy in his building as a personal favor. Rent day he shuffles his feet at my door, a boy come for his bubblegum money. When the sink stops up he's over in a jiff with his motorized snake. He works like a demon, albeit with no expertise, averts his eyes as though awaiting blows from kin.

Pete's letting me coast a few weeks on the rent. I'm flat-busted, Catamounts. Send check or money order care of me to – Ha! Ha! I'd never! Honestly, though, there's a reason I'm tapped. I'm owed thousands by a soft drink juggernaut for my work compiling historical data for an in-house newsletter. (See, *Catamount Notes* isn't the only rag in town!) I won't name the outfit but suffice it to say their cola is not sweeter than the other one. The newsletter, *Fizz*, is designed to amuse distributors with FunFacts, or FakeFacts, as I tend to concoct them. Prez Truman downs an entire bottle of the famed elixir before giving the heave-ho to Fat Man. Mister Sidney Vicious has some sent up to his Chelsea Hotel suite the night he smites the fetching Spungeon. I haven't a clue where I get this crap. There must truly be a collective unconscious, all syrupped and bubbly, but not as sweet as the other one.

Penny Bettis from the soft drink outfit called today to say they might cut my check next week. This is how I know it's Friday: Penny calls to deliver false hope. I've never met her but she has one of those cozy phone voices people cultivate in lieu of truth. I don't blame her for it, it's protocol, and besides, I prefer ease to honesty. Isn't that in our DNA? I'd like to think that with the proper woman I could reach denturehood and beyond swapping comforting obfuscations. Of course, she'd have to know jazz dancing and be willing to bundle her calves in wool for my load. Today I pictured Penny doing leg-lifts by her desk while she offered up a FakeFact of her own.

'Accounting has your invoice,' she said. 'They're ready to process.'

'You said that last week,' I said.

'Last week was hell, honey. You don't want to know.'

'Maybe we could get dinner and you could tell me.'

'You sound cute, but I'm taken.'

'Who is he, Penny?'

'None of your business.'

'Is he feverish for you?' I said. 'Does he weep at the altar of your fat pussy?'

The line went dead. So did my hopes for timely remuneration. I tend to take things too far, Valley Cats. I figure I'm still chatting the woman up and she's filing charges. It's always been this way, as many of you might recall. Somebody chucks a snowball, I'm scouring the schoolyard for rocks. The bully just wants to shove sadness around, shake me down for spare change, I'm looking to scrape out his eye. I lack a sense of proportion. I have no sensitivity to sport. I'm the aggrieved rider on the grievous plain. I'm still pissed about the parade.

* * *

A missive from the man himself! It arrived this afternoon, penciled on what folks once called penny postcards, though they cost near two bits by now. Two bits! Two bits! I'm a cowboy of coins! Never mind, I'll transcribe in full:

> Hey, Miner:
>
> Cut the crap. Whatever you think you saw you didn't see. Nobody wants to read your babble, anyway. Catamount Notes is a forum for decent people to celebrate the ongoing celebration of their lives. Hence my decision to omit your update. Save it for the Teabag Review, okay? Or maybe the Scumbag Review would be better.
>
> All Best,
>
> Fontana
>
> P.S. Who the hell is Jazz Loretta? What in Jesus Christ are you talking about?

I pored over the postcard, hoped to precisely ascertain its tone, deconstruct its guiding logic, tease out its myriad tropes, but I lacked the proper training. Hate to say it, Catamounts, but we didn't have tropes at Eastern Valley.

I called Gary at his Retractor Pad, read him Fontana's card.

'You've got him on the run,' said Gary. 'Now's the time to go in for the kill.'

'What are you talking about?'

'I'm not sure.'

'I guess he's pissed at me.'

'What's he going to do? Suspend you?'

'Good point.'

'No matter what happens,' said Gary, 'you must not be silenced. It's like those poets they put in prison.'

'What poets?'

'Those poets. They're heroes.'

'I guess so.'

'Step up. Be a fucking hero.'

'Fine,' I said. 'I'll be a hero. It's not like they can put me in jail for writing updates.'

'You should read the paper, if that's what you think.'

'I do read the paper.'

'You read that fascist one.'

'It's funny.'

'Laugh for me when they put you up against the wall.'

'They better give me a cigarette.'

'Thank you for keeping our rape room smoke-free. What are you doing tonight?'

'They've got some submarine movies on TV.'

'You still like those, huh?'

'They speak to me.'

'No, I get it,' said Gary. 'But what about fighter planes? A jet pilot shot down in the jungle. His hardass mentor hops in to extract him. They've got to blast their way out.'

'Those are good,' I said. 'But I'm talking subs. The panic. The water pressure. Tyranny in a tiny tube.'

'It's all war,' said Gary. 'It all works.'

Good people, as I peruse this latest update, composed, as you can see, in the face of severe Fontanian repression, it occurs to me that I've taken the wrong tack. My aim continues to be an essay into the truth of my condition, and thus, the Catamount condition, but under the current *Notes* regime, which seems willing to support only craven declarations from the Eastern Valley community, it appears I've failed to heed an important lesson. Gwendolyn's foolish comments about symbolism aside, the only weapon against censorship is guile.

How shameful it's come to this. Fontana was not always so despotic. Some of him is made of charm. Even the charmless parts, I believe, were acquired in provinces of real human pain. I could tell you some stories, true Fontana Arcana, about his master's thesis on adolescence in postwar American literature, his brief amateur golf ranking, the handles of White Horse delivered weekly to his house by ex-Catamount Sousaphonist and Pittman Liquors scion Randy Pittman. I could delve into the man's divorce after the teen escort scandal, his estrangement from his prim progeny. A lead is even developing on where he buys those hideous lime-green jeans he favors in the springtime.

Don't get me wrong. I've always had deep affection for Fontana. Back when he roamed the hallways of Eastern Valley there was a sort of compass-less majesty about the man you couldn't help but admire. He'd maybe lit out from one of his busted selves years before, wandered tundras of indecision, kept himself alive in bleak altitudes, battled the elements within and without, but never found that hidden pass to New Fontana.

I could tell you about the time he pulled me into his office for a private audience. It was late in my junior year. I'd been idling near the juice machine with Gary, watching him brandish his thumb nub to make a point. Gary had a lot of theories in those days. He was a fan of ancient astronauts, especially their work in the entertainment industry. Today's lecture hinged on Thurman Munson, the great Yankee catcher of our youth. Munson, according to Guano, had not plunged to his death piloting a twin engine airplane, but was living under an assumed identity, supervising a new secret baseball program in the Soviet Union.

'That's bullshit,' I said. 'I sold his widow a spaghetti spoon for our Weebalo fundraising drive six years ago.'

'Which proves what?'

'She was a widow, man. Munson was dead.'

'Or else he was in fucking Leningrad. Plus, there's no such thing as a spaghetti spoon. It's just the name they gave to some piece-of-junk ladle.'

Now Fontana glided by, on his usual afternoon rounds. The corridors had a cool empty beauty he must have savored. His polo shirt was nearly the teal of the walls. A pair of golf cleats, slung from his neck, swayed on their laces.

'Boys,' he said.

'Sorry,' said Gary. 'We'll go to the library.'

'No,' said Fontana, 'just listen to this.'

He read from a paperback wedged in his hand:

> 'They said, "You have a blue guitar,
> You do not play things as they are."

The man replied, "Things as they are
Are changed upon the blue guitar."'

Fontana snapped the book shut, stroked his cleats.

'Wallace Stevens. Not bad for an insurance executive.'

'My cousin has a blue guitar,' said Gary. 'A Gibson Explorer.'

'Are things changed upon it?' said Fontana.

'Yeah, when he plays it through a Marshall stack.'

'Funny child,' said Fontana, spun himself on the tiles, a clumsy hoofer's twirl. He always seemed his weakest forcing whimsy.

'Miner,' he said.

'Yes, Mr. Fontana.'

'Follow me.'

Fontana had a Velcro dartboard in his office, a wire basket full of golf balls. A framed postcard painting of an old-time gunslinger hung on the wall behind his desk. Fontana caught me studying the man, the nickel-plated pistols shoved in gabardine pants, the mournful whiskers.

'That's Bat Masterson,' he said. 'Lawman, quick-draw artist, killer. He was also, in later years, an accomplished sports journalist. Died typing.'

'Well-rounded,' I said.

'Bet your ass,' said Fontana. 'Sorry. Language.'

'I don't mind,' I said. 'You should hear my father.'

'Take a load off.'

Fontana slid down in his district Naugahyde. I took a swivel stool near the window. A sun-whitened book was propped against the heavy pane: *What the Aztecs Knew*.

'What did the Aztecs know?' I asked.

'Pardon?'

'Aztecs.'

'Oh. This old Canadian in Mexico gave me that book a long time ago. He said it would let light in. He wasn't wrong. Look at that beautiful day.'

Out the window Chip Gallagher's father Batch mowed the ballfield, rode high on his machine, trailed oil smoke. His windbreaker snapped, fluttered, presumably in wind.

'Good old Batch,' said Fontana. 'Know what he's doing?'

'Mowing the ballfield?'

'He's making the smell of fresh-cut grass.'

'Oh.'

'We've never really conversed, have we?'

'You've told me to go back to class a few times.'

'I don't remember.'

'That's okay.'

'I should remember. That's the thing. I want to be involved in your lives. Or I think I do. But then, really, when I look into my heart, I'd rather be on the driving range, or getting drunk, or my wick dipped. Is this shocking you?'

'Some nights,' I said, 'I picture myself naked, covered in napalm, running down the street. But then it's not napalm. It's apple butter. And it's not a street. It's my mother.'

'Right,' said Fontana. 'I knew I could talk to you. I read your file. You're one of those not uncommon cases. You don't really fit into any category. You're pretty bright, but no student. You hate jocks but you do appreciate a good sporting event. You deplore violence, except against the state. You can probably scrap okay, too. You're sort of bitter, but beyond the more stupid varieties of rage. You think of pussy all the time. Not just pussy. Breasts. Butts. Even the occasional schlong. It's all a flesh swarm in your mind. You think you'd like to be some kind of artist, but you have no idea what that means, and you're afraid you're too dumb, which could be true.'

'That's in my file?'

'No, just scores and grades. Extracurriculars, tardies. The rest is extrapolation. Professional guesswork. How am I doing?'

'Perfect score. Were you like me in high school?'

'No, not at all. In fact, I think I'm more like you now.'

'That's weird.'

'Maybe. Maybe not. Our ages are not our ages, you know? Adolescence, post-adolescence, it's not just a matter of body hair. They're philosophical positions. I wrote a thesis about this once. Sort of. Didn't finish. Should have finished. Goddamnit, Miner, most of these kids at school here, I hate them. They're all phonies. I want to rebel against them. They don't understand me. How do I connect with them?'

'You can't.'

'That's what I thought. There's no way, really. And really, it's not my fucking job. My job is to make sure you go to class. That you don't blow dope on school grounds. Speaking of which, I know about the maintenance shed. Stay the hell away from there.'

'Copy that.'

'What's with the jargon? The argot? Are you crestfallen you don't have a war? A police action? Something muddy and devastating? Some absurd carnage you can hang your disaffection on?'

'Affirmative.'

'Do you know how idiotic that is? How horrible napalm is? Or was? Or is?'

'Sir, I do, sir.'

'Your father, he owns that catering hall, the Moonbeam, right?'

'That's right.'

'Nice place.'

'We're proud of it.'

'Oh, are we? That's good to hear. Now go to class.'

'I have a free.'

'I took you from your free? I'm sorry for that.'

'It's okay.'

'You can tell people what we talked about. I don't give a damn. I'd rather you didn't, but it's your call.'

'I think I'll leave it here.'

'A wise and generous decision.'

Gary was still waiting by the juice machine.

'What happened?' he said.

'The maintenance shed is a no go.'

'Shit,' said Gary.

Point being, Catamounts, I could write reams on my former confidant Fontana. But he's a different man now. He's not that tender teen trapped in a slack duffer's body we used to secretly celebrate. His stewardship of the *Notes* has warped him somehow, and now my updates will languish unread unless I can muster all the cunning muzzled voices require.

Allegory, parable, fable, these are the smuggle ships of freedom, the cigarette boats of daring ideas. I speak of tales too countless to enumerate, about yard dogs, for instance, or independently minded sand pipers, which may appear, at first glance, whimsical, if not a bit opaque, but which upon further reflection reveal themselves to be songs of fierce resistance, or blueprints for revolt.

This being the case, allow me to close my update with a little story. It means nothing, not a damn thing, wink, wink. Don't read too much into it, Principal Fontana, *capice*?

It's just a simple tale, a mere folk legend, for the kids:

Once there was a little girl who owned a little mouse named Teabag. He lived in a large metal cage in her room. This little girl loved Teabag with all her heart, loved to stroke his tiny head with her finger as she fed him crumbs of Camembert cheese, which is pretty pricey, even in mouse portions, especially for a child on a fixed allowance of seventy-three cents a week.

Then one day the girl got cancer. Her father, a doctor, administered the chemo immediately, but it was too late. She died that day. There was so much to do between all his weeping and grieving, so many arrangements to make – flowers, a titanium casket, a suitable poem – it was a while before the father remembered Teabag at all. The poor mouse had been weeping, too, going hungry in his cage. The girl had left no instructions for his care.

Nothing for it now, the father thought. He was a busy man, this doctor, much in demand. Rich people depended on his barbiturate prescriptions. He took Teabag's cage to the sidewalk, raised the metal door.

'Good-bye, little fellow,' he said.

The father knew the mouse didn't stand a chance in this wide nasty world, but what mouse did?

Teabag wandered the neighborhood. The bigness of things was ever so frightening, all those bicycle wheels and curb grates and trash pails, the awful percussion of shoes, those pounding wingtips, high tops, boots, not to mention the singles bars and how do you talk to women, anyway?

Teabag found an upended paper cup near the mini-mart, scurried inside. There in the cool dark of the cup he squeaked out the name of the dead girl again and again, licked at flecks of coffee dried on the walls of his ready-made cave. The flecks made him nervous. He had a sad nervous hole in his heart. Now, suddenly, he felt himself being lifted upwards. His paper shelter swiveled in midair. Teabag gazed into a pair of eyes the color of stale filberts, slivers of which the little girl had also fed him on occasion. The face around the eyes was bathed in blood.

'I'm Fontaine,' said the face through its viscous red web. 'Why do you weep, little mouse?'

Teabag started to tell this creature Fontaine about the little girl, her father, the Camembert, the chemo.

'Stop!' said Fontaine. 'I don't want to hear it!'

'But it's all true,' said Teabag. 'It's what happened to me.'

'That's not the point,' said Fontaine. 'It's not celebratory, see? It's too negative. It's even kind of sick. Chemo? Camembert? It makes no sense!'

Whereupon Fontaine squeezed the paper cup. Mouse guts squirted to the pavement. Our poor hero was now but a smear of fur, even the grief pinched out of him. It was a foul day for allegorical critters everywhere, and another cruel victory for Eastern Valley Alumni Association-sponsored censorship.

Well, Catamounts, I hope you enjoyed my little 'meaningless' story.

Tell it to the tots. They're brighter and braver than you may care to believe.

A Sort of Forlorn Smirk

Felines of the East, I rejoice to announce the birth of a spanking new bank balance, courtesy of Penny Bettis at the cola outfit. The check was cut last week and now I've got a cupboard full of noodles, reasonable wattage in every room. Is this perhaps what it's like for some of you more respectable Catamounts, with your pension plans and golden parasails, that sense of sated languor, as though Fate, suddenly, and without solicitation, had offered up her stippled shins for your tongue's worship?

Not too shabby.

This must be how our very own Phil Douglas feels. Philly Boy, congratulations on your continued success at Willoughby and Stern. You've always been a persistent guy, Phil, a real plugger, whether the task at hand was to find a hole in rival Nearmont's vaunted line, or a fag to bash after the Friday night game. Though not the most talented athlete at Eastern Valley (this honor obviously belongs to varsity deity Mikey Saladin) you were always the most brutal and adamantine of Catamounts, an avatar of the jock warrior code, if you will, which I'm sure you will.

I'm also fairly certain at least a few of our contemporaries shared my fantasy of cornering you in Eastern Valley's dank shower room and firing a hollowpoint round into your skull. We could picture the startlement in your eyes, the suck and flop of your dead-before-it-hits-the-floor body hitting the floor, your brain meat chunked, running out on rivulets of soapy water across the scummed tiles, clogging up that rusted drain the school board never saw fit to replace. Your pecker would be puny with death.

We'd never do such a thing, of course, not like those suburban murder squads of today, those peach-fuzz assassins in mail-order duster coats who lay down suppressing fire in cafeterias. I remember watching TV with Gary during one recent standoff, that magnet school in Maryland where those dodgeball refugees exacted payback with Glocks and grenades. SWAT teams scoped for headshots while the TV shrinks railed against video games.

'Video games?' said Gary, fingered the carb of his bong. 'Try school!'

We'd ordered in fish tacos. We were watching the horror, as one anchorman put it, unfold.

'Fuckers did it,' said Gary. 'I mean, I don't condone what they did, ultimately, but, ultimately, they did it.'

'Totally, ultimately,' I said.

'Balls to the wall, baby!' said Gary, let go with a war whoop, or maybe a war gargle. All the old salty agony.

'Captain Thorazine,' I said. 'Good to have you back, sir.'

'Teabag, son,' said the Captain, 'lock and load.'

But our vengeance by proxy vaporized in an instant. Some correspondent hunkered near the bike rack delivered the news via video phone: the duster boys had killed the only black kid in the school, called him the N-Word, Nigger, too, shot him in the gut.

'No!' said Gary. 'No! No!'

'God, no!' I said. 'God, God! No, No!'

'They ruined it!' said Gary. 'Why did they have to be racists? The bastards ruined it!'

The bastards did ruin it. Their pure hate was tainted now. We pine for avengers. We get bigots, thugs. Only love survives contamination, Catamounts. (Man, if I'd had this on paper at the aphorism slam in Toronto . . .)

So, Phil, my dear Mister Philly Douglas of Willoughby and Stern, locker-room sadist, source of my very nickname (another time, alums, another time), please don't worry about my tender little shower murder fantasy. We who may share it never posed a threat. We have no weapons, no nerve. We're gentle rejects.

Besides, good Catamounts, I'm getting on with my life, getting to the brunt of it. Today I woke early, near noon, brewed some coffee in my mother's antique Silex, watched a tiny bird outside my window dance a little dance on the air conditioning unit. I felt a great communion with this creature, hummingbird, sparrow, whatever the fuck it was. What we both have is today, I thought, until we smack into deck door glass, or fall from the sky twisted up with some avian virus.

The milk was bad but I poured it in my coffee anyway.
Make do. Like the Donner party.

I've been doing a bit of toilet reading about those people-eaters. I keep a little shelf of books about history's horrors in the can. A few pages on the ravages of smallpox, or the cruelty of Pizarro, I'm steeled for the day.

This morning a din came through the bathroom wall – stabs of noise, the sound of human laughter. Those kid neighbors Kyle and Jared were maybe on another speed binge. One of them, Kyle, I think, told me they were grad students, though there isn't any college nearby. They grind it out past dawn a good deal, their rants growing shriller by the hour: the birth of combustion, the chromosomal make-up of chimpanzees, the reason for rainbows, war. I don't mind. Kids must coddle their excitements. Soon enough the normies have you surrounded. It's all barricades, bullhorns. Come out, come out with your wonder abated.

Now the laughter came softer through the wall. The sun was maybe funny to these fellows. I could picture the ashtrays, heaped, the smeared mirror in daylight. Fly high, babies! Guts aflame, beak-smash looming, fly baby birdies, fly!

A sudden fatigue fell over me. Sudden fatigue syndrome?

I put myself down for a nap.

I've always been a peaceless sleeper, not to mention a bully in the rack. I used to shove Gwendolyn around, snatch pillows out from under her head. I had no idea I was doing it. One night, maybe dreaming of dragons, I socked her in the nose.

'You fuck!' said Gwendolyn, switched on the lamp. 'What are you doing?'

Blood had gathered in the lovely groove above her lip.

'I have no idea, baby!' I said.

Somnambulistic innocence only takes you so far.

People get fed up. Gwendolyn got fed up. She'd laid out so many reasons she was leaving I figured there was probably only one: the brute I become in slumber.

Maybe it's punishment for past sins, or else I just nap too much, but I've been having a tough time falling asleep these days. Those car alarms out on the boulevard don't help. That whine, that wail, tripped by the merest graze. *Touch me and I'll scream. I swear, I'll fucking scream.*

56 Dusk and I'm up again, take cold coffee to my desk. My computer snoozes with ease, the bastard, but when I set my mug down with too much force the monitor pops into brightness. What hath God wrought? I am become death, destroyer of worlds. Show balloons?

My dear sweet Doctor Ryson, why Principal Fontana feels compelled to forward my updates to you even as he refuses to publish them is a question better left to psychoanalysis, but I do appreciate how you've taken time out of your busy schedule performing unnecessary hysterectomies to get in touch. I'll copy out your letter here for the enjoyment of curious Valley Kitties:

Dear Mr. Lewis Miner:

Though I can't say I remember you from our Eastern Valley days, I can conclude, after perusing the material Principal

Fontana sent me in my capacity as former President of the Student Body and current President of the Alumni Association, I'm rather relieved I don't. You see, Mr. Miner, you strike me as a lonely, misanthropic man whose worldview has been considerably narrowed by Fear and Insecurity. Have you ever traveled, ever loved, ever experienced excitement, ever done anything kind for anyone? Perhaps if you had you wouldn't be so quick to brag about your autoerotic activities and the images which fuel them. You'd know that there are real women attached to your pathetic fantasies, real women with real feelings, real families, real dreams. I'm not here to legislate desire, of course, and far be it from me to tell people what they should do with their bodies in the privacy of their own minds, but I do wish to impart to you the pain you've caused others, or would have caused others had Principal Fontana not been wise enough to refrain from publishing your material in Catamount Notes.

I hope you'll take this in the right spirit, Mr. Miner. Though, as I mentioned, I have absolutely no recollection of you from our high school years, Principal Fontana assures me you were a classmate of mine, and I remain optimistic you will someday develop into a decent, giving member of our Catamount community.

    Sincerely,

    Stacy Ryson, MD

Very savvy, Stacy. I must admit I didn't realize when I accepted your campaign pencil all those years ago you'd be elected President for Life. A pity I wasn't notified. I'd been under the impression Eastern Valley was a democracy. Serves me right, I guess. I never took those advanced civics classes, or any kind of honors course at all.

Maybe that's why you don't remember me. Allow me to offer you a refresher course on the subject of Lewis Miner, that pale anxious fellow perched a few seats behind you during four years of homeroom. Probably you were too absorbed in those last minute emendations to your assignments to ever notice me, but there's a chance you heard my name read aloud one of the seven or eight hundred times attendance was taken by Ms. Tabor.

Or else perhaps you recall the occasion you fainted at the water fountain in Corridor C? I certainly won't forget it, how you took that dainty sip, so careful not to let your lips touch spout, the way your bulging knapsack swung back as you straightened and seemed to fling you like a stuffed doll, which you somehow resembled in your penny loafers and sailor's shirt.

But physics did not fly you tileward, Stacy. Biology did the job. I'd seen the tremors in your hands, the glittering devastation in your eyes. (Were you eating enough? Sleeping at all?) Yes, others were more intimately involved with your rescue that day, but just for the record, it was yours truly who suggested someone send word to the nurse's station. Let this also stand in the official log: how our eyes met with such guarded and lovely meaning as they wheeled you away on the gurney.

God, I worried for you, Stacy, which I'm certain I mentioned a few weeks later when I asked you to the Halloween Dance. You replied that though you volunteered after school to work with the demented, you made it your policy not to date them. That was quite a quip, Stacy. It made me admire you all the more, so much, in fact, that I went home and masturbated with a giant bread bag on my head, nearly died. My poor father found me gasping for breath in the basement. He ripped away the suffocating sheath but his fingernails, dirty from fixing the toilet, cut my face, which resulted in a terrible infection.

So let's not play the pain game, Stace. My guess is there's more than enough to go around.

Have I loved? I've loved. Witness the aforementioned Gwendolyn. I've liked with serious gusto, too. Need I name names, Catamount names? With apologies to the following for violating their privacy, try these on for size: Sarah Chin (kissing, baring of torsos), Denise Gray (fondled, fingered), Sharon Roland (heavy and/or genital petting), Bethany Applebaum (all and sundry).

Bethany, I guess we were what folks in more superficially innocent epochs called sweethearts. We popped each other's cherries down the Shore after the prom, both of us gooned on Sambuca while that motel TV filled the room with game show. Neither of us, as I recall, deserved a prize.

Where have you been hiding yourself, Bethany? Last I heard you'd gone off to Cornell, that fancy college renowned for its wooded suicide ravine. You did send me a letter from school, notarized by Jeanine, your resident dorm counselor, concerning my jerkhood. Maybe your points were valid, Bethany, but, really, we never had that much in common, not enough to warrant the assassination of my tape deck with your nail file when I dumped you on the drive back from the Shore.

We both knew it was a pre-emptive dump. There was no reason to take it out on my music. Were you planning to be my faithful wife in Ithaca?

Do I look wily to you?

But enough carnal chronology. I cite these names, Stacy, only to assure you that, yes, indeed, I have experienced the tender caress of hands on my body, hands other than my own.

Have I traveled, Stacy? I've been to lands. Not to strain your credulity, nor contradict your searing characterization of me as tiny-minded townie, but I've had my brushes with the crowd fabuloso. Moreover, I'm quite familiar with the miracle of jet engine flight. Once I even had a little money (gone), and friends (gone) with lots of money (not gone), those types who pop up in photo spreads of parties to which you'll never be invited. Don't feel so awful, Stacy. I'm off the list myself.

My misadventures in starballing were on account of Gwendolyn's brother Lenny, who'd trained in some of the best movie idol academies in the country. Lenny was too beautiful and not handsome enough for sustained eminence in America. You couldn't really picture him pummeling the Swiss kidnapper, snarling with any iconic authority, 'Goddamn you, you neutral fuck, where's my wife?!' But he did have an odd slant to his lips, a sort of forlorn smirk, that got him good parts fast.

The funny thing is I'd known Gwendolyn for a while before I even realized she had a brother. Or maybe she'd mentioned him and I hadn't heard. I was too in love with her (yes, Stacy, *love*) to ever really know what she was saying at any given time.

We set up house in my shabby but fairly spacious quarters out here in the Eastern Valley, cooked nutritious if slightly over-buttered meals, talked about our future together: a garden of basil and mint, a working stereo, a wooden dish rack for our wedding china, some wee Miners running about in dirty shorts, delighting us with their incisive critiques of sandbox society.

But Gwendolyn already had a child: Lenny. When he wasn't seducing teenage production assistants or having mild cocaine seizures or picking fights with the least connected person at any given gathering, Lenny sobbed on the phone to his big sister. Hours slid by as I watched my ball team lose on mute and listened to Gwendolyn purr her encouragements: 'Lenny, you just need to relax and take care of yourself. Lenny, your job is to be Lenny. Please, Lenny, you are so talented, you'll be betraying us all if you don't honor your dream.'

Lenny was a schmuck but he did honor his dream, which was to be a famous schmuck. Once he'd copped some statues for his fey portrayal of Tchaikovsky his ascent was quick. His public persona depended on his near-incestuous love for his sister, so Gwendolyn and I became members of his entourage. One tabloid item even had me getting juiced and trying to shoot Lenny in the nuts out of jealousy. The juiced part was true. So was the jealousy.

Lenny had a burning need to keep me busy, far away from his sister. He found me a script-doctoring gig for the son of a legendary producer. The old man was renowned for his deeply American toupee. His kid had written a movie about all the times he'd blown his father's friends in the pool house for Valium, cocaine.

My job was to punch it up.

'Our hero needs a buddy,' I told the kid.

'I'm the hero and I don't need any buddies. I need a fucking three-picture deal.'

My doctoring was surgical, heroic.

'You destroyed my script,' said the kid.

'Let's just pray I got all of it.'

That pretty much ended my stint as a healer.

Lenny, Gwendolyn and I, we'd fly to Paris or Madrid or Mexico City for the weekend. We saw many parts of the world, but just for a few hours, a few days, drunk, still drunk, jet-drunk. It all ended in Lisbon, which was a shame, because I loved that city of fish stink and stone fountains, ornamental balustrades. While

Gwendolyn coached Lenny for his role as Young Salazar I'd walk the *bario alto*, stop in cafes for a *pingo*, or, if Lenny had a night shoot, hit a club called Captain Kirk. I'd befriend the Azorean bartenders, who'd sell me fake hash, point me to the real Fado.

Those rare days Gwendolyn wasn't required on set to provide psychic suckling for her brother, I'd take her to this restaurant I'd discovered near the bus station. You could get fried sardines with their tails stuffed in their mouths and if the waiter had a good mood going he'd tell you all the evil he did in Angola. This aproned fiend appeared intent on making us shudder, especially Gwendolyn, who'd wriggle in her chair as though worried he'd rape her right there on the table, those old junk buses chuffing by. She wants to be raped, I remember thinking, hating myself for thinking that, cringing from myself in my head, then cringing from the man, hating him. Then not hating him, but noting him, as I'd noted the Swastikas. Lisbon was plastered with them – on colonnades, church doors, toilet stalls.

I know, Catamounts, it's an ancient Indian symbol, but it still says 'Heads Up!' to me. I preferred the sunnier sentiment painted in English on a slum wall: *Portugal is Cursed by God*.

'Took them four hundred years to figure that out?' I said to Gwendolyn.

'I do love you, L.,' she said.

She sounded so odd just then, that studied wistfulness borrowed from the pool house fellator's mother, the one who thought skin-popping liquefied gorilla fetus would keep her forty-eight forever.

'Hey,' I said. 'There's a statue of Hank the Nav I want to see.'

I was feeling jaunty, Catamounts. The things of the world had been named, but not nicknamed.

'You're not listening,' said Gwendolyn.

'I'm listening, baby,' I said. 'You *do* love me. I *do* love you. Was there something else? Your feet still hurt? We can skip the Prado.'

'The Prado is in Madrid.'

'Precisely. Sintra, though. That's a must for us. Lord Byron called it the most beautiful place on earth. He had a clubbed foot. His famous poem is pronounced Don Jew-On, for those in the know. That's what Ms. Tabor told us and –'

'Lenny and I are flying to New York tonight.'

'What are you talking about?'

'I had someone take my stuff from your apartment. Thanks for letting me stay there.'

'Stay there? We live together.'

'Since when?'

'Since you moved all your stuff in. Is this Lenny's idea?'

'He needs me.'

'Are you guys getting married?'

'Don't be disgusting.'

'You're the one who fucks your brother.'

'You know that's not true,' said Gwendolyn. 'You're being so goddamn disgusting, Lewis.'

'Why is it disgusting? Who are we to judge? Maybe if I had a brother like Lenny I'd fuck him, too. But I'm an only child. I had to learn to pleasure myself. Jerk myself up by my own jock straps.'

I guess I figured I could win her back with bad comedy.

'Good bye,' said Gwendolyn, peeled off into the crowd.

It wasn't a very heroic note to end things on, Catamounts. Here I was, ditched on the cobbles of a dead empire. Those squat rovers had ruled half the Pope-split world. I'd had the love of a goddess and relatively low upkeep. Now look at us.

Does all of this answer your query, Stacy?

Do I qualify as human, yet?

It was just a goddamn Halloween dance.

Dwarf Star Nubiles

Catamounts familiar with the Miner family agon (I guess this means you, Gary, and you alone) will be happy to know my father has finally called me back. We've fought our wars in the past, Marty and I, mostly over my failure to follow in his footsteps, to 'make something of myself,' an expression I've never understood, as it implies I am both the raw material and the artisan manipulating it, which is kind of silly, not to mention physically awkward, but I don't blame my old man. He didn't invent the English language. (Trust me, you'd know if he had. It probably wouldn't be a spoken language, either. A medium-hard slap on the head, for example, would suffice for 'Hello,' 'I love you,' and 'You're fired.')

My father, as most of you probably know, is founder and chief of Martin Miner Enterprises. His diversified holdings include In Your Cups on Hoyt Avenue ('offering patrons an intimate saloon experience since 1983') and the Moonbeam Catering Hall, where, I recall, Catamount Chip Gallagher married that woman from Dubuque, the one who fed his winning Powerball ticket to their Rottweiler for religious reasons. Apparently she believed the money would distance Chip from his spiritual potential. Chip soon distanced himself from his wife, and, eventually, most of the basic forms of consciousness. That's how I heard it, anyway.

Buy Chip a Cutty Sark down at In Your Cups, ask him yourself.

I admire the hell out of my father, who started with nothing and has lost everything more than once. The Moonbeam is his pride and joy, though it's never done the business of its rival, Don Berlin's Party Garden. This is fitting in its way. Whatever my father has, Don Berlin has more of the same: more house, more hair, more car. They even dated identical twins in high school.

'Prick had the prettier one,' my father said.

These last few years he's been listing towards another catastrophe, buying useless property at inflated prices, but he's never been a man to sit still for moderate and sustained success.

'So many guys,' he told me once, 'they're doing okay. Not too up, not too down. What's that? Kill me you see me doing okay.'

'Okay,' I said.

We agreed to meet at the Moonbeam to work out the details of our détente. I took the bus over there because I don't drive these days. It's a boring story, but the version whose sole asset is brevity is this: I can't deal with cars anymore.

I even went down to the DMV to surrender my license.

'I don't understand,' said the clerk.

'I can't deal,' I said. 'Please, just take the damn thing. You don't want me on the road. You don't know what erratic is until you've seen me.'

'Your record looks clean here,' said the clerk, clicking, mousing.

'They can't believe it, the cops. They're too stunned to stop me. They think it's a dream.'

When I got to the Moonbeam the tables were set for a wedding reception and Daddy Miner was yelling at some Mexican kids in tuxes about how the Moonbeam uniform is a short-waisted jacket and bolo tie, not a fucking monkey suit. I've heard the speech a few times myself, filling in for sick busboys and valets. The Mexicans eyeballed my father long enough to ensure he understood they'd considered violence, rejected it.

'I'm the groom,' one of them said.

My father snorted, wheeled, spotted me at the DJ booth. He stomped across the dance floor, scuffed loafers thumping, his double-breasted bulk iterated by the mirrored walls until it seemed an entire squadron of Daddy Miners was in formation and on the move.

'Don't fuck with the gear. That's sensitive gear.'

'Good to see you, too,' I said.

'Take the bus?'

'Bet on it.'

'How did you get to be such a whackjob, Lewis? Am I a whackjob and don't even know it? Your mother had her moments but she was a product of her era. I'm not buying you a car.'

'Don't want one. Can't deal with them. Speak not of my mother.'

'America is a car country, Lewis. New Jersey is a car state. The Amish are one state over.'

'I'm bucking the system.'

'You can't buck the system unless you're in the system.'

'Reformer's fallacy.'

'Don't talk fancy to me. I sent you to college to talk fancy and you couldn't hack it. What about money?'

'It's the root of something.'

'Don't be a wiseass, Lewis. People just pretend to like them.'

'I'm fine for money.'

'We both know that's bullshit.'

'Had enough for the bus, didn't I?'

'I'm not giving you any money. It's not a principle thing. I just don't have it. The economy's in the crapper. The entire homeland's in the crapper, far as I can tell. Or maybe it's just me in the crapper. Anyway, no benjamins for you, my boy.'

'I don't want your blood money.'

'Blood money? I'm a restaurateur.'

'Watered-down-vodka money.'

'Watch your mouth, boy. That watered-down-vodka money could have put you through college.'

'Anyway, I don't want it.'

'Well, you're going to have to tell me what you *do* want or I won't know what to deny you. Oh, shit, look at those flower arrangements! Roni! Roni!'

Roni is the assistant manager at the Moonbeam, a big pretty girl with a wrecked nose from a grade school newcomb incident. She's an unnatural blonde, sprinkles glitter on her clavicles. Her father was a jockey who walked out when his daughter started to dwarf him, or when he, as Roni once put it, 'gianted me.' Her mother works the breadslicer at the River Mall bakery. Roni's saving up for law school and the Moonbeam will suffer dearly when she leaves. She's a managerial genius, though that doesn't stop my father from doing everything in his power to drive her away. It's his version of gratitude.

'Dang, Marty,' she said now, stilting up on space boots that made her even more enormous, her perpetual parricide. 'Why do you have to yell like that? The flowers are fine.'

She wore a phone jack in her ear. A wire dangled near her chin.

'The flowers look plastic,' said my father.

'They are plastic.'

'That's not the point.'

'What's the point then?'

'Perception.'

'Perception?'

'You heard me.'

'I perceive a lovely arrangement of flowers,' said Roni.

'Injection-molded.'

'You're crazy.'

'You think *I'm* crazy? Look at my kid.'

''Sup, kid.'

'Hi, Roni. Nice to see you.'

'Don't get any ideas about Roni,' said my father. 'Nobody fools with Roni. That includes me.'

'You are a sick man, Marty. I am not amused. I'll be back in the office running your business if you need me.'

'Thanks, Roni. You know I'm just joking, right?'

'Yes,' she said. 'In the refrigerator. It's thawed! I thawed it!'

Roni shook, pinched the wire nearer to her chin.

'Her mom makes her nuts,' said my father.

Together we watched Roni cross the dance floor. It was nearly like a moment, Catamounts, the two of us together there, a dirty old man and his horny not-young son.

'I'll miss her when she deserts me.'

'She just wants to have a life,' I said.

'This is life!' said Daddy Miner with a dominion-gathering sweep of his arm: heat trays, coat check, mop closet.

'So,' I said, 'should we go somewhere, get a coffee?'

'I've got coffee here. I've got big fucking cans of it. Canned coffee is no good?'

'I thought we were going to talk.'

'Canned coffee hinders talk? What are we supposed to talk about, anyway?'

'I don't know. The bad feeling between us. How I've been a disappointment to you. How I haven't –'

'Whoa, hold up,' said my father. 'I don't care about all that crap.'

'You said I had to make something of myself.'

'It was a fucking suggestion, Lewis. Sue me. What is it with you kids today? Do you think my world turns on your happiness? Your success? Do what you please. Just make sure you're alive to wipe my ass when I'm an invalid.'

'I'm alive,' I said.

'Not now. Later.'

'I'll do my best.'

'Fine,' said my father. 'Then we're done here.'

The way I told it to Gary later, it was a kind of liberation. Go forth, Daddy Miner was saying, be your own disappointment. There's a whole wide world to fail in.

It makes me wonder how many of you Catamounts still buckle under expectation's yoke. Your mothers, your fathers, they just want you to be one of the breathers. They've got better things to worry about than your fulfillment. Here are a few of them: What time is the six o'clock news? Will I ever piss with force again? Chicken or chicken salad?

* * *

Me, I was hankering for some eggs by the time I left the Moonbeam. There was a new luncheonette on the corner called The Corner Luncheonette. The cutesy name was worrisome. Maybe they served those tasteless tiny roasted potatoes instead of curly fries. Besides, I have my favorite diners laid out like winking cities in my mind. I'm wary of parvenus. But this one must have been some Flying Dutchman luncheonette, a phantom spoon newly arrived, already a pit, the Formica cracked, the leatherette booths in shreds. The place must have floated in from out-of-state, Cleveland, say, under heavy cloud cover.

I took a counter stool, ordered eggs, sunnyside up, coffee, toast. When the food came all I could do was stare at it.

'What's wrong, buddy?' said the counterman. He looked fatigued, somewhat filthy. Maybe he was a ghost counterman.

'Nothing,' I said.

How could I explain to him the food didn't look quite like food, that it seemed more a model of the meal they might eventually serve you?

Or what about the absurdity of these sunnyside-up eggs, which did, in fact, resemble suns? There were so many books I'd read – mediocre fare, admittedly –

where the home star was likened to a blob of yolk. Which was the original image, I wondered, egg-as-sun, or sun-as-egg? Furthermore, what about those Sci-Fi worlds lit by two or more suns, or two or more moons, even? I licked some butter from my toast.

'Don't like my eggs?' said the counterman.

'I'll get to them.'

'I'm sorry. I didn't know you had a strategy.'

'Is this a real diner?' I said.

'What the fuck are you talking about?'

'I don't know. I'm having one of those moments.'

'Moments?'

'Everything seems a little off. A shade wrong. I thought it was this place but it must be me. I'm misfiring.'

'Are you on drugs?' said the counterman.

'No, are you on drugs?'

'Not real drugs.'

Some summer school girls trooped in with their backpacks and headphones, jubilant nipples puffing through their tank tops. Hilarious, I thought, in homage to Gary, if one can think in homage, and then I suddenly remembered my first literature-induced boner, if literature can include *The Girls of Galamere 5* by Lincoln A. H. Duvalier, a novel about a planet in another solar system where nubiles cavorted in the dying light of a dwarf star. I'd read the book a half dozen times without locating its fundamental flaw: how could a dwarf star sustain nubile life?

Now I dug into my eggs, wondered at the myriad connections the mind could make. Meanwhile, in another sector of my mind not prone to wonderment, I felt some lurid urge to blow the whole mess out onto the smeared steel awning above the Fry-O-Later. I've never paid these noises much heed. Sometimes, alums, I'll be walking down the street, catch myself chanting softly, 'Blow my friggin' head off, blow my goddamn friggin' head off.'

Doesn't everybody, Catamounts?

The voices, I figure they're just a kind of roll call, a homeroom attendance of the soul. Delusional Confidence? Here. Underlying Sense of Worthlessness? Here. Cycle of Emotional Abuse? Step off, motherfucker!

Stacy? Stacy Ryson?

Most of my voices are too vain for harm. There are exceptions, of course, inner tyrants who chuckle at naïve notions of pluralism and fair play, or attitudinal zealots, like those life coaches on TV. One of these latter bellowed from some high moist pulpit of a lobe.

'Gravy boat!' it said. 'Stay in the now!'

I looked up at the counterman, then remembered my father barking those words one Thanksgiving years ago, my mind wandering as it was wandering now, making its maybe-not-so-beautiful-nor-extraordinary connections while a row of aunts and uncles waited for me to pass what wasn't technically a gravy boat but more on the order of a mason jar filled with pan-spooned turkey juice.

'Gravy boat! Stay in the now!'

My father, he's still my deep commander, which is odd because he'd tell you himself his life has been a sham, and not just the sneaking around, the nookie-hunts. All he'd ever wanted was to play his horn in a Cool Jazz quintet. He could wail, too, had been offered a spot with some West Coast whiteboys on the brink of glorious elevator music. My father demurred, begged off, wasted his shot. Yes, those jazzbos spiraled into smack hells of their own devising, but not before slapping down some landmark lite wax.

'Failure of nerve,' my father had once said, the words hard, soothing candy in his mouth.

'That's a good phrase for it,' I said.

'I didn't make it up.'

'No, but it's still good. I usually just tell myself I'm a pussy.'

'Me, too,' said Daddy Miner.

I knew I was in the vicinity of a serious lesson, if not about how to live life, then at least how to put some poetry into your craven retreat from it.

I'm like most of the men in my family, I thought now, or think I thought then, mopping up egg yolk with toast crust, which I've read is a sign of bad breeding. We'll chance anything to destroy ourselves, but we're such chickenshits when it comes to happiness.

Were the women any better? Maybe braver, a bit more eager to pick fights with zoning boards, garbage collection route administrators, or, back in the old neighborhoods, with greengrocers and bookmakers, but what gets called feistiness might just be a fallback mode for the thwarted.

Before she died my mother told me she'd vowed to avoid that curse. She was Hazel Dubnow then, a modern girl like the girls in the modern movies. She had a college degree, semi-brazen lipstick, knew some Keats, a few knock-knock jokes. She'd come by bus to New York City, found a furnished room, an advertising job in midtown, friends who took her to the theater, the philharmonic, to openings, happenings, any kind of occurrence at all.

She made notes for one-act plays on office letter-head, dated account reps she detested, sots who'd suck her breasts in taxicabs, but she could stomach their ineffectual slobbering because she was a tough girl from Pittsburgh and at least these fools had more dough than the apes of the Allegheny. She was always gazing over their shoulders, anyway, off into some future-soft blur where she'd dine on quail and caviar with the wits of her era. These men would bow to her mind before their sensual, precise, perhaps European mouths ever got under her sweater.

Hazel skipped a lot of lunches, saved up for a ticket to Rome, rode through the countryside on the backs of motorbikes with grappa-slugging painters who were probably also in sales, felt Appian drool slide down her chest, flew home. She had ideas at work for ad campaigns, but who wanted to hear them? Not Swint, her supervisor. He shoved her down on his desk one night, commenced something novel, went for her panties, outright. Hazel fought him off, ran down to the street, hailed a cab, resigned by phone the next day.

'Good girl,' said Swint.

There she sat in a coffee shop with some stolen stationery trying to fashion this heartache into a play she'd never finish when Daddy Miner walked in, slid wordless into her booth. That was his big move back then, Hazel told me, to sit down without asking, light a smoke, smile with a worldly tenderness, as though he'd just found what he'd been seeking but wondered now if the journey had not sapped him of his power to love. Who could resist such charms of weariness? The rest, as they say, was history, or herstory, as Hazel would later put it, repeatedly, never quite able to hide the pickle juice pucker it made of her mouth.

Next stop, our very own Eastern Valley, Hazel stumbling through a waking dream, a kerchief on her head for the supermarket like all the other mothers and mothers-to-be. The split-level Marty and Hazel finally decided upon was some jumbo model much admired in the region, and they had more yard than most, and they had me, Baby Lewis, whose developmental fumblings, I pray, brought Hazel enough joy to offset the depression for a while. But Marty was gone for weeks, scouting locales for new schemes to ruin them, and Baby Lewis was probably more chore than beguilement, and the neighbors, even the Jewish neighbors, didn't quite get her jokes.

And you'd think that would be the end of that, but that's never really the end of that, or only in the modern movies. Because Hazel was tough, Catamounts, and, as you might recall, a sorceress. She decided to live her life, but not die of it. That's what she told me, anyway, and what she told me is all I've got to rely on.

She said she became a witness to what she'd come to conclude was her bondage, found books by like-minded women, found women with like minds, too, started groups, newsletters for the groups, a theater collective to perform the plays she wrote for all the groups. Laugh at it now, Catamounts, God knows my father did, but it was dangerous and new to Hazel, and what can you admire more in a person than the will to danger? Sure, her rants could be ridiculous, stridency smothering wit, and yes, she took it too far with me, who wasn't her enemy, just her son who happened to have a cock, but even so, she'd saved herself, or at least altered the terms of her internment.

It couldn't last forever, of course, and after Marty was done finger-banging his wait staff, came home to rest, he noticed that the Hazel who lived in his house was not much like the Hazel he'd hauled out from the city years before. He decided to fall in love with someone else, and did. The ravishing flatware rep would leave him soon enough. He stayed in our house for a while after, never quite the philandering husband again, more a boarder with occasional cuddling privileges. Then came the sad sack condo nearby. I tried to pretend I didn't know what was going on, but Hazel made sure I knew.

'Your father's a fucking bastard,' she said, handed me her new play to read, 'A Fucking Bastard.'

It was a one-act, in verse.

Spite was good succor. Hazel lost weight, wore big shabby sweaters, picked up cigarettes again. Somehow they made her golden, life-like. It was hard going, though. The world she figured she was finally rejoining was long extinct. The women executives at the agency where she'd gotten temp work, more out of loneliness than insolvency, ignored her bra-burner harangues. The Ivy League assistants gave grave mocking nods. The Jewish septuagenarians she met through her wildly inaccurate singles ads still didn't get her jokes. Her groups had disbanded. Nobody would read her plays.

She had the house, though, decent alimony, a few friends left from the old days, divorcees all, puttering around their kitchens, nibbling on unsalted saltines, trying to disentangle themselves from telephone cords. Sometimes I wondered if Hazel had become a lesbian, hoped that she had, but I knew she'd lost the spirit to learn new skin. Hers was rather wan now. The cigarettes hadn't helped, after all. There was wilt, spoilage to her. I figured she was maybe due for another resurrection. Then she invited me over for meatloaf, told me the latest.

Metastatic, she said. It sounded like a funk band.

So, yes, Catamounts, the day finally came and I kissed her cold dead calves, the ones that would never take her anywhere dangerous or new again. Kissed her cold dead calves, I always say, but did I, Catamounts, or do I just say I did? I heaved myself onto her cold dead calves, I'm certain, bolted out of the chair I'd been dozing in when the doctor patted me awake, said to me, 'She's gone,' all that monotony of format in his voice – dim room, dead woman, numb son. Certainly I heaved myself down upon her then, her calves, sobbed into the stubble there. (No courageous vanity for Hazel, no razors, rouge, no mascara.) But did I really kiss her?

'Gravy boat! Stay in the now!'

Who's there? Where's now?

It was still just me, a guy at the end of his eggs, his runny suns.

Good-bye, nubiles. Good-bye girls of Gala –

'They hauled it up from Georgia.'

'Huh?'

'Georgia, I said,' said the counterman.

'What?'

'They bought this shithole diner and didn't even fix it up. Just hitched it to a truck. Authentic. For that authentic shithole feel. It's not your brain.'

'Pardon?'

'It's not your brain. People worry it's their brain. They shouldn't worry.'

'No,' I said. 'They shouldn't.'

His Truth Bazooka

Okay, Catamounts, enough with the morbid stuff, the
dark unanswerables. The monumental questions will
never be laid to rest. For instance, if God exists, why
did He kill my mommy, or even Thurman Munson? Or
how do morons make so much money? Or why were
the Nearmont High Vikings mostly Italian kids,
Armenian?

Gary and I had a good laugh about that today on the
way to the Bean Counter to visit Liquid Smoke.

'Korean and Vietnamese, too,' said Gary. 'And that
Montagnard kid, Vance.'

Gary said Montagnard as though he'd hacked
through jungle with them, worn the sacred bracelet of
the Rahde like Duke Wayne on the Unjust War
Channel.

But we weren't hacking through anything. We
weren't even humping kliks to the next ville. We were

driving past Cassens Park to the old downtown, the sun cooking through Gary's windshield, the ball-courts, ballfields, deserted.

'Remember that time in farm league you shit your pants in the outfield?' said Gary.

'Food poisoning.'

'Didn't we all eat the same thing that day?'

'I got a bad hot dog.'

'Right, I remember. A bad hot dog.'

'What's your point?'

'There's no point. It's a reminiscence, man.'

'Reminisce about something else.'

'Roger that, pants-shitter.'

Catamounts, have you noticed all the empty store-fronts downtown these days? Dugan's Drugs is gone. Manny's Dry Clean, too. Greco's Meats is boarded up with plywood. Eastern Valley Plaza is still humming, of course, all those cappuccinos, DVDs. That fat lady boutique thrives, too. Main is a wasteland, though. Most of the signage dates back to SALT II. That neon jackboot still hangs over the door of Dino's Shoe Repair, but Dino is dead. His sons gutted the store years ago.

The Bean Counter, with its fake antiques and framed clippings from the old *Eastern Valley Gazette*, it feels like a taunt at the dead part of town. I'm not sure which history the Bean Counter means to borrow its ambience from, but it has something do with dark varnish and doilies, paraffin lamps, freight trains packed with gewgaws and taffy and nobody forgetting the *Maine*.

Liquid Smoke's real name is Mira, if one is given to believe nametags, and she's seeking the attentions of a suave older gentleman, if one is given to believe Gary. It's not hard to see why he's smitten. This girl has a straight silk drop of hair like all the teenie sirens on TV. Her bare skin achieves a sort of golden strobe effect when her apron sways out from her halter-top.

Today the Retractor stepped up to the counter and sighed his order in the manner of some jetsetter marooned in New Jersey by circumstance – 'You'll never believe where I had to spend the night!' – a man perhaps suicidally bored by the lingonberry muffin and half-caf hazelnut ice coffee he's about to consume.

Liquid Smoke looked annoyed, filled his order with sullen speed.

'How are the scones today?' said Gary.

'You want a scone or a muffin?'

'No, I was just inquiring after their quality. I've yet to find a suitable American scone.'

'So get the fuck out of America.'

'Do you have a young chap?'

'Like a blister?'

'A beau. A boyfriend.'

'What's it to you?'

'I realize I'm a bit older. My body is probably softer than you've come to expect, but I can make you very happy.'

'I'll keep that in mind.'

'Because the world is both simpler and more complex than a beautiful woman like yourself could ever imagine.'

'Have I seen you here before?'

'I love your coffee.'

'You're one of the crazy Horizons people, right?'

'Depends who you talk to.'

'No, I mean from down the block. Near the old lumberyard? That place, that home for the mental? What's it called? It's called Nice Horizons, right? They come here all the time. It's okay. But don't creep out on me. And don't ask me for the bathroom key. I'm not cleaning up any more crazy person poop.'

The Captain seemed a little shaken. I led him over to the cream and sugar.

'She's just a kid,' I said.

'And we're geezers,' said Gary. 'Washed up at the age Jesus was just getting rolling.'

'Look what happened to him.'

'Fucking Romans. Fucking New Romans, too. You know, the problem with women today is that so many of them have worked out their daddy shit. Guys like me have no shot. Goddamn therapy culture.'

Gary crunched his ice, spat it back into the cup.

The only other customer, an older guy in a vintage New York Giants football jersey, coughed. He was reading the Collected Colette, a lit cigarillo in his teeth. He peeked out from behind his Colette.

'It'll be okay,' I said to Gary.

'No, it won't.'

'It won't?' I said.

Gary stood, gazed out the window.

'Didn't they used to sell dope back behind Dino's?'

'Gary.'

'Not for me, man. I'm just taking sociological note.'

Outside, a man stopped at a traffic light leaned from his jeep, blew something chunked from his nose to the blacktop. A few state troopers stood under the awning of Abel's Bagels, hooting. One drew his pistol, mimed a shot at the snotsman. Gary peeled the cakey lid off his muffin, took a bite, handed it to me.

'Best part,' he said.

'Let's go,' I said.

'Not yet.'

'New plan?'

'I'm going back to the Gary thing,' said Gary. 'It's who I am, what I'm about.'

'You've never stopped being Gary.'

'Never will, brother,' said Gary, walked back to the counter.

'Mira,' he said.

'What.'

'My name is Gary.'

'Hello, Gary.'

'I've got to go to the bathroom. May I borrow the key?'

'You know the rules.'

'I won't poop anywhere, I promise.'

'Now you're definitely not getting the key.'

'I came here because I think you're beautiful.'

'That's nice.'

'I didn't even want the muffin, or the coffee.'

'That's stupid.'

'I'm not that scone guy I was before. I'm not from the Horizon.'

'If you say so.'

'Would you like to go out with me sometime?'

'Where do you want to go?'

'My apartment?'

'That's not really going out.'

'For you it would be.'

'I don't think so.'

'Okay. How about . . . I don't know. Dinner?'

'You've got money to take me out?'

'I've got money.'

'What do you do, Gary?'

'It's a long story.'

'You sell drugs.'

'No.'

'Then tell me.'

'I thought my mother and father raped me. Then it turned out they didn't.'

'And you got paid for that?'

'I did okay.'

'That's wild. But what if they did do it? Do you still get paid?'

'No.'

'Damn.'

'So?'

'So what?'

'Will you go out with me?'

'I don't give a fuck.'

'Cool.'

We left with Mira's phone number, if you're given to believe women who give them out. Digits, I think the Mikey Saladins of the world call them, not that he'd need them, a handsome giant with soft hands and otherwise bat speed. What does a man like Mikey need with numbers? A hero like that, women simply appear, unbidden, in his bed at night, with calves of moonstone, or so I have heard. Or heard myself tell myself.

We retired to the Retractor Pad to celebrate. Gary filled his bong with some puce sports drink. We took our party to the terrace, which is one of the perks of retraction, along with an ice-making refrigerator, heat lamps in the john. We'd hauled this half-rotted park bench to the terrace and we lazed upon it now, watched men load trucks at the mayonnaise factory across the street.

'I had this way ancient uncle,' said Gary. 'I asked him how he got to be sixty-seven, or whatever. He said, "No condiments." Can you believe that?'

'Mustard,' I said. 'He must have used mustard.'

'No mustard. Maybe some pepper.'

'Pepper's not a condiment. It's a spice.'

'You say tomato.'

'What?'

'Cultural relativity.'

'Relativism.'

'It's all bullshit.'

'What about perception?' I said.

'What about perceived relativity?'

'What about this,' I said. 'Say you've got some fake 99
flowers that could pass for real but you know they're
fake. What have you got then?'

'Shit, man, let me answer that question with another
question. Do you think Liquid Smoke is smokin'?'

'Her name is Mira, Gary, and yes, I do.'

'I think I could make a life with her.'

'You just met her.'

'I feel like I've known her a long time. I don't mean
in a dumb mystical way. Or maybe I do. I just know
that I've taken a bad path so far. The thumb thing, the
drugs, the stuff with my folks. This Smoke situation
could turn my life around.'

'Maybe.'

'You don't believe me?'

'No, it's just that I've never seen you with hope
before.'

'Don't worry, I still think we're all fucked.'

'Good.'

We sat wordless for a while.

'You know,' said Gary, 'when Liquid Smoke, I mean Mira, when she mentioned Nice Horizons, it reminded me of something. Somebody said Doc Felix works there now. Doesn't even draw a salary. They just let him live in that dump. My lawsuit destroyed him.'

'Serves him right.'

'I feel responsible.'

'He did it to himself.'

'I don't know. I'm starting to have these dreams.'

'The dope dreams?'

'No, like my mom with all these candles. Fiery dildos and childos and whatnot.'

'Felix made that stuff up. What's a childo?'

'How do I know if he made it up?'

'Gary,' I said, 'you're a retractor.'

'Don't label me. I hate labels. What if I retracted the retraction? Then what? I'd still be Gary, right?'

I followed his gaze to the terrace wall. He'd tacked up one of his old stick-figure diagrams. The figure marked Son was on his knees before the figure marked Father. Blue seeds flew out Father's member. Gary took a long draw from his hip-high bong. His Truth Bazooka, he'd called it once. We'd both winced when he said it. Now he sucked in smoke as though it were air, his last, perhaps, before a leap into the sea off some lush, poisonous atoll. I pictured fish, bitter-blooded, glittery. Hammerheads on patrol. Pink, living coral. Pink, moaning coral. The moans of the coral sounded like chimes.

Door chimes.

'Shit, that's my sponsor!' said Gary. 'Deal, Gary, deal!'

Gary's sponsor Hollis is an asp of a man in soft Italian shoes. He fits my notion of a Christian pop producer with his over-pruned beard, those tinted shades he favors, his collarless shirts. He was a coke dealer in a former life. Now he claims to be in real estate, though most of his 'closings,' according to Gary, occur at clubs after midnight.

Hollis is not what you'd call the nurturing type, and I wonder how good he is for Gary's recovery. Gary said all the gentle sponsors were taken, that he offered Hollis the job because he felt bad for the guy. Everybody thought Hollis was evil, one of those mistakes of the species, steered clear. Nobody would ever identify with his feelings, which I gather is a big part of the healing process. At meetings most nights, according to Gary, Hollis would just sit there crushing his Styrofoam cup.

Others talked about the fear goading them to drink, snort, shoot, binge on cheese dogs.

'I'm in a lot of fear,' they'd say.

Hollis would just crush another cup.

'Hollis is not afraid of fear,' he'd declare, out of turn. 'Hollis is afraid of fun. Fun is what fucks Hollis.'

I've met Hollis more than a few times but he never remembers my name. I assume it's because I am one of the unsaved. He once told me he could tell I was an alcoholic by the shape of my head. He cackled when he said it. He could have been kidding.

Now Hollis raced past me into the Retractor Pad. Together we watched Gary fumble with his bong out on the terrace.

'How is it out there?' said Hollis.

'Cooled off a little,' I said.

'Not on the terrace, lump. I mean how is it *out there.*'

'Out where?'

'In the fucking darkness, pal.'

'It's not so bad.'

'Larry, is it?'

'Lewis.'

'Lewis. Do you know, Lewis, that I can look right at you and tell by a single glance you are consumed by demons of nearly unimaginable ferocity? Do you know how I can ascertain this?'

'The shape of my head?'

'Primarily, yes. Do you pray, Lewis?'

'I don't believe in God.'

'Who said anything about God, twat? Hey, do you like antiques? You'll never guess what I've got in my car.'

'You're right, I won't.'

'A goddamn war mace. It was used by Ostrogoths to split skulls. Fucked-up skulls like yours. Got it in the mail. From an Ostrogoth.'

'I didn't know there were any around.'

'He's an Ostrogoth by choice. You can be whatever you want to be in this country, in case you haven't heard.'

The terrace door slid open and Gary stepped in, his eyes puckered, pinked.

'Good and stoned for the meeting?' said Hollis.

'I don't know what you're talking about.'

'I practically invented drugs,' said Hollis. 'Don't play Hollis, son. Players don't play Hollis, and you sure as hell shouldn't. Let's go. And now that you're all Bakey Bakerton, just shut the fuck up. No sharing until tomorrow. You got me? You better not share. Are you coming, Larry?'

'No,' I said.

'Well, then, you can lock up. And make sure Bishop Bowlpacker here didn't start a fire under that bench.'

'Will do,' I said.

'I'm watching you,' said Hollis. 'I'm noting the shape of your head.'

I went home, studied my head in the mirror. Misshapen, sure, but in the same old ways. I cooked up some dinner, shells and peas, leafed through these magazines I've been getting lately. Free offer. No immediate obligation. Congratulations, you have thirty days to cancel our plan to pluck out your pancreas. How did they get to me? Did I buy something? Sign something? That girl with the clipboard in the park? I'd figured she was just handing out those light-up sweatbands to get a fad going. Didn't they double-check with the credit bureau? Don't they know I'm not good for it?

I guess that's the whole idea, though. That's what Gary says, anyway.

I've read a lot on the subject, but I don't really understand this capitalism stuff. It doesn't seem tenable.

Nice in theory, though.

Then, Catamounts, the shocker. I'm tonguing shell for pea when I read it: 'Actor killed in Acting Mishap.' Apparently, in the dull interlude of a camera jam, Lenny put his prop pistol to his head, pulled the trigger. The blank charge ripped through his temple. God's a lousy comic, a Catskills hack. Give God the hook!

I called Gwendolyn.

Her voice was fuzzy from the pharmacy. She said she had a house full of out-of-work actors groping through her fruit baskets, her pill drawer. Grief-scene fuel. A director who'd known Lenny less than a week had punched a breakfront in the kitchen, torn meaningful tendons.

'Lenny, why?' he'd cried. 'Why did you fuck me?'

He'd had Lenny attached to star in the 'Jew of Malta' set on an alien mining colony.

Mourning rituals were invented hourly. They'd found Lenny's agent in the garage. He'd knifed a strip of felt from the pool table for a bandanna, was weeping his way through choice bits from pioneering black sitcoms. Lenny's personal trainer had dug out Lenny's favorite pair of snakeskin boots, basted them with teriyaki sauce on a no-fat grill. The accountant had stolen paperwork from the study, deal memos, itemized tax returns, hauled them down to the beach with a compound bow, shot them, aflame, into the sea. The poodle was on suicide watch.

'Come home,' I said.

She said maybe she would.

'It's terrible about Lenny,' I said. 'We never got along, but that's only because we both loved you so much.'

'I go now,' said Gwendolyn.

'You go now?' I said.

'Phone off. Funny feel.'

'Whatever pills you're taking,' I said. 'Don't take any more.'

'Any more I take I want. You don't tell it, me.'

'Okay, baby,' I said. 'Just come home.'

'Don't baby it, flatter yourself.'

'Understood.'

Well, alums, it's been a week and I'm still waiting for Gwendolyn to call back. I've put off mailing this update to Fontana thinking I'll have a hopeful, if fragile, conclusion to this installment. I've left messages in Malibu, even talked to a woman named Quince who said Gwendolyn was 'at a loss' and could not be disturbed. I told her to tell Gwendolyn the 'L' in Lewis was for Love.

'You're adorable,' she said. 'You're the one Gwen

ditched, right? Or are you the one who took her to that holistic abortionist and then tried to ball me?'

'Ball?'

'We're saying ball again.'

'Ditched,' I said.

'Good. I'll tell her you called. Oh, fuck.'

'What's wrong?'

'Guillermo's on the patio with matches and gasoline. I've got to go.'

Quince let the receiver drop, bang down on something like a cabinet. I heard grunts, hard breathing, Quince shouting, 'Guillermo, Guillermo!'

Now a fainter voice carried over the receiver.

'Lenny, look! Look at me, Lenny! I'm going to be a star. I'm about to blow up!'

Dogs wailed into the telephone. Hundreds, it sounded like. I'd forgotten about the dogs.

Gary picked me up that night.

'I've got a gift for you,' he said.

We drove down Hoyt, turned off Mavis near the county line, parked near a house on a cul de sac called Drury Court. The place sat back behind some birch trees, a modified ranch. We sneaked up to a shrub-mobbed window.

'Consider this woe compensation,' said Gary.

'I'm not woeful.'

'Just fucking look.'

It was a big room with a shag carpet, antique lamps, a cabinet TV from days when entertainment lurked in the guise of furniture. Fontana was on his hands and knees, yoked to a vacuum cleaner, naked beneath his harness. We could hear the suck and whine of the machine. A whip tip of knotted rawhide kissed his strap-reddened back. Fontana plowed out of view and now came the bare lovely legs of the living-room tiller. I jutted my head past the hedges for a better look.

Jazz Loretta!

The years had been kind to her. Slavish, even. Black eyes still beamy. Her body a pale and beautiful root.

Her sorry domination of the educator Fontana, her slack way with the bullwhip, the giddy-ups, it was not good theater. Probably this pair would have been laughed out of any decent dungeon in the Northeast. But their joy looked true. Truer than mine, the peeper's. I pulled back from the window. The Hoover howled, revved.

Tuna Melt Deluxe

Fuck me, Ostrokitties.

The next batch of FakeFacts is due to Penny Bettis in a week. Landlord Pete will be knocking on the door soon, too. Whither all my bank, Catamounts? Rent, utilities, a fifth of Old Overholt, a few tacos, boom! (Message to the Old Overholt folks: how about a case of your fine rye for this excellent product placement in *Catamount Notes*?)

But I'm not bitter. It's my bed and I'm going to make it. Or, to quote Captain Thorazine: You must bide your time until your time comes, knowing full well, of course, your time may never come. That's the bitch about biding it.

These FakeFacts are killing me, though. When I agreed to this gig I figured the possibilities for cola mythography were endless. Maybe they are, maybe it's me who's reached the frontiers of invention. I'm no genius, after all, just sorry-ass Teabag. But still, ever since I started writing these updates, I've felt this godly hum in the gut. It's all I've got.

Maybe it beats what Stacy Ryson has, which is two hundred-odd pounds of pud-headed malevolence to call honeycakes, or such appeared to be the case the last time I saw her at the River Mall. I'd hopped the bus out there to perv on rich wives from Tobias Hills, drop in on Roni's mother at Slice of Life, cop some snatches of what contemporary amnesiacs call punk rock on those consoles at the record outlet.

Also, I'd found myself in the market for a battery-operated pencil sharpener. There's a top-notch Manila Mo's at the mall. This might seem funny because Manila Mo's is a chain, but good management makes all the difference. Those dreadlocked anarchists who follow the G-8 around like it's a legendary acid band are right about how we've all crawled up to die in the anus of the oligarchy, but don't listen to them when they carp about corporate homogeneity. Go get some Taco King in Nearmont, then get some at the mall, you'll see what I mean. There's a jalapeño fetishist in Nearmont who's going to maim a child with his pepper juices someday.

But back to matters Rysonian and cruel. I'd just

slipped off my Music Mania in-store headphones after subjecting myself to the bloated plaints of Spacklefinger – yes, Catamounts, I do mean that Spacklefinger, the one fronted by our very own Glave Wilkerson, pseudo-poet of Eastern Valley, purveyor of arena rock in deserted clubs near a decade now, whose major label debut, *Sporemonger*, arrives not a moment too soon, as Glave, who might have been an okay dude in high school were he not such a monumental suckass and sister-pimper, is beginning to resemble the very dads his anthems of teen disaffection rebuke – when lo and/or behold, there was Stacy Ryson, strolling down the concourse in mutual butt-grope with a big goon in designer glasses.

I cut them off near a potted fern.

'Stacy,' I said.

She turned, stood, unnerving in her yogic rectitude. I smiled, gave big teeth. They're not pretty, my teeth, kind of pointy, butter-colored, but then I hardly tend to them, not since Gwendolyn left. It's tough brushing alone.

'Do I know you?' said Stacy.

Her goon struck a pose of high moral alert. His head was shaved, shaped like a cut dick, his eyes sealed in smug eyeware.

Damn if it wasn't Philly Douglas.

'Friend?' he said to Stacy, laid his hand on her taut freckled arm.

'Yes,' I said. 'Friend. Old friend. Lewis Miner.'

'Miner?' he said. 'Lewis?'

'Eastern Valley. Class of '89.'

'No shit.'

'I saw you score three touchdowns against Edgefield.'

'Three? Try four.'

'I left early.'

'Didn't you sell me fake speed once?' said Philly.

'That was my friend Gary.'

'My dog died from it.'

'I won't ask.'

'No, maybe it's better if you don't ask, Miner. Like maybe it's better if I don't ask about those updates Stacy showed me. Your homo shower fantasies starring me.'

'Trust me,' I said. 'You're not the star.'

'Phil,' said Stacy. 'Please. That's enough. Lewis, it's nice to see you again.'

'Nice to see you, Stace. You look fantastic.'

'How she looks is none of your business,' said Philly.

'I've got eyes,' I said. 'They do business.'

'I hope you weren't too offended by my letter,' said Stacy.

'No,' I said, 'flattered is more like it. I'm excited about correspondence with someone of your caliber. So, do you still live around here?'

'We're in the city now. We were just in town visiting my folks. Philly and I are engaged.'

'Congratulations. I should send you something, right? A card? Can I get your address?'

'To be honest, Lewis, I thought of my letter as more of a one-time thing. I just wanted to explain my, or, rather, our, meaning women, or, some women, at least, the position we might take regarding your update, had we read it, or rather, had women other than myself read it.'

'You did a wonderful job explaining. I was just thinking about your letter today while listening to the new Spacklefinger LP.'

'That's Glave's band, right? I hear they're getting big now.'

'Spacklefinger rock,' said Philly Douglas.

'They're crap,' I said.

'Come on, Phil, let's go,' said Stacy. 'Good to see you, Lewis.'

'His name is Teabag,' said Philly. 'Don't you know how he got that name?'

'I'm sure Stacy knows,' I said.

'What's the story, Phil?'

'Forget it,' he said.

I guess Philly Douglas suddenly didn't want to tell his fiancée how he'd ordered his buddies to hold me down in the shower room so he could mash his balls into my face. It hadn't bothered me much at the time. I'd been under the impression it was some kind of a hazing ritual. What hurt was afterwards, when I still didn't belong. Funny, but years later I saw this boy on TV who'd also been teabagged contrary to his will. He had a suit against his school for millions. His spirit had died. He couldn't play sports. What a whiner.

'There's no story,' said Philly now. 'He's just fucking Teabag.'

Yes, Catamounts, Philly seemed loath to relive the incident, especially maybe the part where Will Paulsen swooped in, peeled Philly from my face, threw him up against the wall. This would also be the part where Philly maybe pissed his pants. He may have been a football star, a real backfield monster, at that, but he was no Will Paulsen. Goliath never stood a chance, either. Too much mythology at stake.

Now Philly took Stacy by the wrist, tugged her toward a window full of wicker goods.

'Jazz Loretta whips Fontana,' I called out after them.

'Gary loves Liquid Smoke. The pressure from my father was all in my head!'

'What the hell?' said Stacy.

'I'm giving you the news!' I said. 'I'm bringing you up to date!'

'Don't come back here!' Philly shouted past his shoulder.

It was a silly thing for him to say, Valley Cats. No man can tell another man to stay out of the mall. That's not how America works. That's not what the framers intended. Philly must have been flustered, all those dangerous old nut-dangle tingles, plus to meet someone with a legitimate sonic aesthetic. How can he defend a band whose hideous music is rivaled only by its insipid lyrics, a sample of which I've just down-loaded from the *Sporemonger* home page?

I have no home and I'm alone
Too scared to even face me
I close my eyes, close my eyes
Pray to Jesus to erase me
I want to be a nothing man
Because I'm nothing, man
Nothing without you, girl

(Words by Glave Wilkerson
Music by Spacklefinger)

Catamounts, I implore you to shield your young from this pernicious drivel. What happened to hating the state apparatus, or just wanting to be regional Antichrist? Sure, it all gets set to a car commercial in the end, but at least give it a shot. Bang some dope, for Pete's sake, roll in broken glass. Don't flee the melee in your heart. Don't bitch to Jesus about it, either. If that Essene wildman was around today, and, say, head-lining some monster summer tour, you can bet your ass Spacklefinger wouldn't be allowed within five hundred miles of the stadium. There would be a tremendous wall of blood-colored lightning to keep those bastards at bay. That's just my opinion, of course, but I'd also take any odds that if there's one thing Jesus and the Devil agree upon, it's that Glave Wilkerson is not punk. The man has the soul of a college boards coach.

Which reminds me, I've yet to comment on the latest issue of *Catamount Notes*, wherein it was announced my old flame Bethany Applebaum is making a mint helping the doltish progeny of the rich gain admittance to our nation's leading universities.

Bravo, Bethany! Tuck those little one-percenters in all safe and cozy. Keep that ruling class razor wire sharp and shiny!

Bethany, your father was head of the lathe workers local. Would he pop and lock in his grave knowing you've dedicated your life to helping these entitled cretins? You busted your hump to get to Cornell. All that panic and self-cutting, those blood-speckled scrunchies on your arm. Is this your way of giving back to the gatekeepers? Or is your cynicism a huge holy shimmering thing no mortal could view in its entirety at once?

Please write in and let us know!

I walked around the mall for a while. I won't talk about the mall, alums. You know about the mall, the scent of mallness that pervades it. It's the scent of scents canceling each other out. Perfumes, pizza, leather, sweat. How do people proceed?

They had a scientist type in one of my magazines talking about ants. Nobody tells ants what to do, he said. Ants just know what's best for ants.

Moreover, they know what's best by smell.

Maybe that's what Daddy Miner was driving at about the flowers at the Moonbeam.

Plastic roses might confuse.

See what I mean?

Nor do I.

But I must be an ant-guy because I could smell where to go.

Slice of Life is a tiny shop near the River Mall entrance, or, I suppose, exit, depending on your world-view. Either way it's the only place in the whole joint that doesn't smell like mall. I guess you could say it smells like home, if you grew up a long time ago and your mother baked soda bread all day while your father worked the beet fields, or smoked his pipe on the porch and lectured the Labrador on the merits of William Jennings Bryant.

We didn't have that kind of home.

We had pouch dinners and Reagan and such.

Point is, the smell in Slice of Life, that hot bread smell, it will calm you, or at least it calmed me. You know how that squid-like placenta flops out of a woman after her baby is born, all purple and weird? Wouldn't it be better if instead of a mutilated infant octopus a perfect round of sourdough bread slid out?

But perhaps I digress.

There was a big wait at the Slice of Life counter. I stood off near the door for a while, watched Roni's mother work the bread machine. She was a fatter, prettier version of her daughter in a showercap, the same wire poking down past her chin.

'Listen,' she was saying. 'Use the tea towels. You've been using too many paper towels . . . I don't care about the trees, Roni . . . I know, I know . . . but your law school fund is going in the trash with all those goddamn paper towels. Stop using them, Roni. What do you think people did before paper towels? They had lives, you know. They lived lives . . . I know they're more . . . right, absorbent. Absorbent! That wasn't even a word! They invented that word to sell paper towels to people like you . . . I told you, I could care less about the damn planet . . . what's the planet without my Roni in law school? Okay, baby? Okay . . . you have to go, I know. See you later. And tell Mr. Miner to stop staring at you . . . yes, you can tell him straight out. He's a dirty old letch. Okay, Mommy loves you.'

The line had thinned and Roni's mother caught my eye across the counter.

'Can I help you?'

'Just sniffing,' I said.

'Where do I know you from? You look familiar.'

'I work over at the wicker store.'

'Oh, right. I haven't been in there lately.'

'We've got a sale on picnic baskets,' I said. 'Vintage design. You and your sweetheart can ride out to the countryside, eat cherries, read poetry before one of you goes off to die in the senseless slaughter.'

'The senseless slaughter?'

'The trenches. The Boche.'

'You don't really work in the wicker store.'

'I should,' I said.

The bus ride gave me time to shake off my encounter with Stacy and that bastard Phil, not to mention Roni's mother's slander. Who was she to call my father a letch? A man sidles up to claim his Darwinian due and if he doesn't fit the demo he's an outcast, a pervert, a slimeball at best. Besides, she'd never caught Daddy Miner caressing *her* girlfriend's ass near the basement boiler. She hadn't earned the right to call him a letch.

Along these scientific lines I worked through my more virulent feelings about Glave Wilkerson, too. Pretentious mediocrity must have a place in this world, or why would Nature allow for it? We all walk to the beat of a different drummer. It's just that some of these drummers suck.

I got off the bus near Venus Drive, walked the rest of the way to the Retractor Pad. Another dumbfuck in the sunshine: hope, dread, trees. Kids encased in plastic chugged by on miniature mountain bikes. An older shapely woman swerved past on rollerblades. Bronzed, undulant in black Lycra, she clutched a pack of menthol cigarettes, danced on her wheels to something pumped through headphones. It was an admirable kind of ecstasy, hard-won. I wanted her for a lewd aunt.

I had to pound on Gary's door for a while before he answered. He stood there with a beach towel around his waist, his shoulder fuzz damp, his eyes sticky. Love odors sieved out of him.

'Tea,' he said. 'You should call first.'

'I just saw Stacy Ryson. We have some ground to cover.'

'I'm in the middle of something.'

'What something?'

'Nothing.'

'I think we're done,' called a voice from the room.

Gary looked a little dog-like, denied.

'I guess you're done,' I said.

'Guess so.'

Mira sat on the carpet in her brassiere, scraped pot resin with a paperclip. An envelope dotted with the gunk lay near her knee.

'Teabag!' she said.

'Call him Lewis for now,' said Gary.

'I want to call him Teabag. He's gawking at me, I can call him Teabag.'

'I'm not gawking,' I said.

'You're burning holes in my tits, Teabag.'

'That's the liquid smoke you're smelling,' I said.

'Excuse me?'

'Nothing,' said Gary. 'He's just talking nonsense.'

'Liquid smoke?'

'You had to be there,' said Gary.

'I'm here,' said Mira.

You could tell Gary was getting tense. He has those mood veins near his hairline. I threw down for maximum throb.

'Gary likes to call you Liquid Smoke,' I said.

'You're such a little faggot sometimes!' screamed Gary.

'Be nice,' said Mira. 'He's your friend.'

'Fuck that,' said Gary.

He stalked off to the kitchen, started banging things around in there. He came back sipping from a saucepan full of ice water.

'He's not my friend,' said Gary. 'He's a fucking leech.'

Gary took his saucepan to the terrace curtains.

'Hot out? Looks hot.'

'You haven't been outside yet?' I said.

Gary hacked into his cupped palm, regarded the loogie there. These types of moments test a man. Get a tissue? Wipe it on the curtain? Catamounts, what do you think Old Goony did? I'll give you a hint: Gary doesn't have any tissues.

'Earlier,' said Gary. 'I was out earlier.'

'Was it hot then?'

'It seemed hot. Things were all glinty.'

'Glinty,' said Mira from the carpet.

'Sorry,' said Gary. 'I didn't mean that leech thing.'

'Dude, I always pay you back.'

'I wasn't talking about fucking money, man. Forget it. I'm just a little wiggy today. So, Stacy Ryson.'

'She's not a bad person. But she's betrothed to evil.'

'Philly's not evil.'

'No?'

'You need to refine your terms.'

'You think?'

'Fuck knows. Mira?'

Mira was down in her cleavage with the paperclip.

'Mira, what are you doing?'

'Dropped some.'

'We've got to have some girly insight.'

'I'm listening.'

'Would you ever even consider marrying some rich, sleazy, rageaholic normie?'

'Good-looking?'

'Yeah, so what?'

'I don't know. Maybe.'

'Maybe?'

'Probably.'

'Christ, for real?'

'I'm twenty-three. I work in a coffee shop. I don't know my fucking future. There might not even be the concept of marriage by the time I'm ready to tie the knot. And anyway, you two are morons together. Do you know that? What the fuck is a normie? Who are you to use a word like that? You've been going on all day about how most people are idiots. Well, you two are total idiots. So that makes you like most people.'

'Vicious,' said Gary.

'Airtight,' I said.

'Uncalled for,' said Gary. 'All the resin she could scrape. No strings. That wasn't even sex we had, Mira. I can get that sweaty and unhinged by myself.'

'Go ahead,' said Mira.

'Why bother? You have my number.'

'What the hell are you talking about?'

'You have my number. I've given you my number. You have all my numbers and codes. I would sacrifice my life for you to have one decent enchilada the moment you craved it. That's all. God knows this as much as He knows that I don't believe in Him. I don't believe in Him as a favor to Him. The way you should spare a parent too much of your affection at an awkward age.'

'You're fucking ridiculous.'

'You don't even know.'

Gary let his beach towel drop. He had on a pair of garish bikini briefs, some slashing design based on barber poles, peppermints.

'When did you start wearing those?' I said.

'It's European, fool.'

The briefs bore stains, after-leaks of one sort or another. He put out his hands for some deep knee bends.

'Why did you cut off your thumb?' said Mira.

'Sawed it off,' said Gary, huffed into another squat.

'What for?'

'His mother wouldn't let him watch the late show,' I said.

'Not true,' said the Retractor.

'That's what you told me.'

'It's what you wanted to believe.'

'What, then?' said Mira.

'I desired a phantom limb. A physical corollary to my psychic condition.'

'Is a thumb a limb?'

'When you give it to your mother on a napkin it is.'

'You really are a sad sick fuck,' said Mira. 'How about we call your dealer.'

'He's out of town. We could call my sponsor, see what he's holding. It might set a bad precedent, though.'

'Do whatever you feel comfortable doing.'

'I feel comfortable destroying my world for you.'

'Then let's do that,' said Mira. 'Teabag? Plans?'

'Plans?' I said.

Catamounts, do you know that diner over near Van Meter Road? The Garland, it's called. Big shiny morgue of an eatery. It was the Paladin under former ownership. I used to go there for the Sunday special, buckwheat pancakes with blueberries. Now it's the Garland and what you want is the tuna melt deluxe. They do not serve it open-faced, the awful custom in these parts. An open-faced sandwich is a culinary fib, a canard. The Garland knows this, and the secret of a good melt, too. The cheddar is hot. The tuna, room.

Savor it all with a pickle, coleslaw in a fluted cup. There is kindness and central air conditioning in the Garland. Voices do not rise above the porcelain clamor. Murmurs are prized, nullity the civilized ideal.

I'd come here for my refuge. Newly infatuated couples are repellent. They can't decide whether they want you to disappear or stand witness to their giddiness. They use you like a handball wall. Plus, they stink of nookie. I'd come to the Garland for the tuna melt deluxe and to flip through titles on the broken jukebox in my favorite booth. Odes to surf and sun, a token punk tribute to said odes, twangy pleas for liver transplants from deliquescing Nashville millionaires. The jukebox had some Eighties headband anthems on it, too. These last summoned visions of Gary and me marauding around Eastern Valley in my father's Dodge Dart, the cheap speakers hissing up synths, drum machines. That artificial music had authentic feeling if you went fast enough.

A few weeks ago I'd been here at the Garland when I'd noticed a woman in the booth behind me. It was Gary's mother, Clara. Her face was worn, over-rouged, but I knew her right off, asked to join her.

'Sure,' she said.

Colorful folders were fanned out beside her Cobb salad.

'Am I interrupting your work?'

'No, I need the break. This is pro bono anyway.'

'Gary mentioned you'd become an attorney-at-law.'

'That's right. At law. How's Gary doing?'

'He'd love it if you asked him that yourself.'

'I don't foresee that event. He ruined our lives.'

'He ruined his, too. He's your son.'

'I don't dispute that. I have another one, though. He brings me great joy. Funny how Todd has no recollection of Satanic sex rituals.'

'Gary was hypnotized. You can't blame a guy when he's hypnotized.'

'You're a good friend, Lewis. But there's too much baggage right now.'

'Gary will carry it. He wants to carry it.'

I pictured Gary some kind of emotional skycap, a special blazer, a shiny cart for the baggage.

'It's just . . .' said Clara. 'It's just too soon.'

'He needs his mommy back,' I said.

'Then he'd better find a wife.'

'That's kind of cold, don't you think?'

'Maybe,' said Clara. 'Maybe I've always been kind of

cold. I guess as long as I made sure the pantry was stocked and there was enough toilet paper, nobody cared much. I'm not cruel, or mean, or even distant. I'm just cold. I think my body temperature runs low. It's a biochemical thing. I was born this way. The way people are born gay, maybe. After Gary was birthed they thought there was something wrong with him. They whisked him away. Maybe if they'd let me hold him sooner things would be different. Did you notice how I just said birthed?'

'That was kind of cold.'

'This is what I mean.'

'Does Gary's father feel the same way?'

'He really misses Gary. But I can't think about it right now. I don't want to think about it. Gary's okay, right?'

'I guess.'

'Good. I've got to get back to work now, Lewis. Working lunch. Say hi to Gary for me. Or, actually, don't. Say hi to him, but not from me.'

Clara bent back over her folders, her salad, picked at some bacon bits, a sliver of guacamole.

Walking home from the Garland I knew I wouldn't tell Gary about this conversation. What good would it do? Clara didn't want him back in her life. That's supposed to go against nature, I guess, a mother rejecting her son. Even serial killers get chocolate chip cookies, jelly cakes, sent from home. But there's evidence in the other direction, too. I've seen videos of mama pandas sitting on their newborns. They do it a good deal, I gather. The baby comes out looking like a pink mini-frank and, depending on her mood, the mother suckles it, or sits on it, or flings it against the wall. That's why pandas are so rare, I think.

132

A Baby Is Not a Bicycle

Home from the Garland, I found the latest issue of *Catamount Notes* in my mail slot, got myself nooked up on the sofa for a visit with my cougar kin. Some alums had acquired new coordinates of toil on the corporate slave grid. Others were celebrating the advent of poop-smeared approximations of themselves. I'd nearly tossed the issue aside in favor of a longish essay on the return of moral elegance I'd clipped from *MindStyle*, another one of my not-so-free free magazines, when I saw it, that lone boxed item beside the ad for Pittman's Liquors ('Don't even try to get up – We deliver!'). The headline read: TEABAG SPEAKS.

That bastard Fontana! This was worse than the blackball. He'd fiddled with my prose. Here, in its entirety, for those who missed it, is what some ghoulish version of me, concocted in the recesses of Fontana's obscenity of a mind, supposedly wrote:

Hi, everybody! It's Lewis Miner, class of '89, and I'd just like to send a shout out to all you Catamounts and let you in on what's been happening to the old Teabag. I'm doing real well working for a big soft drink company (free sodas on me, friends!) and I've got a nice spread out here in Eastern Valley. I still see some of you Catamounts around town, which is always a pleasure. Mostly I just want to say whassup to Principal Fontana, who got me through some rough spots back in the crazy old days. I'll never forget you, Dr. F.! Peace out, Teabag.

The 'peace out' was an especially nice touch on the part of 'Dr. F.' (How's that dissertation coming, dickfart?) Damn near diabolical. He might have destroyed me in so many ways but he opted for the foolproof: wholesale update rape. Nice try, Fontana, you would-be plow mule, but I will not be broken. One cannot violate verity without consequence, pal.

Catamounts, I was near about to seek out Fontana with some sort of bludgeoning implement when the telephone startled me out of my blood dream. It was Gwendolyn. She sounded far away, her voice tinied down, an ocean or prairie between us. It was how I knew she was near.

'I'm at the airport. Come pick me up.'

136

'It'll take me a while,' I said. 'Why don't you find a taxi? You can afford it.'

'No, I want you to pick me up. Don't rush.'

Airport transit lounges, Gwendolyn once confided, were the only places she'd ever experienced tranquility.

'To be not anywhere,' she'd said. 'Self-contained. Nobody, not even Lenny, making demands.'

Lenny dead, maybe life from here on out was just one long skim latte by the gate.

Gwendolyn had no idea I was in pedestrian exile these days. The airport, it was definitely going to take a while. A few bus rides later – moral elegance, it turns out, never went away – I saw her across the terminal, looking morose in a tube top of festive suede.

'Gwend!' I said.

A national guardsman tracked me from his checkpoint. His cammies, with their neon flecks, appeared designed for casino combat. I wondered if the fucker was profiling my T-shirt. Would I have time to explain that Anal Jihad had been a reasonably bitching South Jersey hardcore band before this guy had me gagged, prone?

Catamounts, I don't have the clothes for the new conditions.

'Gwendolyn,' I said. 'Over here.'

We found some tables near the express food counter. It offered the same food as the regular food counter, just slightly undercooked.

'Taxi cabs are out there,' I said, pointed past the sliding doors. 'See? Those are business travelers. They're forming a line. Some will share a ride into the city. Most of these rides will be exercises in awkward silence, but maybe a few will spark further encounters. An exchange of cell phone numbers. Drinks at the hotel bar. A bold caress at last call. A steamy ride up the elevator. Next thing, somebody, a wife, a husband, in Tucson, say, or even just Albany, has been betrayed. And for what? A momentary cessation of loneliness?'

'You've never been on a business trip, Lewis. You've never been called away on business.'

'I'm ready at any time. Let's get out of here. I feel like I'm being watched.'

'You probably are with that stupid shirt.'

'They had some good songs.'

'Who?'

'Nobody. How are you?'

'How do you think I am? Lenny's dead, Lewis. I can't believe it.'

'It's kind of unbelievable,' I said. 'It's horrible. Look, I know I've already said this but –'

'I've been wandering around here for hours. It's not the same. I don't love airports anymore.'

'People change.'

'Flying in I was next to this monk. He looked kind of like Lenny, but with a beard. He was one of those young monks. He had the robe, the rope belt. He smelled very clean. I don't mean soap clean. Like inside. Like instead of blood he had celery juice or something running through him. Wheatgrass juice, maybe, but not that harsh. More like celery juice. I kept waiting for him to take out special monk food, but he ate the meal, the plane meal. Can you imagine that? A monk? I was mad at him for it. I thought it would muddy up his celery blood. He was writing furiously in a spiral notebook, too, some kind of letter.'

'Why do people always write "furiously"?'

'Shut up, Lewis. You are so fucking insensitive. Just listen to me.'

'Okay. I'm listening.'

'So the monk was writing this letter, not furiously, just writing. Happy? Anyhow, I kept peeking over to read it but his arm was in the way. I caught one part, though. It said, "Brother Michael should stick to brewing ale. He's a fucking clown." I swear to God it said that. Don't you think that's a mean thing for a monk to write? I wanted to ask him what it was all about but he seemed so pissed off. I thought maybe I could tell him about Lenny being dead and maybe he could get some perspective on his rage. I mean, poor Brother Michael. What did he do to deserve this?'

'Do you think the man was really a monk?' I said.

'He had the fucking robe on!'

'No, I just mean –'

'How the hell should I know? Stop interrogating me. I don't want to talk about it.'

'We don't have to. Whatever you want to do.'

'I want to get the fuck out of this airport.'

We took a taxi up the turnpike. Gwendolyn rummaged through her canvas shoulder bag, churned up a bright heap of things: cell phone, cigarettes, magazines, candy wrappers, a tank top, a pair of socks, a thin stack of crisp fifties. The money fanned out against her forearm. A few bills stuck to her skin.

'Look at me,' said Gwendolyn. 'Sweating like a pig. Do my armpits stink?'

I leaned in for a deep whiff.

'I like it.'

'Of course you do, Lewis. Here.'

Gwendolyn peeled some bills from her arm, rubbed them in her armpit, tossed them into my lap.

'What's that for?'

'Car fare. Palimony. Whatever you like. I could do some with my ass, too.'

'Please.'

'Actually, I'm a little low on cash.'

'Do you want to stay with me? Until you know what you're going to do?'

'No, I'm booked at a hotel in the city. We'll go there first. Then you can take this cab home. I just wanted to see you for a minute. And I already know what I'm going to do. I'm going to call up the Board of Monks and report that guy. If he's not a monk they should know about it. If he is a monk they should still know. Either way, he's impersonating an emissary of Christ's love and that's totally fucked up.'

'Somebody has to do something,' I said.

Gwendolyn had a room at one of those hotels downtown where the movie stars stay. Porters in track suits and headsets charged out the smoked glass doors. Come moonfall these men were DJs, but for now they were here for the luggage, the baggage.

'You want me to come up?' I said.

'That's sweet, but no. I have friends meeting me here.'

'Anyone I know?'

'Maybe read about.'

'I see.'

'I don't mean that in a harsh way, Lewis. You know how it is. These people aren't comfortable around strangers. They feel threatened by the average citizen.'

'Now I feel better.'

'I'll call you soon. Enjoy the ride back to Jersey.'

She kissed me on the nose, dipped herself out to the curb. I noticed a new tattoo on her calf, a likeness of Lenny, wreathed in daggers and roses. A tiny pod of bile cruised up my gullet, scout ship for a puke armada. I felt sick, guilty for it. Just as Gwendolyn reached the doors I stuck my head out the cab window.

'Cunt!'

Gwendolyn wheeled.

'Did you hear that?' she said.

'Homeless,' I said, tilted my head up the block.

Gwendolyn shrugged, darted into the darkness of the lobby.

'Man, you lucked out,' said the driver.

'I don't know what you're talking about.'

'I heard what you called her.'

'You heard nothing,' I said, folded a fifty into the plastic tray. When I saw the driver hadn't noticed, I snatched it back.

I walked around in the swelter, the stink, stood stunned at an intersection where a crowd had gathered around a baby in a baby stroller. Citizens debated a course of action. A young woman walked out of a nearby deli with a bottle of Belgian water.

'That's my kid,' said the woman.

She sounded kind of Swedish. A big bum wrapped her up in his arms.

'What are you doing?' she cried.

'You're going to jail,' said an old lady. 'You can't leave your baby out here. This is America. We could have killed it.'

'That's right!' somebody shouted.

'A baby is not a bicycle!'

'I don't understand!'

The mob pressed in on the woman, her baby. I thought they might kill them both. A radio car pulled up to the curb.

'Keep moving,' said the cop inside.

I kept moving, Catamounts.

*   *   *

A Teabag-sighting in the big city is a rare occurrence these days. My last extended sojourn was over a year ago, when I took the bus in from Eastern Valley to hear the writer Bob Price read. I'd been a fan of Bob ever since his first book. It's hard to find anything good to read and I told him as much in a letter to which he never replied. I didn't mind. I wasn't looking for a pen pal. I just wanted to tell the guy he'd done a good job.

The reading was at this downtown bar filled with Nazi memorabilia – flags, armbands, broadsides, identity cards – which the bartender assured me was kitsch.

'Heads up,' I said.

Bob looked sharp in his leathers, read from his story collection *Vegas, Baby*, brought the house down with his prize-winner, 'Good Hands,' the tale of a pregnant teen who dreams of softball greatness even as her world falls apart and she's forced to shoot her emotionally abusive father, then wheel him around in a wheel chair for the rest of his life, or at least the rest of the story.

When the reading was over Bob stood at the bar. We all lined up to buy him beer.

'Mr. Price,' I said.

'Bob,' said Bob.

'My name is Lewis Miner. I wrote you a letter a while back.'

'Oh, yeah. You're the guy with the snake.'

'No, that wasn't me.'

'That was a really cool letter. It meant a lot to me. Sorry I didn't write back.'

'You must be busy.'

'I wouldn't say that.'

'Anyway, I just wanted to say you were great tonight. I'm glad you read "Good Hands." I always thought that story was one of your –'

'You got any cash?'

I'd been working for my father at the Moonbeam that week. I flashed Bob my take-home wad.

'Beautiful,' said Bob. 'You're with me, buddy.'

We took a cab across the river to a place Bob knew, this Dominican dive that served domestic beer, international cocaine. Bob led the way, nodded us past the door goons. He took my money, scooted into line at the DJ booth. I stood off near a dingy red curtain, watched Bob chat with a stringy-haired Eurasian-looking guy behind him. Bob pointed me out for the fellow. They both laughed.

The curtain slid open behind me. A woman stepped

out. She had some kind of gypsy look going with her loose skirts, her beret. Past her was a dim alcove, like a voting booth without the levers. The snorting chamber. This wasn't Sodom, after all. You couldn't just huff rails at the bar. The woman had a nice smile but all I could see were the coke stars in her eyes. The pain of her pathetic life took several hundred million years to reach me. I had my own terrible light to emit.

'I look at you,' said the woman, 'and I see a jealous man. A strict man.'

'Not me. You've got the wrong guy.'

I began to imagine how I'd call Gwendolyn in Hollywood, tell her I'd fallen in love. Maybe Gwendolyn would see the error of her ways, catch the redeye home. She'd find me in bed with this woman. We'd all get high, have a three-way. No needles, though. That would be the rule.

'Yes,' said the woman, 'you are a jealous man. It's easy to tell these things. You are also a handsome man, but you know that already. What are you looking over there for?'

Bob Price was near the DJ booth, about to procure the bounty of the marginal economy. I figured I'd get my drugs and send Bob packing, go back to Beret's place. Fuck three-ways. Fuck my take-home wad. We could have a good life together, me and Beret. Hard, but good. Our children would have rich cultural legacies.

'I'm just looking over at my buddy,' I said.

'You mean acquaintance. I can tell these things.'

'No, he's my buddy.'

'You lie to yourself,' said the woman. 'Sad for such a handsome man.'

'Look where we are,' I said. 'Aren't we all lying to ourselves?'

The woman took my hand, kissed it.

'I never lie,' she said. 'What is your name?'

'Lewis.'

'Luis. My brother is named Luis.'

'They also call me Teabag.'

'Why do they call you that?'

'Long story.'

'Do you like to be called Teabag?'

'Usually not.'

'Why don't you tell them to stop?'

'It's too late.'

'Yes,' said Beret. 'It's much too late. Your so-called buddy is calling you.'

Bob saluted from the corner of the room. He stood there with the stringy-haired guy. The soil samples had been collected. It was time to board the surface module, head for the home globe. I kissed the woman's hand, made for the door. A big kid with dazzling neck gold scoped the corner through the door slit, shoved us streetward. The night sky was moonless over the warehouse roofs.

'This is Zev Kwan,' said Bob. 'We're going to his place to listen to some old hardcore.'

Bob caught me gazing back at the steel door of the bar.

'Something wrong?'

'I was into that chick,' I said.

'What, the coke whore?'

'She's a person.'

'We're all people. She's a coke whore person.'

'Then what are we?'

'White fucks,' said Zev Kwan.

'Where's the hope?' I said.

'It's in my pocket,' said Bob.

We went to Zev's place a few blocks away, did a hundred dollars worth of what was probably baby powder in about seven minutes. The stuff worked wonders for a while. Maybe it was real blow, after all. Zev hauled out his prizes, first pressings of forgotten hardcore pioneers: Painful Discharge, Containment Theory, Semblance of Order. I believe he had some

Anal Jihad, too. Zev wept recalling his first show. He was eleven, his father just dead in a car wreck.

'They poured beer on my head and kicked me in the chest and loved me,' he said.

Bob and I tendered warm nods. Then Bob started talking about his literary career, lambasting this or that critic, or some jealous colleague he suspected had nixed him for a fellowship. It was a bit hard to take, not least of all because I'd never heard of these people and Bob went on as though they were household names.

'Maybe in ten, fifteen years, people will get what I was up to, Miner. But not if these idiots are still around. The gatekeepers, the fucking gatekeepers. That's why I write for the dead. And the unborn.'

'What are you up to, exactly, Bob?' I asked.

'Excuse me?'

'What is it the gatekeepers don't get?'

I didn't hear all of it due to the grinding of my jaw and what I took to be an impending heart attack. Zev had wandered off and now he returned wearing a tie-dyed union suit, a Cub Scout scarf knotted at his throat. He said nothing and began to whack away at his record collection with a field hockey stick. Black shards flew the painted floor.

'Fuck analog!' he said. 'Fuck the warm sound!'

'We're out,' said Bob. 'Zev's gone odd.'

We booked out of there, Catamounts. It was sun-up and the streets were full of vampire interns slithering home to change for work. No coffin sleep in the new-old-new economy.

'Take care,' said Bob, hailed a cab, ditched me in the poison dawn.

There was something fallen about Bob, but I'd still like to track him down, buy him another beer.

We were buddies one night.

More FakeFact Fun

It was too early for coke bars, Catamounts. Besides, I had a feeling Beret had long quit the scene. I caught an afternoon bus back across the river.

I waited for Gwendolyn to call, waited for days.

I wandered my rooms eating gherkin-and-butter sandwiches, drinking beer, radios going in every room. There was news about the war, news about the news. There was news about some dead celebrity's head. It had been frozen for future news.

I called Gary but he wouldn't pick up. I pictured him with Mira in his peppermint panties. Catamounts, was that so wrong? Maybe if I concentrated long enough I'd sense when he'd spent himself, the way people sometimes feel the sudden death of a far-off friend shoot through them, suddenly.

* * *

I fondled myself to fruition eleven times in one day, matching a personal best I'd set in the ninth grade. Sex addiction? Boredom? Despair? They say there is nothing beyond language, and mostly they're right, save the spunk-stiffened balls of paper towel beneath my bed.

Old mark matched, I twitched for a time in semi-waking dream. The hero of my sleep was called The Kid, the best professional masturbator in the East. The Kid took the night train to Kansas City, checked into a grand hotel. He dropped his valise on the bed, snapped it open: jars of fancy pomade, a stack of elegantly monogrammed jerk-off towels. There was a knock at the door. A boy stood there, a neighborhood boy.

'They said you was here.'

'Here I am.'

'Teach me,' said the boy. 'My pa taught me some, but he's dead. Teach me what you know.'

'First you've got to put a picture in your head. And not your ma.'

'Never knew her.'

'Good then. Get a picture. You got a picture?'

'Yes, sir, I do,' said the boy. 'Now what?'

'Never mind now what,' said the Kid, tossed the boy

some coins. 'Go get me some sandwiches. Come back with my change and I'll show you the rest.'

'Thanks, Mister!'

The Kid lay back on the bed, loosened his belt.

'So tired,' he whispered at the wall.

Maybe it was time to settle down, buy that land by the river bend, woo Wilhelmina, the schoolteacher.

How much whang could a man spank in this world?

Meanwhile, on the other side of town, in a room above a barbershop, the Kid's only rival, an enormous man named Buttercup, stropped a borrowed razor. His mother would be coming soon to shave him down.

The phone rang, the showdown postponed.

'Wakey, wakey, eggs and bakey.'

'Who is this?'

'My daddy used to get me up on Saturday mornings like that. Or else he'd say, "Drop your cocks and pick up your socks!" Cocks plural, mind you. Guess you can take the man out of the barracks . . . anyway, I preferred the former.'

'Fontana?'

'How are you, Miner? Long time no update.'

'You bastard,' I said. 'Don't Miner me. How could

you print that trash with my name on it? If I knew anything about the legal system I'd sue your ass. I'd have your ass in some kind of judicial sling.'

'Calm down, Lewis. You need to get out more.'

'Or maybe buy a mule harness.'

Fontana let that one settle.

'Did you hear what I said?'

'I heard you,' said Fontana. 'Don't think I didn't see you boys out there, either. Thing is, I don't give a damn. You were the one in the bushes. I was the one having fun. Remember that. There's nothing they can do to me now, anyway. I'm calling you for two reasons. One is to let you know that I've resigned as editor of *Catamount Notes*.'

'You're kidding me.'

'You can send your screeds to Stacy Ryson from now on.'

'Stacy Ryson?'

'I think she's going to throw it all up on the world-wide net or something.'

'Well, maybe I'll have better luck with her. New times, new blood. Fresh voices from the edges of experience. Of course, she's sort of rearguard in her way, but maybe –'

'Lewis.'

'What?'

'Do you have a job?'

'If you'd ever read my updates you'd know the answer to that question.'

'Fair enough. But really, man. This is an alumni bulletin we're talking about.'

'I know what we're talking about. It's the principle, Principal.'

'Fair enough.'

'Stop saying fair enough.'

'Stop writing updates. For your mental wellbeing.'

'I'll consider it. What was the other reason you called?'

'I need to ask you something. Do you know Hollis Wofford?'

I told Fontana I didn't know any Wofford, but Hollis was a name I'd heard. It was the same Hollis, Catamounts, Gary's sponsor, the coke-dealer phrenologist and Friend of Bill who still maintained loose ties with Satan. Now that Fontana has resigned his editorship, I figure it's your job, Stacy, to worry whether the truth I'm about to divulge, that it was Hollis who jumped Fontana the night he staggered into Brenda Bruno's, belongs in *Catamount Notes*. The beatdown wasn't a matter of cash or powder, either. It was a love deal gone sour. Triangular, or Mexican, with Jazz Loretta at the hinge.

'Christ, I love her,' said Fontana, and I was beginning to feel my old affinities for the man, his respect for the heart's ordeal.

'I don't blame you,' I said.

'What the hell does that mean?'

'It means we're talking about Loretta,' I said.

Dearests Jasmine, Brie, no offense, but Loretta was always the kindest and most radiant Jazz Lovely. Her legwarmers were hand-knit, too. Gathered in the gym for your recitals we Catamounts always knew that in Loretta we had the female equivalent of Mikey Saladin, somebody better than us, sent down maybe to guide us, or else to teach us not to wish past our gifts.

Fontana swore he'd never touched her in her school days. He hadn't seen her for years, forgotten all about her. Then one morning a vision of pure light in a denim dress waltzed out of the Sprout Master with fresh carrot juice, and though this fantasia seemed oddly familiar, he rolled up curbside in his Datsun, announced he was new to town, asked for the way to the Nearmont driving range.

'Jeez, Principal Fontana,' Loretta said. 'That's a killer line. No wonder you have such a reputation.'

'What reputation is that?'

'Melancholy, kind of tragic. Failed-poet-like.'

'That's just my act. I'm really a drunk. And all poets are failed poets. Get in.'

'Why would I want to do that?'

'So you can tell your friends about your weird day. Creepy old Fontana gave you a ride.'

'I don't think you're old.'

'Prove it.'

They drove laps around the block while Jazz Loretta sipped her juice. It was one of those exquisite May mornings, Fontana said, azaleas in the plaza blooming, the sky nearly Caribbean. Fontana was a prince of suburbia in his lime green jeans. They drove and talked and Fontana soon discovered that Jazz Loretta was not pure light, after all, just pure person. She had a real estate license, a kid. The bad marriage was behind her. Hollis had beaten her during and between his binges. Now he was clean and eerie and court-restrained. Loretta had a new life, a gym membership, a book club. She still liked to dance, do other stuff Fontana probably wouldn't know about.

'Try me.'

'Horseplay.'

'Roughhousing? Like what I used to have to break up in the cafeteria?'

'No, I mean bridles, saddles. You know.'

'What do I know? I'm fifty-five years old.'

'Oh.'

'Well, maybe I do,' said Fontana. 'I've often wanted to pull a plow. Be a beast of burden. A water buffalo, something like that.'

'We should start a farm,' said Jazz Loretta, sucked up the last of her carrot juice. Or maybe she slurped it. Or maybe she'd already drained the damn thing. Fontana never specified.

Fontana did admit he'd been seeing Loretta off and on for a few years since that day. Now Hollis looked to be wedging himself in again. He'd called Loretta, said he had money for the kid, told her to swing by Brenda Bruno's, where he was closing a sale. She knew that meant he was working the bar with his little packets. Loretta was wary and Fontana volunteered for the pick-up. Soon as he climbed out of his car, Catamounts, Hollis fell upon him with his war mace, his Ostrogoth Express. The blow would have caved Fontana's head had he not ducked, some vestigial shirk from a stint mentoring manboys in the Northeast Kingdom of Vermont. Still, the mace grazed

Fontana enough to drop him on the blacktop in a heap of throb and blood.

'You think I'd give that bitch another red cent?' Hollis shrieked. 'You're more of a fucking idiot than I figured. You're also a raging alcoholic. A fucking active. I hate actives. Look at your head, you old pickled twat!'

There was more but Fontana missed it from the roaring in his ears. Hollis blazed off in his huge tinted car. Fontana stood somehow, stumbled into the club. That's when Gary and I had steered him out again.

'You were calling for Loretta,' I said. 'But you'd come alone.'

'What is this, kiddy detective hour? I got creamed in the head. I didn't know what I was saying.'

'Where'd you go, though? You just took off.'

'I'm not sure. I woke up on my sofa covered in mud.'

'Nice.'

'Look, I'm sorry about the Teabag Speaks thing.'

'Whatever.'

'No, really. It was wrong. I do stupid things like that. It's sad. It's just me trying to prove I'm appropriate. They've relieved me of my duties, they've got an acting principal in there, and still I want to prove to the school board that I'm appropriate. I want everything difficult to just go away. But it's me. I'm the fucking difficulty.'

'It's okay.'

'Listen, will you keep an eye on Hollis for me? Just give me a heads up if he starts doing war dances. I have a feeling he regrets not finishing me off.'

'I guess so.'

'You're a good kid, Miner. I always liked you. I know I've been erratic. It's this Loretta situation. I just have to calm down. I'll see you at Don Berlin's Party Garden.'

'What are you talking about?'

'The reunion. Five years of classes. Didn't you get the mailing?'

'No.'

'Oh, right. I scratched you off the list in a moment of spite. Your buddy Gary, too. I'll tell Stacy to send some out to you guys.'

'Don't bother.'

'Why not?'

'I'd never go.'

'Come on.'

'Fuck that.'

'I'm the MC.'

'Have a blast, dude.'

'Dude. I don't cotton to dude. I'm still your principal. I'll always be your principal, no matter how chummy we may get.'

'Copy that.'

There was much to ponder here, Catamounts, and there still is as I type this update. I'm worried Stacy Ryson may prove an even worse prude than Fontana, *Notes*-wise. Also, I'm not so certain I want in on this Hollis mess. The man has an Ostrogoth war mace and a severe beef with Byzantium, so to speak. News of this impending reunion bothers me, too. Updates, the occasional run-in with an ex-classmate, that's one thing, or, if you must get technical, two things. A full-on Catamount clusterfuck is a possibility I'd rather not even consider. The only thing worse would be a class party at the Moonbeam. Thank God for Don Berlin, his entrepreneurial mastery over Daddy Miner.

Better not to panic until I finish the next batch of FakeFacts. Penny Bettis has been riding me hard for new material. I delivered her some a few weeks ago with a note apologizing for my comment regarding the size and holiness of her organ, received this curt reply: 'Send more FunFacts, but also please go to Hell.'

The new batch includes some corkers: Charles

Manson kicks back with a freezer-cooled bottle after a Spahn Ranch orgy, composes a song on his acoustic guitar called 'The Pigs are Alright.' Senator Joseph McCarthy pours some cherry-flavored over ice and notes a troublesome reddish tinge. Former Councilman Glen Menninger sips nervously from a liter of New Diet the night he plots his embezzlement of nearly two point three million dollars in Eastern Valley development funds.

This last bit may not fly with Penny Bettis. Glen Menninger is not what they call in the ad world a life form, nor is he, as far as I know, a thief. But he is a politician, so you've got to figure he's done something horrific. That's my theory, anyway. Besides, when Glen was editor of the school paper he killed an exposé I wrote accusing Superintendent Murnighan of torching the field house for the insurance payout. Glen wanted proof like we were real journalists or something. It was just the damn school paper, for God's sake. Fuck Glen Menninger. That's a theory of mine, too.

Anyway, Catamounts, it's late now and your faith-ful updater is getting sleepy. I'll send my FakeFacts off to Penny in the morning. Sometimes I wonder if she knows I make them up. Sometimes I wonder if she cares. It makes me sick in a way, because I do believe in the truth, in historical accuracy, the light it can shine on our shadowy puppet play of an existence and all that. Our nation wallows in the dark too much, eating cheese puffs, touching ourselves. We think we're not fat and that we're a nation. It's sad, and I know fools like me are partly to blame. But I console myself with the thought that *Fizz* is an in-house newsletter. It's not as though kids see it. What kids do see is that copy of *Catamount Notes* you've left beside the toilet in that wicker magazine rack, the one you maybe bought on sale at the River Mall. These young malleables make their little number twos and pore over all your Catamount lies about what enchantments await a faceless node on the global motherboard, what comforts are guaranteed to those who gleam with this belief: that we are all of us blessed with talents, skillsets, and if we just stay the course, apply a little elbow grease, ride out the bumps and grinds of decreasing economic indicators, life will shine like our new 'professional' kitchens.

Dream on, worm bait.

No Closer to Resolving the Mays Debate, or, Why I Even Bother

A man so old he's got his baby teeth again stood
behind me in the supermarket today. He clutched a
sack of potatoes, wore a baseball cap that read: 'Ask
About Our BJs.'

Catamounts, I note this merely as precaution.

Objects too close may be a mirror.

'Nice hat,' I told the man.

'Is it a ball team?' he said. 'Found the thing lying
around the house. One of my grandkids must have left
it on the last visit. Odd name for a ball team, though.
The BJs.'

'They're good this year.'

'Expansion team? I never heard of them. I only
follow the National League. They have what's his
name, Saladin, with the steroids.'

'Silly rumor,' I said.

'Don't care either way,' said the man. 'It's the heroin what worries me. What are the kids going to think when a junkie jacks a hundred dingers?'

'Good point.'

'I watch a lot of sports. I'm a veteran, too. I was at Normandy.'

'The Greatest Generation.'

'The what? Oh, that's a load of crap. We weren't so great. Most of us were morons like you or me. We got lucky. Hitler beat himself. Bet you don't even know who Hitler was.'

'Which Hitler do you mean?'

'You're a funny young man. What's your name?'

'Lewis.'

'I'm Auggie. Auggie Tabor.'

'Any relation to Judy Tabor? The teacher?'

'That's my daughter.'

'I had her in high school. How is she?'

'She's fine. She's living down in Jacksonville, Florida. Right there on the beach. Married a rich fellow, a developer. Looks nineteen with her tan and her new tomatoes.'

'Excuse me?'

'Augmentation of the ta-tas.'

'Jeez, I can't imagine that. She was always so

serious. She's the one who taught me about the absurdity of existence.'

'Little Judy's much happier now. I never liked her reading all those depressing books, those Frenchies and such. She's frolicsome by nature.'

'Well, say hello for me.'

'Going down there in a few months. Her stepson is teaching me to surf.'

'Okay, then, guess I'll see you around, Auggie.'

'A pleasure. And by the way, I lied.'

'What's that?'

'I know what a goddamn BJ is. I was at Normandy, for Christ's sake.'

Bad news on the deadbeat front: my landlord's clan held a council, voted Pete meek. Shamed, undone, he's fashioned a new persona: bagman, baby tough.

He banged on my door this morning in a dark silk shirt.

'Pete,' I said.

'Pay up,' said Pete.

'You know I will,' I said. 'What's gotten into you?'

'Nothing's gotten into me. You owe, you pay. I forgive you for taking advantage of me when I was but a neophyte, but I'm stepping up now. I'm owning my ownership. I'm a landlord. From a long line of land-lords. I have ways of settling this situation. I'm hooked up. Hooked up with interesting people. Hollis Wofford, for example.'

'I know Hollis Wofford,' I said.

'So he tells me. Hollis is a partner of my family now. We've joined economic forces. That makes him, by extension, your landlord, too.'

'You should steer clear of that guy,' I said. 'There are some who consider him an evolutionary cul de sac.'

'I don't know what that means,' said Pete. 'And I don't take advice from renters.'

'I can't believe this new attitude, Pete. I'm a little shocked.'

'I advise you to get over your shock.'

'Look,' I said. 'I want to pay you. I always do pay you, eventually. But you can't threaten me. Ever hear of tenants' rights?'

'You need a lease for that.'

'I have a lease.'

'Ran out last month.'

'I thought we had an agreement. An understanding.'

'A nod and a handshake won't cut it these days. Do I refer to my SUV as a horseless carriage?'

'I'm not sure I follow.'

'The earth turns. Terms evolve. What passed for civilization before is an abomination to us now. Nostalgia is fear smeared with Vaseline. Think about it.'

Pete turned, stalked off down the street, a new languorous gangster strut. He stooped to tie his shoe and I saw the bulging sheen of it tucked in an ankle holster: his cell phone.

I heated up some split-pea soup in the kitchen, thought about it. Maybe I could call Gary, borrow from his retractor trust. It's a bitch to owe your best friend money, Catamounts. The awkwardness is bad enough, and then you have to pay the jerk back. What about Penny Bettis? I could beg her for an advance, throw in some extra FakeFacts, gratis. Clark Gable gargled with the stuff to stifle his halitosis. Skip James cut a rival pimp with a broken bottle of it. Or how about a TrueFact: it rots your fucking teeth.

I called the Retractor.

'Hey, man,' I said. 'Just calling to see how you're doing. I was thinking of you today. How are things with Mira?'

'We've been making the beast with two separate parts that don't touch at all.'

'Sorry to hear it.'

'She's playing hard to find. She shows up late at night. What's wrong with me, Lewis? Guys my age have careers, children. I'm being toyed with by a twenty-three-year-old. I'm a joke. It's the young skin. That's all it is. Too bad she's not fourteen. That would have been something. Something wrong, but still. What was that?'

'What?'

'The sound you just made.'

'A laugh. I laughed.'

'Is that a new laugh?'

'That's my laugh.'

'You've been working on a new laugh.'

'The hell I have.'

'Fucking poseur,' said Gary, hung up.

The phone rang a few seconds later.

'It's definitely a new laugh,' said Gary.

'Listen,' I said. 'I need to ask you a favor.'

'How much?'

Tonight the evening news ran some footage of Mikey Saladin. The man stood shirtless, bandaged, before the press corps. These vipers hissed about a trade, their dry invisible tongues slithering over Mikey's great veiny arms, his granite abs, though I can't prove it, of course, their tongues being invisible.

'I'll always be a Jersey boy,' said Mikey, 'no matter what uniform I wear.'

A viper from the network of record inquired about retirement rumors.

'Retire from what?' said Mikey. 'From baseball or from banging your wife?'

'And what about banned substances?' said another.
'Have they enhanced your performance?'

'About as much as that twelver of Schlitz you drink every night has enhanced yours, you fat fuck.'

His insolence was warranted, Catamounts. These media fiends think their microphones are electric shock sticks. Sick of their softness, they hope to jolt their betters. Bat Masterson would be appalled. He'd strap his irons back on, catch the next coach to Abilene.

As for Mikey Saladin, he might be old for an Estonian ice dancer, but not for a power-hitting short stop. His slugging percentage is up because of anabolics, growth hormones? How about wisdom, maturity, the resolution of a grueling custody battle? Go ahead, drive Mikey from the game. Banish what shines, revel in the antics of dullards. Not only Mikey will suffer. Think about the kids from his Sacrifice Fly Foundation. I suppose you'd prefer they were back on the streets so you could buy your party favors from them, rent their hot little mouths on the West Side Highway. You'd best pray Mikey Saladin doesn't catch you. The man has no mercy for your kind.

Some of you are maybe wondering why I persist with these updates. A few of you, perhaps, pass the whipped potatoes at table, remark: 'Is Teabag a fucking twit, or what?' (Or would, if you had any inkling of my futile toil.)

Worry not, Catamounts. I might be a twit – I'm uncertain of the parameters – but I do not labor under any illusion my updates will grace the pages, or, scratch that, the screens, of our beloved alumni bulletin. Fontana was correct in his prediction that *Catamount Notes*, under the Ryson regime, would be an electronic affair. I received an email today announcing the site was officially live. The same old lies. Now they are linked to other lies. You can leap between them.

Instead consider these ramblings an antidote, the anti-update, continuous and true, if not always factual. Someday, perhaps, my missives will serve some edifying purpose. Archeologists will look to the Teabag Letters as a source text in their quest for Catamount meaning. Our lives and dreams may feel insignificant now, but the future could dispute our puniness. Menninger may become a universal synonym for glad-handing sleazeball. A Jazz Loretta might denote a sort of woolen legging. Our descendants could very well reside in a domed city-state called New Fontana, with statues of Mikey Saladin in every public square.

Or, of course, not.

Many are the ages of man that have meant nothing at all, as Ms. Tabor once put it in Introduction to World Literature. Maybe she was crashing hard on diet pills, but she had a point.

It matters little in the end, Catamounts.

Even the semi-forgotten times have had their Teabags, their town criers, totem carvers, scribes, skalds.

Hear ye, hear ye, the Jaguar King died in the sickle moon, the year Reed-Seven. The honey jars numbered ten and two. Leif Leifson jumped from the dragon ship, slew many shitloads of Jutes.

These are the Catamount dead: Dean Longo (OD, disillusionment), Enrique Herrera (drunk driving, loneliness), Will Paulsen (drunk driver, bad luck), Tina Chung (cancer, radon), Shandra Baum (cancer, anger), Chip Gallagher (cirrhosis, pending).

* * *

Tonight I took a walk down Venus Drive, cut through the woods to the Pitch-N-Putt parking lot. The stars were out, what stars we get in our dirty sky. Some old golf carts stood near the field house, more for after-hours ball retrieval than for play. Nearmont has an eighteen-hole course and a state-of-the-art driving range. The Eastern Valley Pitch-N-Putt, with its culverts of broken glass and unmowed greens, must have been designed expressly for trespassing, teen sex, vandalism.

Gary and I used to come here to drink beer and smoke bones and talk about the future, when we'd drink beer and smoke bones with girls. Gary was going to be a rock star, or a rock journalist, maybe both.

'I don't want to be a superstar,' he said. 'Just a star. I want to have influence. I want to be the visionary all the hacks steal from.'

'Why would you want to be that?' I said.

'It's cooler,' said Gary. 'Maybe I won't even start a band until I'm twenty. You shouldn't even attempt to rock until you've run the gamut of human experience. All of my records will include essays I've written about why the record rocks.'

'I don't know if that's such a good idea.'

'Wilkerson liked it.'

Glave was a joke to us even then, but he did have a

nice Les Paul Sunburst, and Gary had jammed with him once in Glave's basement.

'He's got chops,' said Gary. 'But no heart.'

'No heart,' I said.

'But chops,' said Gary.

Sometimes others came to park and smoke with us. Randy Pittman would drive up in his Pittman Liquors family liquor van, offer us in-state vodka, bitch about his vicious father. He had a plan to run off with his Sousaphone, join the Navy marching band.

'I need the discipline,' he said.

One night he came by with a bottle of apricot schnapps and we got sick on the stuff while he told us how his father really wasn't all that mean, just a little tweaked from his tour on a patrol boat in Vietnam. Old Man Pittman was only a cherry when another piece of new meat caught a bad case of nerves. Everybody got scared Charlie would hear the sobs, the whimpers. A corporal named Van Wort slit the kid's throat, dumped him into the Mekong. Randy's father made Randy swear to keep the whole thing secret, but Randy figured he could trust us. We didn't know anybody in the Navy, and who'd believe us, anyway, a couple of ass clowns from Eastern Valley?

'What a load,' said Gary.

'True fucking story,' said Randy.

'Well, the patrol boat's a nice touch, but really, I doubt your dad told you all of that. For one thing, guys who were actually in the shit talk squat about it. That's just how it is.'

'I'm his son.'

'He still wouldn't tell you.'

'You can't speak for everybody.'

'No, I can't, dude, and neither can you.'

'What the hell does that mean?'

We never really got to hear what that meant because suddenly there was a loud crack from out past the woodline.

'Shit,' said Randy Pittman.

The kid was bleeding from all these tiny shallow holes in his chest.

We drove him to the Eastern Valley clinic in my father's Dart. Randy bled all over the seats, but they were vinyl and I didn't mind. He wasn't dying and this was a nice vacation from our usual Pitch-N-Putt bone routine.

The way the doctor figured it, or whoever the guy in the white coat who tweezed out the buckshot was, somebody had fired on us from far off. The pellets had petered out right as they hit Randy. The police never found the shooter, though they did undertake a token manhunt, once through the trees with a flashlight. They also issued a sketch of the suspect, a suave-looking black man with slicked-back hair. We had no idea where they came up with that one. It looked copied from an old Duke Ellington album sleeve.

Later we figured it was Georgie Mays who'd fired on us, this nutjob from Nearmont who'd been bragging all week about his new shotgun. He'd never be brought to justice, though. Georgie's family went back to revolutionary war times, descended from the guy on the Nearmont town seal, Matheson Mays, who either spied on the British or spied for them, scholars had never decided. Matheson Mays was hanged before he could clear up the debate.

It didn't matter now. The man was on the town seal and the Mays name was under municipal protection. Besides, everyone was too riled up about the gangs of dead black jazz geniuses apparently roving our district with heavy armaments to give the Mays connection much thought. You may recall Glen Menninger's editorials in the school paper about the need to balance tolerance with safety, arguing we should err on the side of safety. I wrote a short rebuttal, which he tried to pull, big surprise.

But most of our times out here were not so eventful.

It was usually just me and Gary and maybe Randy Pittman or Dean Longo. We'd sit around and talk about the unrelenting boredom of our town. The unrelenting ferocity of the world was a different problem. Only Dean Longo found a permanent solution, a bag of dope that, according to the coroner, would have killed a rhino. I think about Dean sometimes, not that I ever knew him so well, because we all dabbled in rhino death, and Gary did more than that, got himself a habit that was scary and embarrassing at the same time. We were all so grim and invincible then. I guess we figured we were trying so hard, there was no way we could die. But you can always die.

It took me an hour to walk to In Your Cups. The notion of a car seemed newly appealing. Maybe my father was right about this being a car state, a car system, and how you can't buck a system you're not in, or under, that's not bearing down on you.

Daddy Miner was behind the bar with Victor, the new bartender. I considered sharing my ontological breakthrough with the old man, but I'm not an utter fool. I'm not an utter anything. I pulled a stool up to the leather-padded bar. Down the far end of it Chip Gallagher appeared to be having a lover's spat with his double Scotch. I decided to leave him to it, asked Victor for a beer.

'That's not on the house,' said my father.

He was twisting a key in the register. He twisted it some more and the key broke off.

'Goddamnit!'

'Don't know your own strength, Mister M.,' said Victor.

'No, Victor, I do know my own strength. I'm a weak piece of shit. This key is just a weaker piece of shit. They don't even make them out of metal anymore. I don't know what this is. Some kind of alloy.'

'That's still metal,' said Victor.

'What are you, a fucking smelter?'

'No, but I blew one at a club once.'

'You people are always bragging,' said my father. 'I've had more flap candy than you could shake a stick at. You don't hear me yapping about it all day.'

'Yes, I do,' said Victor.

'Well, I'm the exception. I'm the exception which proves the rule.'

'What's the rule again?' I said.

'I don't know,' said my father. 'I'm all confused now. I can't get into the register. I wish I could just smash it open. Get me some steroids. Like that Saladin kid.'

'That's just gossip,' I said. 'Mikey's the best player in the game.'

'Yeah, but the question is, which game? It's not baseball anymore.'

'You're dead on, Mister Miner.'

'Thanks for agreeing, Victor, but you still can't have Wednesday off.'

'I'll work Wednesday,' I said.

'We don't need a barback.'

'I'll pour,' I said.

'Sure you will.'

'I know the drinks.'

'You think that's all this is?' said my father. 'A rang-a-tang can learn the drinks. It's not the drinks. It's knowing what to do when the shit goes down. It's about quiet strength. A light but firm touch. Ask Victor here.'

'Touch lightly but firmly,' said Victor.

'What is it with you people and innuendo? You're out, you're proud, I'm proud, calm down. You don't have to reduce everything to the baloney pony.'

'You don't have to leer at every woman under seventy who walks in here.'

'I said I was the exception,' said my father.

'Okay, then I'm an exception, too,' said Victor.

'Fine. We're both exceptions.'

'But don't use the phrase "you people." You haven't earned it.'

'You don't know what I've earned,' said my father.

'Let me pour,' I said.

'Absolutely not,' said my father.

'Dad, nothing ever happens here. Everyone's pleasant.'

'That's how they lull you.'

'Who?'

'The bringers-down of the serious shit. And I can't be here to protect you. I have a vast empire to survey.'

'Okay,' I said. 'Forget I asked.'

'I may need you at the Moonbeam soon. I'll let you know.'

'Fine.'

'Maybe I won't, though, if that barracuda Don Berlin keeps it up.'

'How's that?'

'Nothing.'

My father went back to his office, fled the rush of suits from the bus station. These were family men, or else anxious types who'd lost their nerve, their wolf moves, for the city bars. One of them I'd seen before, a bond specialist who favored worsted vests. He sat in the corner talking to a familiar cascade of hair.

'Mira!' I called.

Catamounts, I must confess I had thoughts of carnal betrayal vis-à-vis Gary when Mira came over to greet me, that thrum she gave off, her tawny arms hooped in silver, the voluptuous green wit of her eyes. People say the truly beautiful don't know how beautiful they are. People also say the meek shall inherit the earth, that anybody can be president, that someday they'll make androids you'll want to fuck. Maybe they will, but where are you going to get the money for the androids? Those prices, you might as well be president.

'Teabag, how are you?'

'A-okay, Liquid Smoke.'

'Are you going to buy me a drink?'

Victor swept by with a bottle, topped off Mira's vodka tonic.

'On the house.'

'Thanks, V-Man.'

'V-Man?'

'We go back. I was here last night.'

'With Gary?'

'No, not with Gary.'

'Oh.'

'You know what I read yesterday? Well, I didn't read

it, but the man who told me, he read it somewhere. You know starfish?'

'Is that a band?'

'No, I mean, like, starfish. The ocean creature.'

'Resting on the ocean floor.'

'Right. This guy told me you're not supposed to call them starfish anymore. It's, like, derogatory. You're supposed to call them sea stars.'

'Why is that?'

'Because they're not really fish. They're something else. Mollusks, maybe. That type of genus. I don't know the technicalities.'

'That's weird,' I said. 'But I guess it's reasonable. If they're not fish, I mean.'

'Fucking thought police,' said Mira.

I laughed. It wounds me to admit it, Catamounts, but my laugh did sound different now, a tad fakey. Was it due to some reaction when it hit the atmosphere, a sine-wave vapor-type deal? Damn me for not paying more attention to Mrs. Strobe sophomore year. I guess I just tuned out after I aced that quiz darkening bubbles at random. Mrs. Strobe kept me after class, hovered over me in her serape, her heavy jewelry, told me I had a future in science. This scared me, Catamounts. I kept picturing myself stuffed into a mist-shrouded pod, genetically spliced with Vinnie Lazlo.

I tanked the rest of the semester.

'Still seeing Gary?' I said to Mira now.

'Here and there. Mostly there. Now and then. Sometimes. I'm still intrigued by him, sort of.'

'So, what's the problem?'

'He's a basket case, maybe? You know what he's been talking about? Retracting his retraction.'

'I know.'

'Will he have to give the money back?'

'I have no idea.'

'I told him he should go find Doc Felix, confront him.'

'That's crazy.'

'I told him he should bring you along. He's not well. He needs an interest. Something beyond the pursuit of immediate gratification. A passion.'

'Like model boats?'

'Not a hobby. A passion.'

Mira scoped the room, maybe for the starfish man.

'Real boats?' I said.

'Keep thinking, Teabag.'

Catamounts, I walked home from In Your Cups filled with visions of Mira's hair sweeping across my skin, my lips buried in her sweaty golden rabbit butt. Shameful, sure, but just a vision. My loyalty lies with Captain Thorazine, and besides, Mira didn't seem too keen on me. I chalked my lust up to Gwendolyn's proximity. She still hadn't called, and her hotel wouldn't put me through.

I guess I'm not famous enough for standard operator service.

How Cowboys Could Be Sad

It occurs to me, Catamounts, sitting here composing this latest update, that someday, if and when the collected works of Lewis Miner ever see the light of day, some futuristic editor-type might attempt to assemble these dispatches in a certain manner, to, for example, tell a story, or else effect some kind of thematic arrangement of interwoven leitmotifs: Work, Love, Masturbation, Gary.

This would be a grave mistake.

There are no themes, no leitmotifs. There is no story.

What's all this story-telling stuff, anyway? Stories pour out of us daily, and most of them might not unfairly be lumped under the taxonomic heading: More Boring Than Your Neighbor's Spork Collection. Ever notice how whenever anybody says, 'Hey, have you got time for a story?' or 'You simply must hear this story' or even, in that down-to-business style of today, 'Quick story,' you find yourself wishing some wheezing and pustular people-snatcher would burst through the wall and carry you off to some dank cave to feast on your viscera?

There's a reason you wish this.

Nobody likes a story, especially a good one.

Nobody likes a story, that is, unless he's in it. Are you familiar with that searching twitch on people's faces when you relate some tale to them?

Where am I in this? they are thinking. When is he going to get to me?

Maybe it wasn't always this way. Maybe when the Cro-Mags sat around the cookfire scaring the crap out of each other with yarns about saber-tooth tigers, or even pustular people-snatchers roving the outer dark, those in the audience had the opposite in mind: Please, please, pantheon of local animistic deities, please don't let me be anywhere near this story.

But it's all very different now.

It must be the video games.

My trouble, Catamounts, is that I am very much in this, at least as far as Hollis Wofford is concerned. Last night, back from In Your Cups and my boozy, dreamy walk beneath the lights of the county road, I found the man waiting on my stoop. He seemed steeped in painful thought, wore mustard-colored driving gloves, rolled a bottle of mineral water between his palms. He'd parked up on the sidewalk, more statement, it seemed, or automotive jeer, than bad parallel job.

I wondered if he had his Ostrogoth war mace in the trunk tonight.

'Hollis. What are you doing here?'

'I'm sitting,' he said slowly. 'I'm chilling. Maxing and relaxing. Cold-lamping, as the poet once said.'

'Did you want to see me about something?'

'Just checking on one of my properties.'

'I heard the news. Congratulations on your new business venture. How's your old business venture going?'

'You're very cheeky, Larry. Actually, I was just conferencing with your neighbors. Have you met them?'

'Briefly.'

'I'm trying to help them achieve a moment of clarity.'

'You're selling them drugs.'

'Some people have to hit bottom before they can . . . well, hell, you know. Look at you. Look at your head.'

'There's nothing wrong with my head.'

'Looks like a hippo's hemorrhoid.'

'I'm a buck turtle.'

'Come again?'

'Does Gary know you're here?' I said.

'What's Gary got to do with it? I just figured as long as I was here I'd wait around, see if I could talk to you.'

'I didn't even think you knew who I was.'

'I don't. Not really. I know you're Larry or Teaball or something. I know you talk to that fuck Fontana.'

'He was my high school principal.'

'My wife's, too. You know my wife Loretta. She knows you. Sweet and dumb, she said about you. I think those were her words. But Gary tells me you're some kind of writer. I always thought writers were smart.'

'Not the dumb ones.'

'I could tell you some stories. You could write them down, make a mint.'

'Sure that's a good idea?'

'You could change my name,' said Hollis, tucked his shades into the collar of his collarless shirt. 'I could be Wallace. Wallace Hofford. Does that sound too Jewish?'

'I don't need your stories. I don't even like stories.'

'Screw you, then. I'll get a pro. Loretta always said I had good stories.'

'Aren't you under court order not to see her?'

'Justice is fallible,' said Hollis.

He peered into the water bottle as though proof of his belief were in it. Or maybe he was just enjoying the bubbles.

'I should really go inside,' I said.

'That would be your personal choice.'

'Was there some message you wanted me to relay?'

'A message? Relay? How does that work?'

'Do you want me to tell Fontana anything?'

'Tell him to stay away from my wife,' said Hollis, and for a moment I thought of Lenny, how he'd never been able to sell a line like that. Poor dead Lenny.

'Ex-wife,' I said.

'Only in a legal sense. I still fuck her sometimes. I still know what to say to make her cry and hate me but need me more than ever. Doesn't that make her my wife?'

'That's sick.'

'Sick? You ever been married?'

'Almost.'

Hollis cackled, stood.

'I will, for real, kill the fuck,' he said. 'If it comes to that.'

He started down the stoop, clipped me with his

elbow on the way to the curb. Schoolyard stuff. Bullies grow up, too. Grow old, stay bullies. Buy cars, car insurance. Borrow tools, have biopsies.

Ensconced in his machine, Hollis lowered the passenger window, saluted, a sort of wistful Sieg Heil, gunned into speed.

I knocked on Kyle and Jared's door. Jared answered, shirtless, jittery.

'We'll turn it down,' he said.

'Turn what down?'

'The music.'

'You're not playing any music.'

'Oh,' he said.

'I was just checking in. Hollis was hanging out with you, right?'

'Hollis. Yes, Hollis. Six letters.'

Jared stuck his hands in his armpits, gibbered under his breath.

'Are you okay?' I said.

'Me? I don't know, man. How can I know if I'm okay? How can I make that judgment objectively? I'll tell you what I do know. That meteor, the one that took out the dinosaurs? Kyle and I were just talking about it. A rock from space. A piece of masonry, right? A piece of free masonry. Are you following? Stop me if this is obvious to you. Corn comes from the Andes. Andy Griffith was the sheriff of Mayberry. Omar Sharif was in *Lawrence of Arabia*. Mayberry. A-berry. Arabia. Coincidence? This is shit nobody's looking at right now. This is shit they'd kill us for if they knew we knew.'

'I won't tell anybody,' I said.

'I haven't even told you yet.'

There was a message from Gwendolyn on my answering machine. Alums familiar with my feelings for this woman will not be surprised to learn I fell to my knees and kissed the perforations of the speaker as her frayed voice squeezed through them, ran my tongue along the rims of those tiny holes. I'm a man of great emotion, and I'm not afraid to show it, especially when I'm alone.

'Lewis,' she said. 'Oh, Lewis. I'm here at the hotel. And you're there, aren't you, Lewis? Oh, you must despise me. I despise me. But not like you must despise me. I've treated you so bad.'

'Badly!' I shouted at the machine.

'I should have just left you alone. But part of me still wants to be with you. But that's the part of me I don't want to be part of anymore. Talking in circles,

I guess. Sorry. Or, no, these are more like parallelograms. Or those things, what are those things? That overlap? That are somehow separate but overlap? It's something from geometry. Oh, I don't know. I'm so tired. I just want to curl up in my room tonight. My room is three fourteen. Isn't that bizarre? Lenny's birthday was four thirteen. Nothing happens by chance. This room is my haven. I'm so damn tired, Lewis. I've been going out every night. Lenny's old friends. I miss you, kind of. I still want you in my life. Or, I still want to think of you as somebody who's in my life. Do you remember when we met? Toronto? The aphorism slam? I want to say we were so innocent then, but we weren't, were we? We knew what we wanted. You wanted to fuck me. I wanted to win the aphorism slam. I love aphorisms. They're so terse. Is terse the word? But here I am yammering. Shows what I know about terse, right? Oh, fuck it, I did love you, Lewis. I wanted the little things with you. I was scared of the world. But now I know I like the big things better. I learned that from Lenny. He knew how to reach up for the brass balls, the big ring. And now that he's dead, I have to honor Lenny. I have to carry on his legacy. Does that sound crazy? Maybe it's crazy but it's the way it is and I'm –'

The machine cut her off. The beep blasted my ear.

'What?' I shouted. 'What are you?'

I found the number on my Caller ID, dialed it back, told the desk Gwendolyn's room number. The clerk put me right through.

'Hello?'

'What the fuck was that?' I said.

'Oh, hi, Lewis.'

'Nice speech.'

'Sorry. I guess I got a little carried away. What did I say?'

'Come over, you can listen to it. I've got it on tape.'

'Jesus, you have that on tape? You wouldn't do anything with that, would you?'

'Gwendolyn,' I said. 'You are not famous. Nobody cares. Nobody even remembers Lenny. He was a blip.'

'He was not a blip, Lewis.'

'Yes, a blip.'

'He was my brother.'

'The radar man doesn't care, Gwendolyn.'

'Radar man?'

'The fucking blip tracker!'

'What? Oh, Christ. It's okay, Lewis. I forgive you. It's good for you to air your grievances. It's good for you to clear the air of your . . .'

'Grievances?'

'No, fuck, I can't think of the word. I smoked too much pot. Trying to come down off the –'

'I still love you,' I said.

'Oh, Lewis.'

'No, wait.'

'Wait, what?'

'Scratch that.'

'What do you mean?'

'Something just clicked. When you said, "Oh, Lewis." I felt this seismic shift.'

'I thought it was a click.'

'I don't still love you. I don't still love you at all.'

'Really?'

'Really.'

'Say it again.'

'I don't love you, Gwendolyn.'

'I can't believe it. I'm shocked.'

'I advise you to get over your shock.'

'Lewis?'

'Yes?'

'Come to the city tonight.'

Catamounts, I wish I could say that was the end of that, but I guess I was still dreaming of our future together, our basil, our mint. Maybe I was my mother's son, living in the fog of tomorrows, shutting my eyes for the retinal burn of snapshots never snapped. Why couldn't Gwendolyn just settle for me? Don't we all settle, Valley Cats? Haven't you all settled, weighed the trade-offs, shaved down your desires for what was there, what worked, what wasn't actively bent on your destruction? Resigned yourselves to the ear hair, the nipple hair, the watery farts, the fat behind the knees? The shoes in the doorway, the dishes in the sink? Isn't that what love is all about? Don't the experts tell us so? Don't the people on the street concur? Don't we all settle, barter our fevers for a partner, a mutual fondler, a talking animal companion? Catamounts, why couldn't she settle for me?

Because she's a dumb selfish cunt, I thought. Because she's a sick, sad, broken thing who can only love what won't love her back.

I caught the last bus to the city.

Gwendolyn's room was mostly bed, beige. Wall art on the walls. Sea scenes, Aegean. A cactus on a shelf. Soft rock drifted from the clock radio on the bedstand. Thick candles flickered, lilac, chemical. Gwendolyn led me to the bed, laid me down, undressed me, herself, straddled me, raised a slender glass pipe to her lips.

'What are you doing?'

'Smoking crack. They call this the glass dick.'

I knocked the dick from her mouth. It bounced off the bed.

'Smoke crack on your own time,' I said. 'Not when we're having break-up sex.'

'Sorry.'

I took her in my arms and we rocked softly to the soft rock for a while. Gwendolyn licked my neck. I bit her hair, her breasts, slid down and nibbled, swirled, easy with the teeth, hard with the tongue. I hadn't eaten pussy in a while. It's like falling off a bicycle. You never forget.

'Lewis,' she said. 'Oh, Lewis.'

'Does that feel good?'

My tongue was strong, Valley Kitties, a suave darting thing. Gwendolyn began to buck and shudder.

'Oh, Lewis, yeah, Lewis. Shit, yeah.'

'You like that?'

'Oh, Lewis! Lewis!'

'Who's Lewis?' I said, leapt into a squat. 'My name's Lenny! I'm your dead brother Lenny! I'm dead but I can still suck pussy like a pussy king!'

'What the fuck!'

'Lenny! Lenny!'

I stroked up my load, fired it point blank into her eyes. The act startled both of us, I think. She blinked the spunk away, rolled over. The bed bobbed. I stayed in my squat, studied the mole on her back.

'Uh, oh,' I said.

Gwendolyn pressed her face into the pillow.

'Go,' she said.

'Baby, I'm sorry. I took it too far.'

'You stupid bastard. Took what too far? You're insane.'

'The parade!'

'The parade? Just get the hell out of here. Before I hurt you.'

'Baby, we've hurt each other too much already.'

'I don't mean that way. Baby. I mean so you bleed.'

I dressed, crossed the room to the door with the slow mournful swagger I'd practiced for this day. Pride and heartache. How cowboys could be sad. Two-bit cowboys full of bone-hard sorrow. For because of what people do to each other. For because of all the loneliness in the world. Now a sudden sob thrashed through me, some moist beast flippering up through my chest. It doubled me up and I sank to my knees, inched back over to the bed. Gwendolyn stared up at the TV bolted to the wall. Her cheek still bore a sticky sheen. I shoved my head in her lap.

'There, there,' she said.

'Oh, fuck . . .'

'It's okay.'

Huge slabs of me, my whole gelatinous baby Tea being, flobbed out on the counterpane.

'Cry it out, Lewis.'

'You cry,' I cried. 'Why do I have to cry?'

'I'm all cried out. I've been crying for months.'

'Fuck you.'

'You tried that already.'

I could hardly breathe for the tears, the snot. I tried to flush the burn from my eyes, glanced up at Gwendolyn, the delicate swoop of her jaw, her plump lips, her nose, her beautiful nose, Hazel's nose, really, my mother's nose, more flared. I'd noticed the resemblance before, of course, but in the throes of new love you drive such thoughts from your mind. Probably now I'd convince myself I'd only ever loved her for her nose. This absurdity would vanish, too.

The man on the TV talked feverishly. The picture switched to a shelled village somewhere. Corpses lay in heaps near a stone well.

'I guess that puts things in perspective,' I said.

'You'd think it would. But it never does.'

'I go now,' I said.

'Be good to yourself,' said Gwendolyn.

It was an odd thing for a person about to smoke crack alone in a hotel room to say, but I believe she meant it.

That was the last I saw of her alive, Catamounts. I've seen her tons on TV, though.

I rode the elevator down with a famous white rapper in a black mink body suit.

'I'm Teabag,' I told him.

''Sup Teabag.'

'Got the name in school. It was kind of random. I wasn't even the weakest kid. Vinnie Lazlo had no hands.'

'Happens, yo.'

'That's exactly it,' I said. 'It's no big thing. It's just what happened. You have to be able to say what happened.'

'Word.'

'Dig this,' I said. 'We delude ourselves to get through the day. Like, I might say to myself, "Lewis" – because that's my real name, Lewis – I might say, "You got this life deal under control. Your ship be rollin' in, kid." Or, like, you might say, "I'm real, I'm hard. I just happen to be white."'

'Say what? You know who you're talking to? I'm hillbilly hard, yo.'

'Okay, bad example. But you get my point. We delude ourselves. But one day the delusion doesn't work. It's like a Chevy that won't turn over. It's a cold-ass day and your ride will not turn over.'

'I was with you until the Chevy, Teabag.'

'It doesn't have to be a Chevy.'

'You best pull your shit together, Teabag.'

The door slid open and the rapper stepped out to greet his retinue. He wove through the room, juking and kissing, bumping bejeweled fists, running his hands on the women, pinching up morsels of satin, skin. When he reached the door he turned and caught my eye, lowered his diamond-encrusted shades. I thought he was going to call to me across the lobby, say something gritty, uplifting, some brotherly admonition to stay strong, or rock steady, or even just stay in school. But he was pointing at me, whispering to his bodyguard.

I found a side door, fled.

Nice Horizons

How could I know that rapper was on his way to an
awards ceremony where he would win the People's
Prize for Best New Entertainment Package?

'I'm just proud to be the people's package,' he said in
the paper the next day. 'That's why it means something.'

Home that night I took a series of showers, hot,
warm, hot, finished up with an icy blast. Penance for
that baste job on Gwendolyn's face, I guess. The parade?
My God, Gwendolyn was right, I must have been insane.
Part of me, anyway. The part I should have kept cuffed
to the bedroom radiator, begging for another moldy
crust of pumpernickel.

Tea, the tender monster.

Better test those binds again.

I dried off, slipped into my vintage imitation silk
smoking jacket. It was something I'd bought years
ago to don in moments of extreme psychic agony. I'll

pretend I'm another kind of man, the sort to sit with a snifter of Armagnac, muse upon his luck in the latest stock market crash. I've always been lucky in the stock market, Catamounts. I've never lost a cent. You all get one guess why.

Later I sat at my desk, worked on my poem about the splintering of consciousness in our rootless age. The poem's been running in my head for some time. The beginning goes like this:

> Consciousness/splinter(ed)
> This is the rootless age

I'd been having some trouble with the rest of it. The trouble maybe stemmed from its atrociousness. I booted up my laptop instead, cruised those lonely information fire roads for some legwarmer lovelies, but even my yarn harem offered no solace tonight.

There was a deadness in me now.

I needed something to take my mind off my mind. There was nothing to smoke or drink in the house, nothing sugary to shove in my mouth. I couldn't bear to watch TV. What if they had those corpses again and they still didn't make me feel better?

I thought maybe I'd feign sleep.

* * *

Sometime during the night a figure appeared in my bedroom, hunched on a chair near the door. I heard breathing, short and sharp, saw something enormous pumped in shadow on the wall.

'Kid?' I said.

The figure drew still. Moonlight through the window caught a piece of polished brass, a bracelet on a hairy wrist.

'You know me?'

'You're the Kid,' I said. 'You took Buttercup in Kansas City.'

The Kid didn't answer for a while.

'Guess I done took them all,' he said at last.

'Why are you here?'

'Tired, I reckon. Reckon I'm tired.'

'How much whang can a man spank?' I said.

'Ask myself that question every day.'

'Why not just stop?'

'And do what?' said the Kid. 'This is all I know. Since I was a youngster, an orphan, and Mr. Feegle brung me in, taught me the game. I can do it any way. Fast, slow. Forever, quick. Forty times in a row.'

'Forty?'

'In Fort Worth it was forty.'

'God. I thought eleven was good.'

'There's no shame in eleven.'

'Still, forty.'

'Wish I could just wipe it all clean from my mind,' said the Kid. 'Wish I could just start over. I'd never touch the damn thing again.'

'I may know somebody,' I said.

'Somebody who?'

'An angel. Guardian.'

'Never had much respect for celestial types. They get everything handed to them.'

'This guy's good.'

'We'll talk again,' said the Kid. 'Sorry about the mess.'

'What mess?'

I reached for the light switch. Illuminated, I was alone. My smoking jacket was draped on the chair near the door, a pair of slippers underneath. Just another hallucination, Catamounts? I got down to my knees, felt around until I found it, a small sticky puddle on the hardwood. The Kid's mess?

It tasted like me.

The rest of the night I dreamed of Lenny and Gwendolyn. They took lazy walks across a lake of fire. They made love on a molten patio.

'I'm a schmuck!' Lenny shouted as he came.

There was a musical number. Azorean boys in top hats sang a song called, 'Honor Your Dream.'

I never got to hear the end of that song. Somebody was banging on my door.

Gary stood on the threshold in a fishing hat.

'We're going in,' he said. 'Our objective is to infiltrate and neutralize the forces of my mental oppression. I'm calling it Operation Thunderstruck.'

'It's like morning right now, man.'

'What is the spirit of the bayonet?' said Gary. 'To kill is the correct answer, but take your time.'

'Gary, when are we going to stop talking like this?'

'You mean like everything's pretend? Like we can't face the truth of our lives as we live them?'

'Yeah, that.'

'Today,' said Gary. 'Today's the day.'

Nice Horizons, in case you've never noticed it, Catamounts, is that place set back in the marsh grass behind Mays Lumber. I kept an eye out for Georgie Mays as we drove by the woodpiles. I'd heard he worked at the lumberyard, or at least spent his afternoons idling near the tool shed, waving a jigsaw at his many invisible foes. Some Catamounts may recall how

Georgie once stalked a history professor from Rutgers for publishing letters which proved his ancestor Matheson's Tory sympathies. These were long missives, the earliest known Catamount updates, if you will, many addressed to Benjamin Franklin's monarchist son. Charges of treason didn't bother Georgie so much as the professor's insistence on the phrase 'erotic overtones.' He'd mailed the academic some feces of indeterminate origin in Ziploc bags, picked up the man's children at their Quaker pre-school.

'Tell your daddy no Mays man ever had a taste for cock,' he told the little ones, ditched them in a cornfield near a high-voltage transformer.

They'd put a winking metal device on Georgie's ankle after that little escapade.

There was no sight of Georgie today, just some flatbed trucks, a few men drinking liters of cola from a plastic cooler. I couldn't make out the labels from here.

Some Catamounts may not be aware of this, but the cola wars continue to this day. Folks have just forgotten, moved on to more comprehensible conflicts. Believe this, though: the centrality of cola in our transnational life will be affirmed in future tracts. Citizens swilled caffeinated sugar water, experts will explain, while enjoying digitally enhanced entertainment. Their dim repetitive culture was the work of 'artists,' who employed 'imagination.' Regeneration would not come for many years, and only in the wake of utter annihilation –

'What are you jabbering about?' said Gary.

'Me? Nothing.'

Nice Horizons was about a quarter mile on, a complex of dark glass and wood built at steep healing angles. We pulled up to the main office, sat parked for a few minutes.

'What's the idea here?' I said.

'I'm not sure,' said Gary, tapped his thumb nub on the wheel.

'I figured you had a plan.'

'My plan was to be spontaneous.'

Gary dialed around on the radio, found some dance track on a techno station. 'You can't have it both ways,' a man intoned to a mournful beat.

'I hate this friggin' shit,' said Gary.

'You don't have to go in there,' I said.

Gary shrugged, fingered the bass lure hooked to the mesh crown of his hat.

'What's with the angler duds?' I said.

'Does it look retarded?'

'Don't use that word,' I said.

Catamounts, I'm not sure how many of you recall Fred Powler from our Eastern Valley days, but if you do, and knew him for the joy-bearing boy he remained even while being pelted with bombardment balls, you wouldn't abide the way people toss the R-word around, either.

'Okay,' said Gary. 'I'm sorry. Not retarded. How about lame?'

'Totally,' I said.

'Good,' said Gary. 'I'm going for sympathy here.'

I followed the Captain into a dim lobby. Cheery awful smears lined the walls. Fingerpaintings, mostly, and some that looked toed. A sign hung near the fire exit: 'Mandatory Hug Zone.'

'Freak city,' said Gary.

The woman at the reception desk fixed us with her friend-of-the-damaged smile. We watched it fall in stages from her face.

'Gary?' she said. 'Lewis?'

It was Stacy Ryson's sister, Tiffany! She'd been a few grades behind us, so some Valley Cats may have what they call in the photography world a degraded image of her. Picture a gangly girl with a lousy haircut who nobody realizes will be beautiful one day, though Gary and I, we always knew. We considered her high hilarity even then, hounded her in the library every chance we got, picked out dirty books about sluts in petticoats for her perusal, offered her our weed, which she always refused.

Her sister Stacy got all the glory – Class President, Merit Scholar, Rotary Club Student Prize – but Tiffany was, by my lights, the superior Ryson. She'd written a sonnet about her yeast infection, liked to lug around a cello she couldn't play.

Once, a bitter winter afternoon, she followed us out to the maintenance shed, watched while Gary and I sucked on his one-hitter. We stood in biting wind, passed the shiny bullet pipe between us.

'It's so cold out here,' said Tiffany. 'Is it worth it? Smoking the pot?'

'To me,' said Gary. 'Yes.'

'I like the way it makes you guys smell,' she said.

'You can smell it?' I said.

'Everybody can. My sister says you guys are the true fools of society because you don't even know what fools you are.'

'We know,' said Gary.

'Do you have hallucinations? Do you see whirling

colors or skeletons rising out of the ground? Or, like, on the football field, is there a giant nipple?'

'This is just pot,' said Gary. 'Shake, at that.'

'You should try some,' I said.

'No, thanks,' said Tiffany. 'I like feeling things the way I feel them.'

'That's insane,' said Gary.

'I'm cold,' said Tiffany. 'I'm going in before they catch us.'

'You're always welcome here,' I said.

'I know I am,' said Tiffany.

She never followed us out again but we all stayed library friends. We were like a secret gang, but only during frees. She'd draw pictures of us in her sketch-book, interview us in whispers for her tell-all book about Stacy, *Perfect Sister*.

Gary and I were graduated that year and I guess we forgot all about Tiffany. Now here she sat at the Nice Horizons reception desk. She looked about the same, too, except for the pukey streaks of color in her hair, the thick crucifix knotted to her neck.

'Is it really you guys?'

'It's us,' I said.

'I always think of you together and here you are together.'

'We're like an ancient prophecy,' said Gary.

'I don't know about that,' she said.

Her hand darted to the wood at her throat.

'What's that?' I said.

'What does it look like?'

'I know, but, like, actually?'

'Did you get all Goddy on us, Tiff?' said Gary.

'Not on you. On me. In me.'

'I thought it was some Goth deal.'

'It's the real deal,' said Tiffany. 'Just like my savior.'

I felt that nervous smile on my face, the one I tend to get around people who believe in things.

'I'm here to see Doctor Felix,' said Gary.

'He doesn't see people. He works with the groups. Do you have an appointment?'

'I've got to see him,' said Gary.

'It's his day off. He's in his room. I'll call him. He knows you?'

Gary looked both annoyed and relieved that Tiffany seemed to have no grasp of his history with Doc Felix.

'He knows me.'

'We're always welcome here,' I said.

Tiffany must have missed my reference to that day by the maintenance shed. The universal sign for bone-toking, thumb and forefinger pinched up to my lips, didn't help much, either. There's a chance I looked to be choking on my hand.

'Are you okay?' said Tiffany.

'He's fine,' said Gary. 'He's just an awkward guy.'

'No,' I said. 'I was just remembering when we . . . oh, forget it.'

'I've forgotten most of it,' said Tiffany. 'I recall just enough to thank Jesus every day for saving me.'

I've got nothing against religion, Catamounts. It's idiotic, but so's most television, and I've watched about twenty-five thousand hours of that, the idiotic kind. Educational, maybe nineteen hours, tops. Daddy Miner and Hazel never took me to synagogue, but I did go to Catholic mass once with Dean Longo when we were nine or ten. I didn't mean to go, I was bouncing a ball in his yard when the whole family came out in their nice clothes, piled into the car. I just squeezed in after them. They were a big family with a big family wagon and Mr. Longo didn't notice me.

I loved all the pretty glass, the priest with his wine and snacks. When I later discovered I'd eaten the body of Christ I got scared, told Daddy Miner the whole story.

'Don't worry,' said my father, 'that wasn't the body of Christ.'

'It wasn't?' I said.

'He was much taller.'

A few years later all the other Jewish kids in town were gearing up for that momentous day when they'd get cash from strange uncles and synth ballads would be played in honor of their ability to sound the Torah out phonetically.

'What about my bar mitzvah?' I said.

'It's bullcrap,' said my father.

'Gary's getting one.'

'Mazel Tov.'

'If L. wants to, let him,' said Hazel. 'Maybe he needs something to rebel against later.'

'I didn't have one,' said my father.

'That's what I'm talking about. So now you rebel against me.'

'Please, Hazel.'

'Well?' I said.

'Well, what?' said my father. 'Are you telling me that every day after school you want to go to another school and learn a language that sounds like people with bronchitis?'

'Marty!' said Hazel. 'We're talking about thousands of years of tradition. Patriarchal tradition, but still, even I respect it on some level.'

'Don't confuse the issue,' said my father.

'What's the issue?'

'Lewis,' said my father. 'You know how when we go to grandpa's house he has that cow tongue cut up on a plate?'

'Tongue?' I said. 'That's a real tongue?'

'What did you think it was?'

'I thought they just called it that. That's disgusting.'

'So we agree,' said my father.

'We do?' I said.

'We're going to take this assimilation thing the whole nine. No half-assing.'

'Marty, he doesn't understand you. He doesn't know when you're kidding.'

'He knows I'm not,' said my father. 'I'm a fucking secular American. I nearly shed my fucking blood for the right to be one, too. I scrambled for Cuba. Don't ever forget that. My unit scrambled for Cuba. I was on the fucking tarmac. I was ready for Castro's bullet. And I liked Castro. But more than Castro I liked the fact that I didn't have to eat tongue if I didn't want to. I didn't have to pray to any god, either. Except DiMaggio.'

'Marty, this doesn't make any sense.'

'I sup from the melting pot.'

'There's herring in the melting pot,' said Hazel. 'Gefillte fish.'

'Can't taste it,' said my father, smacked his lips. 'It's all ham hocks to me!'

Hazel laughed for the first time in a while, that laugh like flash lightning she had. I could see them both lit up in it, figures frozen in an old love pose, the way they'd maybe been, before the head scarves and the bad investments, the groped hostesses, the agit prop, baby Lewis, too. A random millisecond of illumination to remind you of the daily dark.

'Fine, forget it,' I said, went back to the basement, maybe to evacuate Saigon.

Which is really just to explain to you, my fellow alums, why I never got bar mitzvah'd, which I'm sure most of you (minus the Jews) never wondered about anyway, but which may also, perhaps, provide some context for my mixed feelings apropos Tiffany's new dead boyfriend. Part of me was happy she'd found peace, grace. Another part wished she'd stuck with her weirdo grandeur. But at least her hair was still shitty.

She puffed a lock of it off her forehead now, spoke low into the phone.

'Karl,' she said. 'Doctor Felix. There are two men here to see you . . . Well, yes, I do know who they are, in fact . . . just by coincidence . . . okay, hold on a minute. He wants to know what it's about.'

'It's about the mystery of the mind,' I said.

'It's about all the money he used to have in the bank,' said Gary.

Tiffany conveyed both interpretations.

'Follow the hallway to the end,' she said. 'Knock on the last door.'

The last door, it sounded so ominous, Catamounts, reminded me of the days before we discovered parking lots, when Gary and I used to play those dragon games after school. Our dungeon master, Todd, Gary's older brother, had no passion for the fabulous, the strange, for hidden rivers, ruby-walled caves. He believed our games should mirror the humiliation and despair of everyday life. We never slew giants, won treasures, wove spells. We'd just tool around in the forest, get jumped by trolls and such, each roll of Todd's queer dice another pike tip tearing through our cotton armor.

'You're both dead,' Todd would hiss from behind his laminated screen. 'Killed by drunken orcs, no less. Pathetic, but that's life. Nasty, fucked-up, short. Get used to it. I'm going to roll now to see what kind of vermin converge on your corpses. Why don't you guys get me a nice glass of ginger ale.'

Later we'd invent new personas, meet the same shitty fate all over again. One day Gary said, 'Screw this.' We went outside to shoot hoops.

'Don't blame me,' Todd called out after us. 'I'm not God. I'm just the dungeon master.'

Walking down the hallway of Nice Horizons I wondered what menace lurked behind door number last, a slab of blond wood with a dry erase board hanging from a hook. Gary knocked, and just as he did, I read the note penned in neat lunatic script near the edge of the board: 'Doc, sorry I missed our last group: I took your advice and it worked, but it hurt like a bastard. Best, Alvin.'

Gary paused, knocked again.

'Enter,' said a voice.

I followed the Retractor into the dim concrete box. A penitent's cell: desk, bed, tiny TV. My old dorm room, the one I'd inhabited for half a semester before realizing there was nothing I could misconstrue in college I couldn't misapprehend in the real world, had more amenities. A lean bearded man sat backwards on a swivel chair. He bobbed slowly, chest snug upon the springy pad, a frothy beige shake in his hand. The room smelled of Pine-Sol and pipe tobacco, cherry-scented.

'Remember me?' said Gary.

'The broken boy who reamed me good,' said Doc Felix.

A tendon in his neck twittered as he spoke. His eyes stayed locked, peerless. Felix had a majesty to him I had not expected. It couldn't just be the power shake. He seemed some kind of sage in his ruin.

'That's right,' said Gary.

'You took everything I had. What else do you want?'

'Got a beer?' said Gary.

'There's no alcohol here. This is a medical facility.'

'Got any medicine?'

I laughed.

'Who's this guy?' said Doc Felix.

'Teabag.'

'You had to bring a goon? Are you that scared of bad old Felix? And why does he have that fake-sounding laugh?'

'It's my real laugh,' I said.

'Sounds a little worked to me,' said Felix.

'He's not a goon,' said Gary. 'He's just gotten fat.'

'Thanks,' I said.

'Don't you remember Teabag?' said Gary. 'I used to

go on about him in our sessions. Remember, the guy who was holding me back?'

'Thanks again,' I said.

'Burned my notes,' said Doc Felix. 'I'm going to drink my lunch now. Feel free to sit down.'

We perched on his narrow bed. The quilt stretched over it was stained, ancient. It had a rodeo on it. Cowboys on bulls, broncos.

'That blanket goes back,' said Felix.

'Looks it,' I said.

'You can see my early spurts.'

'Is that what those are?'

'Mementos,' said Felix. 'Tribal markings. Tree rings.'

'Don't you want to know why I'm here?' said Gary.

'I know why you're here.'

'Why am I here, then?'

Gary's voice bore the whiny vibrato of an arrogant child, the kid he used to be, the one about to get caught out for breaking the vase, spraying the schnauzer's balls with silver paint. It was tough to watch old Goony this way, but a buddy sticks by through all phases of the asinine.

'You're here,' said Felix, 'because you're worried that maybe everything was true, after all. Everything except the retraction. You're here because you've been having the dreams again. You're here because you're realizing that what your mother and father did to you cannot be undone just by denying it happened, by saying, "Oh, my, I'm so sorry. I must have had it all wrong!" So, you want me to make it okay again, like it was for a little while, until it wasn't okay anymore because you slacked off and drifted away from my care. That's why you're here.'

230   Gary gnawed at his nub.

'So now what?' he said.

'Now what what?'

'I need your help.'

'It's too late.'

'I'll give you your money back.'

'I don't want the money. Whoever has the money is weakened. It's like a bad amulet. Do you understand?'

'I have to know what really happened.'

'Do you have a time machine?'

'No.'

'Then you'll never know what happened.'

'I dream about the goats,' said Gary. 'Octavian, my twin. I have to get past this.'

'Nobody gets past anything.'

'Or work through it.'

'Nobody works through anything, either.'

'Then I have to accept it.'

'Who could accept such a thing?'

'Learn to live with it, then.'

'That's what you're doing.'

'But what about the pain?'

'Love it or leave it,' said Doc Felix.

'That's it?'

'No, that's not it.'

'What else?'

Felix swiveled away, drank down the rest of his shake.

'May you be gang-fucked by flyblown wildebeests.'

Shop-N-Pay

Hell of a day today, Catamounts. So damn close to promising. Already by noon I'd polished up some FakeFacts, put a dent in the dishes, even banged out a few push-ups on the kitchen floor. The sweet burn lingered in my shoulders for hours.

It seemed your faithful correspondent had turned over a new leaf, or at least wiped some larval slime off the old one, was, in any event, readying himself for a new Minerian epoch, one notable for relative efficiency in the industrial sector and widespread cultural giddiness.

A long boom was in the offing, a mood I could ride into early evening.

Then the mailman came with the mail, for which he's not to blame, handed over the usual sheaf of bills, bill notices, final bill warnings. My whole life is either due or past due, Valley Cats. Forests are falling for the burgeoning need to threaten me.

There, hidden in the grim bundle, was the card:

Time Will Take You On!
The Eastern Valley Alumni Association Presents
A Togethering
Five Years of Classes: 86–90
Don Berlin's Party Garden, Rt. 17
Drinks and Dinner Served
Master of Ceremonies: Salvatore Fontana
Special Guests: Congressional Candidate
Glen Menninger, Spacklefinger

Catamounts, let me be certain I understand the big plan. We're all to drive over to Don Berlin's and hop on the cosmic scales, weigh our failures, our follies, our fat asses, all of us, Glen Menninger, even, Stacy Ryson, Mikey Saladin.

All of us, minus the dead.

Minus Miner, too, if I can help it.

I called my father, asked if he had any work at the Moonbeam for the night in question.

Daddy Miner said he had a dinner for the United Federation of Shamans scheduled, could use an extra hand with the bus trays.

'You hear about Berlin?'

'Another wall?' I said.

I feared my father had heard about the Togethering, would berate me if I told him I wasn't going. Nothing pisses him off like people trying to avoid awkward social encounters in rented halls, even somebody else's rented hall. You have to care about your industry as a whole.

'Not Germany,' he said now. 'New Jersey. Don Berlin.'

'No, what?'

'Rumors, is all. I've got a guy at the health department. People are talking. Code violations at the Party Garden. Oh, how the mighty have fucked up.'

'They're going to shut him down?'

'Probably not,' said my father. 'It's just talk. I'm sure it'll all work out.'

'Buy them off?'

'It doesn't work like that.'

'How does it work?'

'How does what work? I have no idea what you're talking about,' said my father, hung up.

He called back later on a pay phone, said he thought his lines were tapped.

'The health department?'

'It's a government agency.'

*　*　*

Alums, I'm a bit worried about Gary. He hasn't been himself since our visit to Nice Horizons, if Garyhood can be defined as a kind of viscous swirl of big-hearted sadism blended with thick chunks of auto-destructive habitude and the merest tincture of regret.

Doc Felix, once again, has screwed old Guano up but good.

I'm not sure how to help him, either.

Last night I walked over to the Retractor Pad, took my usual spot on the terrace bench. Below us, on the loading bay of the mayonnaise factory, a commotion. A stocky guy in coveralls stood on the platform, called out to the factory doors.

'Come out like a man!' he said. 'Come the fuck out and get your man-beating!'

'It's our lucky day,' I said. 'Ringside seats.'

'Asshole,' said Gary, got up, took his bong inside.

We sat in the living room and watched TV, an old cop show. Men in checkered suits batted each other into big spools of wire on a factory floor. Maybe the incident pending outside was based on this episode.

'Assholes,' said Gary, clicked over to a show about sea life. Something furred, five-spoked, filled the screen.

'That's a sea star,' I said.

'What, are you fucking my girlfriend, too?'

I kept my eyes on the coral reef. The eyes are windows into men's boners, and I feared Gary would see mine. I heard the click of his Bic lighter, the charry suck.

'You know I'd never do that,' I said.

'She'd never let you do it,' said Gary.

'What's the difference?'

'The difference is everything.'

Noises rose up from the factory dock, something soft heaved down on something hard, corrugated metal, maybe, followed by a high human wail.

'Man-beating in progress,' said Gary.

'Some scientists in the asterozoic community,' said the television, 'have ignited controversy regarding the name of this enchanting creature. The starfish, you see, is not a fish at all.'

'The fuck it's not!' said Gary, poked back behind him at the book shelf, snatched down a thousand-page biography of Elvis I'd once given him for his birthday, whipped it. The book hit the plastic base of the television, bounced to the carpet.

'That would have been genius,' I said.

'Go fuck yourself,' said Gary.

'Hey,' I said. 'Calm down. What's with you? I'm not your enemy.'

'You're an enemy of feeling,' said Gary, got up, stalked off to the kitchen.

I sat alone for a while, watched hairy things float and flutter.

Today Penny Bettis called to tell me *Fizz* had been discontinued.

'Nothing personal,' she said. 'Company cuts.'

I told Penny what a shame that was. We jawed for a while about the many vital journals going under these days, how a virtual silencing of the American conversation had ensued. Or maybe it was just me jawing.

I think Penny Bettis had already hung up.

I called my father and asked for more shifts at the Moonbeam, told him how a few days ago Pete had barged past me into the apartment, run the tap, inspected the plaster on the walls.

'Place should be ready in no time,' he'd said.

'Ready for what?'

'Decent tenants.'

'I'll see what I can do,' said Daddy Miner now. 'By the way, a friend of yours called here. Guy named Bob Price.'

'What the hell did he want?'

'Said he wanted to volunteer in the kitchen. Something about research for a book.'

'What did you tell him?'

'I told him I'd been misrepresented enough in your mother's plays. I gave him Don Berlin's number.'

'Good.'

I went for a walk around the block. I needed air, new vantages. Moonbeam stopgap notwithstanding, I knew I was pretty much screwed. When does it end, Catamounts? I'm no philosopher, but when does it fuck- ing end – this carousel, or whirligig, or whatever spinning thingamabob it is which whips us with terrible speed back to the same hopeless place we started? Is life just this ceaseless cycle of weariness and fright, or is there some luxurious interlude I've somehow missed?

Responses appreciated!

Now a van puttered past, a dented heap tricked out with stickers and crepe, a multi-directional bullhorn bolted to the roof.

'Vote Glen Menninger for congressman! He has money! He knows people who have money!'

Through the windshield you could see shiny claws on the wheel.

'Vinnie!' I called. 'Lazlo!'

The van pulled over to the curb. Vinnie curled himself out the window, hopped to the sidewalk.

'Miner, how are you?'

'Jesus, Lazlo,' I said.

Have any Valley Cats seen Vinnie Lazlo lately? All this time I've been drinking too much and cursing the inevitable he must have been at the gym. He's a freaking Adonis with forks coming out of his sleeves. I asked him about the forks, too. We were never buddies but there was always something understood between us. Maybe it goes back to the locker room, the day I got my Teabag tag, Vinnie whinnying under the sink while Philly and Friends pinned me down and Philly shimmied up my chest, his balls some pink tuberous bulb sprouting from his clenched fist.

'Teabag that faggot!' Brett Meachum had said.

My head pincered between Philly's knees, I felt the smooth bulb wrinkle, bob loose in my eye.

'Look, he likes it!'

'Dickslap him!' somebody else, maybe Stan Damon, called.

'Dude, now *you're* being a faggot!' another called.

'No, I'm just saying dickslap him.'

Vinnie must have seen Will Paulsen burst in then, throw Philly up against the wall, give him that hard chop to the gut. Philly slid to the tiles and his cronies fled.

'You're fucked,' Philly moaned, crawled off.

That's when Vinnie Lazlo waved his weak hooks, clicked out from under the sink. I wonder if he noticed the nod Will gave me before he left the locker room that day, the nod that said I saved you this time, stranger, but now I must make my lonesome hero's journey of a thousand heads, or whatever, and anyway we are all of us fucked, we are all of us always fucked on this so-called road of life, pitted and rutted and rife with fiends as it is, so do not believe for a moment you have truly been saved from anything, for the road never ends, only you end, another meat sack heaped on the berm.

I think that's what the nod meant.

Maybe it meant something else.

'I do have hands,' said Vinnie now. 'Very high-tech. Flexible. But I missed the hooks. Truth is, chicks go for the hooks. I wear the hands when I have to, the hooks when I can.'

'You look great, Vinnie.'

'Thanks. I'm a decathlete. I play the mandolin, sculpt. I do all the things the handed do.'

'Yeah, I've been sculpting a lot lately.'

'Same old Teabag. How's Gary?'

'He's okay.'

'No three-ways with the folks these days?'

'He's working on it,' I laughed.

I guess Vinnie always hated Gary for cutting his thumb off. Maybe Vinnie took it as a taunt, though I know Gary wasn't thinking of Vinnie when he did it. God knows what Gary was thinking. I'm still partial to the late show theory.

'Vinnie,' I said, 'are you working for Glen Menninger?'

'Volunteering.'

'Why?'

'I believe in his vision.'

'But he's a dick.'

'He could be a great leader.'

'Man, I'd vote for you long before I'd vote for him. I'd vote for Stacy Ryson. I did vote for Stacy Ryson.'

'This isn't Eastern Valley, Tea. This is reality. This is down-and-dirty politics with real lives and actual ideas at stake. Menninger's the man for our times. He has money. He knows people who have money.'

'Yeah, I heard you going on about that from the van. That's kind of a weird slogan, don't you think?'

'I don't mean to be rude, Tea, but the only people who think it's weird are the weirdos themselves. People living in a fantasy world, a world without legitimate reasons for torture and all the cars run on strawberry ice cream.'

'Interesting.'

'I don't mean to get on my soap box, but I was born without hands. Look at me now. I made it. Fuck the victims. I mean, victimhood.'

'Your dad is a bank president.'

'I know what my dad does.'

'Just saying,' I said.

'Your dad owns a bar and a catering hall.'

'So?'

'You look pretty fat these days.'

'Thanks.'

'Just saying,' said Vinnie. 'Anyway, I should get going. Here, take some literature. We can always use another hand.'

Vinnie didn't crack the smile I expected. He'd always delighted in dumb allusions to his condition. But that was the old Vinnie. He was dead now. The new Vinnie slid back into his van, pulled away from the curb. Where the same old Teabag stood. The fat bastard who'd forced a chuckle at the expense of his best and only friend.

God, Catamounts.

Blow my friggin' head off.

* * *

At the Shop-N-Pay I walked my typical circuit, down cleaning goods, up party food. The synchronicity puts me at peace. The sports drinks are the same unnatural hues as the toilet cleansers. The snack chips come in canisters like those for the scouring powders. Maybe I'm nostalgic for that simpler time when synthetics aroused such jubilance, before the food freaks began clamoring for actual food, fruit from the trees, roots from the earth. I'd always hoped we'd get down to one item, an energy bar, say, which, after eaten and voided, could be suitable for use as spermicidal lubricant. Or, with a few molecular nips and tucks, deodorant. No more mushy pears, lettuce the texture of wet tissue paper. Shunt those to an uncooled corner. Shelf-space would be reserved for the one product in its principal flavors: wicked, awesome, phat, phresh, skyberry.

When I turned the corner I caught sight of old Auggie Tabor beneath a woodcarved sign that read, 'Bagelria.' Auggie licked his finger, dipped it in a balsawood barrel, brought it up sprinkled with tiny black seeds. I gave him time to suck himself clean before I called his name.

'Hey, fella,' he said. 'How goes it? You're not going to tell them about the poppy seeds, are you? I love these Jew donuts they got here but I'm keeping off the carbs.'

'I've got your back.'

'That's kind of you.'

'Talked to your daughter lately?'

'Sure did. She had her cantaloupes taken out. They were leaking.'

'Sorry to hear it.'

'No, it's all fine. Listen, you know anything about computers?'

'Little bit. Not much.'

'Something's wrong with mine. Won't wake up. How'd you like to make twenty bucks?'

Auggie drove us to his big rotted house on Drury Court. We crossed his dead lawn to the door.

'Just a sec,' he said. A chipmunk carcass lay on the porch near the welcome mat. Auggie tugged a house key from its desiccated mouth.

'Pretty damn clever, right?' he said. 'Who needs those foam rocks?'

The foyer was dark and stank of egg salad. Down a high narrow hallway a dog gate opened to a sunlit kitchen, a swirl of earth tones, old chrome. The only new appliance was the most impressive, a state-of-the-art Italian stove with a row of complicated-looking knobs for grilling and broiling and maybe transporting pork roasts to other star systems. A book lay sideways on a small shelf above it: *The Lonely Gourmet: Fine Dining for Shut-Ins*. A picture of his daughter Judy stood beside the book. She looked just as I remembered her, pale, scrawny, the eyes of a mystic, meaning's penetrant. Another, smaller photo was slipped into the frame, a bikini babe with sun-streaked hair, high tan breasts like lacquered stones. She held the waist of a staid-looking man in terry cloth as they strolled along a shoreline.

'It's like I have two Judys,' said Auggie. 'But both of them are still Judy. Neither visits.'

'She was a good teacher,' I said.

'Her mother was very proud of her. Come here, take a look at my machine.'

Auggie's computer sat on a butcher block near the kitchen window. I tapped the space bar and the monitor lit up.

'Thanks a mil,' he said.

'You didn't need me for that,' I said.

'No, you've been a big help. How about some osso buco? Shouldn't take more than a few hours. We can talk. I can tell you about Normandy.'

'That's nice of you, Auggie. But I've got to get going.'

'No, please, let me repay you.'

'It's okay, I've got to run.'

'But I've got stuff to talk about!' said Auggie.

He seemed pretty shaky, alums, this shut-away man with stuff to talk about. Maybe I saw myself in sixty years, and no memories of a catastrophic beach landing to keep me company.

'Don't you have a newsletter you can write to?' I said.

'A newsletter?'

'That's how I do it.'

'Do what?'

'Deal with it. The silence. The terrible silence under all the jabbering of the world.'

'The terrible silence,' said Auggie. 'That's it. I hate the terrible silence.'

'Write an update. Tell them what's going on.'

'Tell who? Aarp?'

'Do they have a newsletter?'

'People bitching about prescription drugs.'

'You have to be crafty.'

'You mean slip the other stuff in there all sneaky?'

'Exactly.'

'Is that what you do?'

'My newsletter won't publish me. I write for the dead.'

'The dead?'

'Well, not the dead. The unborn, or the just born, or something. Anyway, you should give it a shot.'

'Maybe I will. Maybe that's exactly what I'll do. You sure you don't want to stick around for dinner?'

'Better not.'

'Good enough. I've got some writing to do. Take care. Sorry I dragged you out here, but I'm glad I did.'

'Me too, Auggie,' I said.

It was kind of exhilarating to meet a kindred spirit, Catamounts. God knows how many latent Teabags are out in the world, their inner updaters untapped. It's tragic, when you think about it. Here's a man who keeps his house key in a dead rodent but never worked up the courage to share this safety tip with his fellow retirees. I pray he's found it now. Maybe I've found my calling, too.

Updater facilitator.

Out on Drury Court I followed the curve of the sidewalk, looked for Mavis to mark my way home. Some of these houses seemed familiar in the high heat. Maybe I'd haunted a few of them in this kind of shimmer when I was an itty-bitty toddler, pre-Tea, still uncategorized, uncasted. Get this, Catamounts: I have a snapshot of yours truly nude in a wading pool with Stacy Ryson. We're nearly two and I'm pointing at her pooty. It's like Hitler and Stalin back when they signed that pact. This picture was taken during a period of tense negotiation, too. Our parents were deciding whether to be friends. I guess the Miner clan couldn't cut it.

Now I passed a man on his lawn in a lawn chair. He drank beer from a foam beer holder. A child tottered in the grass near his feet.

'Miner!' came a voice, and I turned back.

The man was gone, the child chewing foam.

'Miner!'

The voice was coming from the house next door, a place I knew, its peeled shingles and chipped siding, Fontana's ranch, The Hi IQ. The window where I'd watched Fontana in his harness was boarded up. Most of the others, too.

'Miner, get over here!'

The voice was coming from the rose bed, the transom behind it.

'Come around, I'll let you in.'

I jumped the wooden gate, jogged around to the back yard, a thin patch of crab grass bound by high pickets. A cellar door lurched open, knocked over a grease-caked grill. Fontana's head popped out of the dirt, shaggy, almost puppety, something you'd maybe pound with a mallet at a street fair.

'Leave that shit,' he said.

I let the grill lid fall to the grass.

'Come down to the storm cellar.'

It was really just a basement den. Damp carpet. Bumper pool. The sink in the kitchenette brimmed with dishes. Paperback books littered the floor, old pocket-sized editions, novels, social criticism from the early Sixties. A hardback copy of *Vegas, Baby* propped the leg of a card table where the room dipped a bit. Fontana had duct-taped his Bat Masterson postcard to the wall. A rhinestone-studded bridle dangled from a hook beside it.

Fontana wore a patchy beard, food-stains on his polo shirt.

'Beer?' he said, fetched us some Mexican lager from the refrigerator.

'Hot as hell out there,' I said.

'Dog days. We've got to savor them. Those last few weeks before school starts up again. Never gave a shit about the heat. I used to sit inside and read. Watch the tube. Listen to my records. It's why I became a teacher. Summer break. Not that I'm lazy, though God knows I am. It's the cycle. That sense of renewal. When you're a kid you go through all those changes. Grownups don't get that feeling.'

Somehow while he'd spoken Fontana had finished his beer. He went back to the kitchen for another, a bag of pretzels, gestured for me to join him on the sofa. A pellet rifle stuck up from the cushions and he took a half-lotus position around it, gripped the barrel, his belly a giant white slug falling over his chinos. I sucked in my own slightly smaller slug.

'I'm losing it, Miner,' he said.

'Hollis?'

'He's been coming around. Parks across the street for hours at a time. Gets in the house somehow. He signed for a package. Opened it, too. A crewneck sweater I'd ordered. Left a note. "Loretta's favorite color – *corpse ecru.*" Is that supposed to be witty? I think what I'll do is not go upstairs for a while. If he breaks in again I can lock myself down here.'

'It's no way to live,' I said.

'Of course it is. It's one of them. But I'm worried about Loretta.'

'Is he stalking her?'

'That term's a bit simplistic, Miner. She says she hasn't seen him. I don't know what the story is.

Probably there are threats, concessions. Periods of uneasy truce, ferocious coupling. I believe your generation calls them hate fucks.'

'How are you figuring the generations?'

'This is all conjecture, though. Loretta still comes here sometimes, but she won't talk about Hollis. Bunker life is wreaking havoc on us. The last time we just touched, caressed. Really pretentious, like in those so-called erotic movies. No roping, no branding, nothing. A real bringdown.'

'I don't need the details,' I said. 'Can't you go to the police?'

'Wish I could, but I'm a libertarian. Anyway, nobody's really done anything yet. I can't prove he broke in here. I guess I could get a handwriting specialist, but shit, I don't know. Have you seen him around town?'

'A while ago. He was talking about killing you.'

'Thanks for warning me.'

'I've been pretty busy.'

'Do me a favor, go to Loretta's. Tell her I need to see her.'

'Why don't you call her yourself?'

'She won't pick up her phone. She knows it's me and she won't pick it up.'

'I'm familiar with the phenomenon.'

'I don't have a lot of blissful moments left in my blissful moments bank,' said Fontana. 'I need Loretta. And I'll deal with Hollis at some point. I'm not going to become a hermit down here. I'm not hiding. I'm just gathering my strength. Go to her, Miner.'

'I will.'

'And here.'

Fontana slid his hand in the sofa, came up with a worn brass rod.

'It's her favorite bit,' he said. 'She'll know I sent you.'

Now he snatched up the pellet rifle, swung the barrel around the room. He stopped at a long mirror leaning in the corner, drew a bead on his reflection.

'You know then that it is not the reason that makes us happy or unhappy.'

'Pardon?' I said.

Fontana fired. The pellet hit with a click. The mirror splintered, held.

The bit was a bulge in my pocket. I fondled the metal, pressed Loretta's bell. Fontana had told me the way, another hump through the valley, my shirt sopped with sweat. I sniffed myself, smelled rotten batteries, garlic, veal. I'd done some free shots of sausage vodka courtesy of Victor, but that had been days ago. The evil, I guess it takes its sweet time leaving. I stood woozy now at the loveliest Jazz Lovely's door, felt a sudden stab of guilt for that evening outside Fontana's window. Doubtless she knew I'd seen her, tilling the carpet, flogging the mule, but then again I was the sweet and dumb one, wasn't that what Hollis had said? Maybe my witness didn't count. Maybe that stab wasn't guilt, either. Maybe it was just my liver giving out.

A boy in a baseball jersey came to the door, whitish hair, pale narrow jaw. Something in his features fetched up Will Paulsen for me. Years before Philly Douglas ever thought to hang brains in my face, Will lived on our block with his mother in a rented house. It had only been one summer, we'd hardly spoken, but I'd wave whenever he rode past, Will a wizard on his undersized ride. I'd watch him do his tailwhips, his barspins. Maybe he'd remembered this, my neighborly admiration, the day of his locker-room rescue, though Will had always been a friend to prey. When older kids tore down our street for some recreational torment he'd ride up, scatter them, ride off. He'd do it mostly with the scary twitch of his forearms, living freckled hammers. Nobody knew where he rode off to afterwards. Probably into the fields behind the power plant. There were high weeds there for a hero to hide in, bury trinkets, make plans.

'Yeah?' said the boy at the door.

'Is your mother around?'

'She's taking a nap.'

'Can you tell her there's someone here named Teabag, or, actually, someone named Lewis Miner, with an urgent message for her from a close friend regarding recent and foreseeable events?'

'I have deficit, you know.'

'What?'

'Can't concentrate.'

'Just tell her Teabag is here.'

'Be right back.'

I took a seat on the stoop, waited, watched a pair of squirrels square off in the yard around an acorn. They looked equally starved, but neither seemed willing to seize the nut. It was hard to get a handle on their motives. They were squirrels. Once my father found one loose in our basement. It did a panicky skitter under some metal shelves. Daddy Miner ordered me to stay back, stalked the animal with a billy bat.

'It's probably insane from rabies,' he said. 'That's why it came in here.'

I wondered then if you had to be insane from rabies to want to enter our house.

The boy returned to the door now, leaned out as though to check the position of the sun. His eyes, light-caught, were Will Paulsen's eyes.

'She said come in.'

The boy led me to the living room, found his most recent mold in the carpet, lowered himself into it. He worked a tremendous corn chip into his mouth, unpaused his video game.

'First-person shooter?' I said.

'What?'

'The game you're playing.'

'Yeah, shooter.'

'Looks fun.'

'It's called Glory Hole. It's about a guy who has to cap people with all these weapons. To save the free world. But the free world hates him because of something he didn't do. But he doesn't care, he's still going to save it.'

'Have you ever felt like capping people?'

'We already talked about this at school. No, Mister, I don't feel like capping people because I know the difference between fantasy and reality. This game is fantasy. Reality is I don't want to talk to you because I'm playing this game.'

'Copy that,' I said.

'Teabag. Oh my God, look at you.'

There she stood at the edge of the room, Loretta, principal lovely of the Holy Jazz Club Trinity. This may come as a shock, Catamounts, but she looked kind of drab here in her home, her home sweats, just another mommy with a ponytail, nothing like the Jazz Loretta of old, or even the one in Fontana's window. What I mean is, with her pouched eyes, her flaky skin, she nearly looked like the rest of us. A trick of the lack of light, I guess.

'Come into the dining room.'

She'd put out some cookies, dry vermouth.

'Sorry, it's all I have.'

'This is great.'

'You're sweet,' said Loretta.

'What about dumb?'

'Pardon?'

'Nothing,' I said. 'Nice kid out there.'

'My pride and joy. He's been having some adjustment problems. I'm sorry if he was rude.'

'Adjusting to what?'

'Himself, I guess.'

'It's funny, he looks a lot like Will Paulsen. Do you remember Will?'

Loretta looked startled, turned away.

'Yes,' she said. 'I remember him.'

It took me a moment to suss it out, Catamounts. I'd just figured the kid resembled Will Paulsen because, well, there's a finite gene pool here on Planet Earth and some kids do. Loretta wasn't helping, either. She wore this faraway look as though she were conducting some kind of inner fire drill, evacuating the premises of herself in a quiet and orderly fashion.

'Does Hollis know?' I whispered.

'Maybe. Maybe not.'

'Does the boy know?'

'Don't think so.'

'I was never really close to Will,' I said.

'Me, neither,' said Loretta. 'Except for a few weeks. We met at a wedding. Or met again. I'd always had a crush on him, since high school. But he was so off on his own, you know? I think I really loved him, though.'

While she spoke her beauty seemed to rush forth to the surface of her suddenly, frazzled, flush, a late party guest.

Gravy boat! Stay in the now!

'Are you okay?' she said.

'Yes, yeah. Anyway, it was terrible what happened to Will. That hit-and-run. Will was out walking, right?

I guess the guy never saw him. But you don't just drive off.'

'If it happened that way,' she said.

'What do you mean?'

'It means what it means. Hollis was out driving that night. Came home with a crushed fender. Said it happened when he'd parked to get smokes. I didn't know cars bled so much.'

'You could have tipped off the police.'

'The boy needed a male role-model.'

'Hollis?'

'He was around. He knew about football. Clock management. The nickel package. The red zone. I try, but what the fuck do these things mean? Anyway, I was a kid myself. I was into Hollis for a lot of money. Pretty strung-out, too.'

'There must have been an easier way.'

'This was the easier way.'

Things were getting a little odd, Catamounts, and I wondered whether I'd ever summon nerve enough to include Loretta's story in my update. I'd never considered censoring myself before, but this was heavy-duty revelation. Modes of chicken-choking are one thing, Valley Cats, murder, deceit, mistaken patrimony, these belong to a darker realm. Or do they? (Note to

Stacy: Perhaps this question could serve as an excellent icebreaker on the new Catamount Discussion Board!) Anyway, I worried I wasn't up to the task, but as you can see, I conquered my fear. An update is an update. The things that happen, even if they didn't happen, are the things that may or may not have happened.

Does that make any sense?

This will: when I took Fontana's brass bit from my pocket, slid it across the table, Loretta laid her pale hand on it, her eyes gone moist, dreamy.

'Poor horsy,' she said.

Extra-Puffed

God smile on you, Stacy Ryson.

God grin and frig you with his giant hydrogen hand.

Your decision to delete my latest update from the Eastern Valley Alumni Electronic Forum is a blessing in disguise. Yes, domestic short-hairs of the geological depression, I know I remarked a while back how resigned I was to my erasure from the greater Catamount dialogue, but after logging onto the alumni page and seeing how simple it was to post an item, I guess I couldn't resist.

Even as I clicked send on the submission form I knew I'd violated some of my Serious Inner Tenets, particularly the one that pertains to my continued reluctance to assume the mantle of hypocritical hyper-normative pussy-hearted fuck. So picture my relief, Stacy, when my only karmic payback was your terse little bitchmail about how all update submissions are pre-screened, that mine had been deemed unsuitable for the Catamount community, which, as you pointed out, includes minors (but not Miners, I gather).

Fair enough, as Principal Fontana would say, and my musings probably are unsuitable for impressionable minds. Heaven forefend they chance upon these outlaw rants, discover too soon all that Sex and Death and Love and Longing out there like glad knaves in life's lurking spots, or even glimpse the tears and jissom on a sad man's pajama top.

Better you hide in your bedrooms, junior Catamounts, with your sleek modular desks, your tungsten-coated gooseneck lamps, all that soothing pointillism on the wall. Better you get cracking on those college admission essays, prevarications three-parts stroke and one-part gloat, if I remember the measurements correctly. Don't forget to mention how much you learned about character canvassing for Glen Menninger last summer, especially after befriending a man named Vinnie, who, though born with terrible mutilations, is an absolute angel on the mandolin!

Don't forget to note how fortunate you were to be sponsored by your father's firm on that white-water rafting trip last August. The vistas were magnificent, all those mountain peaks and Douglas firs – what an eco-system! – and that ghetto boy paddled better than anybody.

Nature is poor people, too!

Don't forget to spell-check your essay before you send it off to Bethany Applebaum for a spit and polish.

She's got connections at Cornell!

Someday, perhaps, a voice will rise among you, a boy or girl with the guts to utter the truth of what occurrences, mighty and tiny, have occurred up to that particular date.

This child will be the Teabag of the new generation, town-shunned, jerk-judged.

Maybe this young bard will seek me out for counsel.

'Listen, boy, girl,' I'll say, 'nobody wants to read an honest update. It's Death's collection notice. Stick to babies, work transfers.'

'But I want to be like you!'

'Don't be a fool,' I'll say. 'I wanted to be like me, too. Look what fucking happened!'

Today I heard a high whine out the window, peeked out past the AC unit to the alley below. Landlord Pete had his boot on a cat, its neck. The poor thing looked sick. It twitched on the cement. Nearby was a mangle of feathers, beak.

'What are you doing?' I called down.

'Tabby's done for,' said Pete. 'Ate a bad bird. There's a lot of them around these days. It's on the news. It's a virus.'

Pete pulled a knife that bordered on sword, stabbed up the bird.

'This would be the perpetrator,' he said. 'The carrier.'

He stood down hard on the cat. I heard a quick shriek, a snap.

'Got the rent?' said Pete.

'I'm really close. A few more nights of work.'

'I'm really close, too,' said Pete.

Later that day an ambulance wailed up to our house. I threw on some shoes, rushed downstairs. I figured they'd need bystanders.

My neighbor Kyle was dead on the living-room floor. His roommate Jared stood over him while the paramedics went to work with fists and paddles. One spoke into his epaulette while he pounded.

'Tell me what he took,' said the other.

'Nothing,' said Jared, pointed to some powder on a mirror. 'He just did a bump. Jesus, it was nothing.'

Kyle's eyes popped open, tore around the room.

'What happened?' he said. 'Am I dead?'

'This is a kind of way station,' I said.

'Shut the hell up,' said Jared. 'Kyle, you're going to be okay. These guys here saved your life.'

'Thanks,' said Kyle. 'You guys rule.'

Then his eyes rolled up funny and he was dead again. The paramedics went at it with the paddles once more.

'Jerks!' screamed Jared. 'You're not doing it right!'

He snatched the paddles away, whapped Kyle's face with them.

His method didn't work, either.

I sat with Jared most of the afternoon while men came and took our statements and other men carried the body away.

'It was just a bump,' went Jared's statement, or part of it. 'He's done mountains of it, fucking Fujis of it.'

The rest of his statement was about how his mother had deserted his family when he was in kindergarten and the last dinner she ever made for him was fish sticks. He and Kyle, they'd bonded over the degree to which they both loved fish sticks so how the hell was he, Jared, ever going to handle the frozen food aisle ever again with all that breaded cod there cold in bins and not break down about the double crazy whammy of his AWOL mother and his dead best friend?

'Hollis Wofford,' Jared added, 'he sold us the stuff.'

The men with notepads traded loaded looks.

Maybe the kid was in shock, Catamounts, if that's your body saying life is not a TV show. Jared shivered and I brewed him some tea, this health brand with a root extract the Druids grew to cure dangerous moods. There was a knock on the door and Landlord Pete leaned into the room.

'You better not have mentioned me or Hollis,' he said.

'I was here,' I said. 'He didn't say a word.'

'I didn't ask you,' said Pete.

'I told them Kyle got it from an old friend,' said Jared.

'Good work,' said Pete. 'I can't tell you how sorry I am. You can't predict. Mysterious ways. Your time is your time. Good kid, Kyle. Nice kid. Let me know. Want something. Call my cell. Take care.'

Jared went to the bedroom, maybe to weep in peace. I stuck around in case he needed more tea.

I guess Dean Longo was on my mind, Catamounts. I hadn't known Dean much better than Kyle, but I'd eaten the body of Christ with him when we were kids, and later, some mushrooms, mescaline. We'd sat around with tequila and speed a few times, too. Sweet depravity, I did know that, the mania for more, more booze, more weed, more powder, more riffing on the nature of the world. I still detested tongue-cluckers, safety fetishists, comfort food fucks, even as I sensed I was sliding towards those soft kingdoms myself.

The bad years before Dean died he lived in the city and I rarely saw him, though Gary did, they shared a place, some studio. They had a band for a while, too, though I believe their principal instruments were the pointy kind, with a plunger.

'Do you think Dean died on purpose?' I once asked Gary.

'I don't know,' said Gary. 'Did he live on purpose?'

That answer screwed with me for a few days, as I guess it was designed to do, but when I finally asked Gary what he'd meant by it he gave me this look like I'd better never ask him again.

Jared went to stay with friends in Jersey City. The fresh dead move too easily in an old house like this. I went upstairs, fell off early on the sofa in the middle of a ball game. Mikey Saladin roped them to all corners, turned a nifty double play.

That night I dreamed of the Kid again. He was an old codger now, years past his championship prime. His victory over Buttercup in Kansas City was the stuff of forgotten legend. A new breed of professional masturbator had usurped him, men and women with enormous genitals and endless reserve who lacked both the craft and poetry of the old guard.

He'd never gone home, the Kid, never bought that land at the bend in the river, never wooed Wilhelmina, the schoolteacher.

She was dead of fever, or had married an owlish young inventor who'd patented a peanut sheller.

He'd heard both things.

The Kid sat now in a hotel room in Vancouver surrounded by several powerful television producers. The Kid's plus fours were fallen at his shoes and he sat there in a silk-upholstered chair, stroked, kneaded himself, to no avail. He wanted to please himself, these men. They'd promised money but he was weary. His prick felt filled with wet sand.

'This is pathetic,' said a producer. 'I thought you said this guy had the goods.'

'He does,' said another. 'He did. He was famous once. My grandfather, when he was a little boy in

Kansas City, he met him. He always talked about it. I'm sorry. I should have known better.'

'This is bullshit. Let's get some heroin. Or hamburgers. Pay the geezer, get him out of here.'

The Kid's hand went dead in his lap. He stared up at the wooden ceiling fan. Its revolutions were the revolutions of his life, his storied life whose story nobody remembered anymore. He'd beaten Buttercup, the invincible Buttercup, others, too. Choad Leonard. Baby Arm Bartlett. Wee Billy Thomas. He'd bested Gertrude 'The Gorge' Mosenthal and White Gravy Drake in Charlotte with a half million in chits on the betting table. Nobody gave a damn anymore. The Jew-hater with the car factory was right: History was bunk.

Days later, coming back from the mini-mart, I noticed boxes stacked on the porch downstairs. A man walked out of Kyle and Jared's doorway with a duffel bag on his shoulder, an inflated inflatable woman under his arm.

'What's going on?' I said.

'I'm Jared's dad,' said the man. 'Just picking some things up.'

'Is Jared okay?'

'He'll be fine. It's not the first time he's lost a buddy this way.'

'Maybe he needs some treatment.'

'He's getting it. The District Attorney's a friend of mine. I asked him to work up some charges, put Jared away for a spell.'

'Your own son?'

'Jared's a bright kid. He'll make a fine jailhouse lawyer.'

'What about rehab?'

'Jared doesn't need to talk about his feelings. He doesn't have any. He needs to learn about fear in the company of true predators. Over time he will become a predator himself, or perish. Either way he won't be the pampered brat he is now.'

'Tough love.'

'There's no love in it anymore.'

The man took his son's things out to his station wagon. I followed with some bags, boxes, helped him tie down the load.

The Colette Man was at the Bean Counter. He was marking up his favorite author with a feathered pen. Ashes from his cigarillo fluttered down upon his vintage football jersey. Who was this guy? He didn't seem the type to live around here. I thought I knew all the types who weren't the type. They tend to be the types I know.

'Hello,' I said.

'What's doing?' said the Colette Man.

'Are you taking a class?'

'Come again?'

'All those notes.'

'I'm home-schooling myself.'

Mira was at the counter pouring coffee for a ravaged-looking man in an oil-stained Stetson.

'Milk it up, there, mama,' said the cowpoke.

I knew this voice, its scratch, its lilt.

'Bob Price,' I said. 'Holy shit. It's me, Lewis Miner!'

'Howdy.'

'You know each other?' said Mira.

'We're buddies,' I said.

'We are?' said Bob.

'We were buddies one night. "Zev's gone odd," you said.'

'What?'

'After you read at the Nazi bar.'

'Oh, right,' said Bob. 'You're that fan who tried to force all that blow on me. Truthfully, dude, I thought you were trying to fuck me.'

'I don't really remember it that way,' I said. 'What's with the cowboy routine?'

'It's no routine. I'm part cowboy. I was nearly born in Nevada.'

'It's so weird to see you here,' I said.

'I remember hearing about this town. Maybe from you, come to think of it. Seemed perfect for this book I need to research. It's called "Americaville." This place will be the model for the East Coast chapter.'

'Are you working for Don Berlin?'

'Pulling a couple of shifts, yeah. I want to capture things from all angles. Professionals, proles, layabouts.'

'You should interview me.'

'Which one are you?'

'Some of each.'

'I'll call you if I need you. What's your name again?'

'Teabag,' said Mira.

'Lewis,' I said. 'Is it going to be a novel?'

'No, I'm done with fiction. I said what I wanted to say. I said it the way I wanted to say it. Nobody will understand what I did until I'm dead.'

'So fucking die!'

The Colette Man stood, dropped his cigarillo in his demitasse, stalked out.

'What's that all about?' said Bob.

'That's Craig,' said Mira. 'He owns the place.'

'What a hard-on,' said Bob. 'It's not like I'm going to apologize for my talent.'

'Hey,' I said, 'I've been writing some stuff myself.'

'That's wonderful,' said Bob. 'I'm immensely thrilled for you. Do you have any cash I can borrow?'

'No, I'm sorry. But, anyway, what I've been writing is –'

'No money at all?'

'Sorry, I'm tapped.'

'Liar. Hack. What time should I pick you up?'

'For what?' I said.

'I was talking to the chick.'

'Come by at five,' said Mira.

Bob left and I leaned over the counter.

'You're dating that joker?'

'Just fooling around,' said Mira. 'He came in here one day and we got to talking. He makes me laugh.'

'He does?'

'Well, maybe not laugh. Anyway, you were kissing his ass.'

'I was just being friendly,' I said.

'Friendly to his ass,' said Mira.

Maybe it was my duty to warn Gary about how Bob Price was setting nookie-traps all about town, but I had more pressing business with the Captain. I bought an iced coffee to go, got going. The ice would be melted by the time I reached the Retractor Pad, but it was the thought that counted. The thought that I'd been nice enough to buy Gary an iced coffee was part of a larger notion I meant to plant in his mind: that he should maybe float me more cash. Gary's handouts weren't lasting. It was time to discuss a long-term loan. I had some phone bills, a letter from the IRS folded in my pocket to prove I had documents pertaining to my finances. I figured I'd show them to Gary, use the word 'finances.' This would make the loan official. Then I wouldn't feel so bad when I defaulted. It would be like screwing a bank, or a credit card company, not your best friend.

Clara, Gary's mother, answered the door at the Retractor Pad.

'Lewis,' she said. 'What a nice surprise.'

Gary and his father, Ben, a balder, bonier Gary, stood together in the kitchen.

'Hey,' said Gary.

His voice was hoarse and he heeded his father as he spoke.

'Everybody okay?' I said.

'Beautiful,' said Gary's father, softly. 'Everybody's beautiful.'

It was pretty awkward, Catamounts. I was definitely the fourth wheel on the tricycle of family reconciliation. These kinds of deep encounters are better viewed from a distance. That's why there's daytime TV.

'I've got iced coffee,' I said. 'I think the ice might have melted.'

Clara took the soggy cup, poured the coffee off into a mug.

'Here you go, Gary, honey,' she said.

'Thanks, Mom.'

Clara smiled and Gary lunged at her, wrapped himself around her waist, curled up to her blue-jeaned belly.

'I'm so sorry, Mommy.'

Coffee slopped to the floor.

'There, there, baby,' said Gary's mother. 'Everything's going to be fine. We're going to be a family again.'

Now Ben began sobbing, bobbed, honked, a spit-laden horn.

'Ben, please, no more,' said Clara.

Ben closed his eyes, heaved. Clara unhitched Gary, shoved him gently against the stove. She pulled her purse down from the refrigerator, led Ben by the elbow to the door.

'Nice to see you, Lewis,' said Clara.

'Yes,' said Ben.

'See you on Sunday, Gary, baby,' said Clara. 'I'll make your favorite cake, with the Life Saver on top.'

The Captain nodded into his palms, wailed.

I stood beside Gary, rubbed his neck. I've never been a big man-toucher, Catamounts, but the moment seemed right to chance it.

'She loves you,' I said. 'You're her son. She's no panda.'

'No what?'

'Nothing.'

'She said she saw you in the diner,' said Gary.

'I should have told you,' I said.

'No, it's okay.'

Gary looked up, his face swollen, cut with an old-time Gooner smile. He rinsed himself at the sink, dried off with a tea towel.

'Fuck me!' he said, popped his temple with the heel of his hand.

'I know,' I said. 'This is heavy.'

'No, I mean, fuck me. Now I've got to get a job.'

'What are you talking about?'

'I gave them the settlement money. The retractor money.'

'All of it?'

'They're not doing so hot.'

'You didn't keep any for yourself?'

'Clean slate.'

'But the money was the clean slate.'

'Felix was right,' said Gary. 'That money was a bad amulet. Whoever has it is weak.'

'You want your folks to be weak?'

'Who cares?' said Gary. 'They probably did molest me.'

He moved to the window, peeked past the curtain.

'Maybe they're hiring down at the mayonnaise factory,' he said.

I pulled out my phone bills, the letter from the IRS.

'What's that stuff?' said Gary.

'My portfolio,' I said.

'What are you talking about?'

'Nothing. Nothing now. I've got to get to work.'

Leave it to Captain Thorazine to throw his money away without asking if I wanted some. What do I care if it's cursed? I'm weak anywise. I'm bedecked with bad amulets. My belly's full of poison birds.

I guess I was pretty pissed, because that night at the Moonbeam, washing dishes for Delbanco Realty's annual gala, I kept thinking how I should have told Gary about Bob Price and Mira, if only to revel in his heartache. Later I started picturing Gary wandering half-dead in the desert after being raped and robbed by roving bandits. Blood seeped from his wounds into the sand. The sun cooked up squishy blisters on his back. Birds, carrion-specialists, swooped overhead. Probably I wasn't that pissed. It was really just a way to pass the time at work.

Then we had a rush, all the folks from Delbanco Realty demanding coffee for the drunk drive home. It was just me on duty, and Rick, the cook, who waxes his mustache, fancies himself a folk artist. There's a color print of one of his masterworks up near the punch clock. It looks like your typical angel poster, everything fluffy, radiant, until you notice all the unspooled intestines, the torn wings. It's some sort of celestial killing floor, all of it framed as though broadcast on an antique television set, the kind with metallic mesh speakers, quaint buttons, knobs. Rick's brilliant, ask me. It's a shame he missed that outsider art craze I recently read about in one of my magazines.

'I should have diddled kids,' he yelled through steam. 'The critics would have loved my paintings then.'

'Maybe it's your subject matter,' I said.

'What the hell are you talking about?' said Rick. 'People go bananas for angels.'

'Not when they're impaled on giant meat hooks.'

'But it's on TV. My paintings aren't real, they're on TV.'

'I understand that,' I said. 'But still.'

Now Roni burst through the doors.

'Rick, we need more flans! We're running out of flans! How many flans did you make?'

'I don't know. Fifteen.'

'There are over a hundred guests tonight!'

'Nobody ever eats flan.'

'These people want their flans!'

Roni's eyes caught mine, or caught mine conducting perv recon on her person. Catamounts, I've since learned from the Colette Man that you shouldn't compartmentalize the parts of a woman as it demeans her totality, but Roni's totality was so damn luscious and immense I'm sure she understood I could only appreciate her in parts, the swell of her calves in those high suede boots, the soft crevasse her bunched breasts made in her blouse.

'I need you in the stock room, Lewis,' said Roni. 'We've got to find more napkins.'

The stock room is not my favorite nook. It's dark, reeks of decomposing animals, but it seemed a cozy mountain villa here with Roni. Enormous cans of tomato sauce and tubs of red powder filled the shelves around us. Hate to divulge a divine Moonbeam secret, but that red powder is actually barbecue sauce. Stick a hose in the tub, voilà, fresh batch.

It took me a moment to get my bearings in the must, the clutter. Roni wheeled and we nearly collided, stood, huffed fraught breath. Light from a bare bulb fell down her hair, caught the glitter in the hollows of her neck.

'Napkins,' I said.

'Napkins,' said Roni.

We kissed, our hands marauders, jerked each other to the floor.

Roni's skirt was peel-away. I yanked her giant ass to my face. I was like a man who refuses to lose the ass-eating contest.

It was maybe an ancient kind of contest where the winner wins a kingdom, the loser loses his tongue.

It was a new moist language I gibbered up into her, too. I flipped her over, concocted more delicate lingo for the other hole. Catamounts, perhaps it's best not to get too graphic, to instead let the subtle play of metaphor carry the day, but I must confess I'd never seen a chick bust a load like that before. Her thick hips were sort of tremoring and her juice just fountained out of her, crystalline, stinky-sweet. Roni moaned, flibbered on the floor, a plump exquisite porpoise. Me, I was Poseidon, horndog of the deep, or maybe the Man from Atlantis.

When we'd finished and I'd messed my Moonbeam-issue kitchen shirt, Roni shot up, started to dress. Done, near decent, she knocked a packet of napkins from the shelf, rocked it in her arms, a paper baby, while I scrambled with my pants.

'Hurry up,' she said.

'I'm hurrying,' I said. 'And don't worry about anything. I know the drill. I won't tell anybody and I won't expect special treatment. I won't act like we're ever going to do this again.'

'What drill?' said Roni.

'You mean we can do this again?'

'We'll see,' said Roni. 'But the special treatment thing is true. No special treatment. Except for this kind.'

'Okay,' I said.

We walked out of the stock room together.

'Where were you guys?' said Rick.

Dessert plates smeared with some foul custard were piled on every surface.

'Lewis was eating my ass,' said Roni.

'Sure he was,' said Rick.

I went back to my station, my weed farm.

'I'd better take these flans out,' said Roni, nearly knocked down Daddy Miner on her way to the dining hall.

'There you are!' said my father. 'And there you go!'

'Bye, Roni,' I called.

'Don't get any ideas about Roni,' said my father.

'Gravy boat,' I said. 'Stay in the now!'

My father smiled his my-son-the-moron smile. I'm sure many Catamounts have fathers with similar grins in their arsenals. Maybe they teach it at the Dad Academy.

'That's right, kid,' he said. 'Gravy boat, and whatever else you said.'

'Stay in the now,' said Rick. 'He said stay in the now.'

'Did I ask you anything, Rick?' said Daddy Miner. 'FYI, you and I have a big-time flan-related confab ahead of us tonight, so don't cut out.'

Roni was gone by the time we shut down the kitchen. She hadn't even left me a note. I guess she wasn't ready for sex outside the workplace. Rick reported to Daddy Miner's office for his bawl-out session and I went home, watched TV.

They were pitching end-of-summer sales on the local station and I started thinking about Fontana in his bunker, wary of Hollis but also eager for his summerlong becoming, his transformation, the eversprouting pubes of his soul. He was nearing sixty, still talking about the grownups. I was half his age, no better. Everybody gets stuck somewhere, though, Catamounts. Maybe this wasn't such a bad place to put down stakes. It's not my fault, anyway, I thought, poured another whisky.

'Consuma Cultcha!' I shouted. 'You done infantalasized me!'

There I was, all liquored up, giggling, making a fool of myself alone in my home, when suddenly Gwendolyn's face filled the screen. Her hair fell in whitish waves and her lips looked extra-puffed, a pout shot straight from a needle gun. There was a wise shimmering ache in her eyes as she held aloft a tiny box.

A pack of laxatives.

'I'm on the go,' she said. 'I don't have time to sit around. Do you?'

Fall of Berlin

Today is Hazel's birthday. She would have been, well,
what? An older old lady?

When she was mostly dead in the hospital I clutched her chapped hand, desperate for those involuntary spasms people take for secret squeezes, farewell twitches. The nurses know better, of course, even the ones who believe in Heaven, wear dumb pins.

I had lots to say after the memorial service.

I said, 'She was the only one who loved me unconditionally.'

I said, 'She believed in my potential.'

I said, 'I'm floating in darkness now.'

It was all about me, of course. Teabag, aggrieved. Never mind the woman we'd just fed to flames.

I was floating in darkness anyway. I'd been floating in darkness while she was nibbling on saltines.

Did she love me unconditionally? Did I love her

unconditionally? Who tests the conditions? Maybe Gary did. But look at Gary. He had to buy his mommy's love back.

Hazel was the universe for a while, then she was the old woman who knew about that mole on my scrotum, who didn't approve of my friends, who took me, probably correctly, as a less cunning corollary to my old man.

Right before she died she was the universe again.

Then just my dead mother.

There are perks to the pain. You have permission to appear saintly, or at least tuned to some extradimensional frequencies.

'It may sound silly,' you tell people, 'but sometimes I know she's there in the room with me. Life, death, it's such a mystery.'

People nod, their eyes water. They want to be part of the mystery. Maybe they wish their mothers were dead so they could be part of the mystery.

They must hate themselves for wishing that, cringe from themselves in their heads. Maybe they go home, call their mothers up, lunge at these women with their baby love. The mothers want to watch a movie, have a light snack, not listen to their progeny slobber. Why can't these kids understand what's understood?

'I love you, too, honey.'

Devotion's twitch, its unvolunteered spasm.

Hazel's calves.

Today is the birthday of Hazel's calves, Hazel's nose.

I've got a candy bar in the freezer in honor of this day.

Fontana called while I was peeling the wrapper. He sounded frenzied, demanded we meet for lunch. I wound the candy bar up in its foil, stuck it back in the freezer.

'The Garland?' I said.

'Good tuna melts, but full of spies.'

We met at the Corner Luncheonette, that Flying Dutchman diner near the Moonbeam. Fontana was antic in the shadow of his sweatshirt hood, as though in his solitude he'd been storing up new frowns and sneers, some experimental grins. He stabbed at the fruit in his fruit cup, stole looks out the window at his ride.

'The car will be fine,' I said.

'Anything happens to me, it's yours. I'm serious. Ginny and Jen, my daughters, well, there are only so many listless embraces I can take from those bitches. The hooker thing, it didn't have to be the end of the world. They acted like I'd done it to hurt them. What, a father's supposed to cut it off? A father can't fuck? They don't get the car.'

'Don't be silly. Nothing's going to happen.'

'Nothing never happens,' said Fontana. 'Psycho followed me to the pharmacy last week. I was getting my Saint John's Wort. Some magazines. Do you read *MindStyle*? They had this article –'

'Hollis?'

'Of course, Hollis.'

'He's just trying to intimidate you.'

'Thanks for the expert profiling. Doesn't matter now, anyway. Or it won't for long. As soon as they catch him I'm safe.'

'Catch him?'

'There's a warrant out. He sold drugs to some kid who died. Kid's parents had connections. This is how society works. People leaning on people. People pressuring people.'

'There's a warrant?'

'That's what Loretta says.'

'Have you seen her?'

'Loretta? She was over the other night. I'm sure Hollis was out in the bushes, too. Like you used to be.'

'Just that one time.'

'You haven't missed much. We're not planting this

year. The fields lie fallow. We've been reading haiku to each other, though. We cooked Swedish meatballs the other night. Miner, let me tell you something. I realize now I can exist. She makes me want to exist. Even the Hollis part is amazing in its way. I mean, how many romances go south because of boredom, distraction? You know, I read in the paper that people lose interest in each other after a few years if they don't breed. It's biological.'

'Junk science.'

'Just what they said about Copernicus. But that's not my point. My point is how many love affairs have the benefit of an outside threat to invigorate them? Well, around the world, sure, tons, you've got your coups, your pandemics, your floods, but here in Jersey? We don't get to screw to the boom of the Ack-Ack guns around here. Not yet, anyway. Probably soon. Where's my car?'

'What's an Ack-Ack gun?'

'Never mind that. I've lost view of my vehicle.'

'It's right there where it was the last time you looked.'

'So it is.'

Fontana took a French fry from my plate, dipped it in the wet dregs of his fruit cup.

'How can you eat that?' I said.

'I eat the world, Miner. It's all tasty. I want to exist, to live, and that makes the world extremely fucking tasty. Also, I haven't really eaten for days. Or slept, for that matter. I'm too excited about existing.'

'Is that why you wanted to meet? To tell me that?'

'No,' said Fontana. 'I had to get out of the basement. Listen, it would mean a lot to me if you'd come to the Togethering. I need moral support.'

'I'm working the Moonbeam that night.'

'Can't you switch?'

'I begged for the shift. Anyway, are you sure you should be out and about so much?'

'No way Hollis will risk showing up in public.'

'He's got friends.'

'Nobody likes Hollis enough to hurt me for him. And I'm not worried about the Togethering. Dark parking lots are that man's domain. Maybe he's already split town. Anyway, you've got to come. What's wrong with you? What are you scared of?'

'Everything.'

'You think you're the only loser this town has produced? We should be jubilant in our disappointment. We should join hands, form a ring. A broken promise ring. Everybody's weeping themselves to sleep, Miner.'

'Not Mikey Saladin.'

'Are you kidding? He hit .232 last year.'

'I didn't know you followed baseball.'

'I don't. It's a load of pseudo-poetic crap, boring as hell. It was invented so frustrated intellectuals could pine for their daddies without appearing too unmanly.'

'I like baseball,' I said.

'I'm just kidding, buddy. Of course I like baseball. But I like French fries dipped in melon juice and giving it to Loretta from behind more.'

297

'I should get going,' I said.

'Live, Miner. There's nothing to it. It's not original. Just necessary.'

I'd had enough of Fontana, Catamounts. Sometimes the idea of a man is sufficient. Fontana was a fine enough notion for a man, but to see him here, sick eyes afire in hood shadow, to listen to his lectures on the art of living, it was more than I could stand.

I stood.

'Where are you going?'

'There's something I've got to do,' I said. 'Be careful.'

Fontana gazed out in reverie upon his car.

'Maybe I don't like baseball,' he said. 'I can't decide.'

* * *

I wandered out to the avenue, Catamounts, to the bus shelter cater-corner from the Corner Luncheonette. The ride to the Department of Motor Vehicles took long enough for me to realize what I was doing. Symbolic implications. Rewards in real time.

It turned out I didn't need to take any kind of test again. The clerk slid my license across the counter.

'Why do we even have this?' he said.

'I couldn't deal.'

'And now?'

'I've been walking in circles. I want to drive in them.'

'Glad I asked,' said the clerk.

That night I stopped off at In Your Cups to celebrate my reinduction into wheelsmanship. Victor spotted me a shooter of that syrupy stuff fratboys drink to nerve them for rape. The TV over the bar showed the view from a news chopper, a forest in flames.

'Half the country's burning up,' said Victor. 'It was a dry summer. Driest on record.'

'It rained here,' I said.

'Nonetheless,' said Victor, appeared proud he'd used the word, unsure how to follow up. 'Nonetheless, we have statistics to prove this was the driest summer on record. It's no surprise. What with the economy. And the terrorist networks.'

'Not to mention the television networks,' I said. 'And that guy in the White House, what's his name?'

'The President!' somebody called from the end of the bar.

Chip Gallagher had the makings of a one-man orgy down there with his boilermaker and his jeans unzipped from his last trip to the john.

'The President,' said Victor. 'Exactly.'

'The President is a fucking monkey,' said Chip. 'They should put him in a monkey house and feed him peanuts and cashews and shit.'

'That's elephants,' said Victor.

'Ah, the free flow of ideas,' I said. 'Democracy in action.'

'Don't come in here with your snide comments,' said Chip. 'This is a safe place for inane chatter and random hooting.'

'Sorry,' I said, 'next one's on me.'

'That's more like it.'

I slid down the bar towards Chip.

'Are you going to the Togethering?' I said.

'The what?'

'That reunion thing?'

'Oh, shit, man. Yeah, I heard about that. Open bar?'

'I think so.'

'Then I guess I'll be there. Is Jasmine Herman going?'

'Jazz Dancing Jasmine?'

'With those fucking . . . what do you call them?'

'Legwarmers?'

'No, those wristbands. Remember those spangled wristbands? She used to drive me crazy with those things. I wonder what she looks like now.'

'No worse than you or me.'

'Amen to that.'

'How's Batch?' I asked.

'My old man? He's dead, dude.'

'I'm sorry. I didn't know.'

'Last May. Caught a stroke.'

'He was a good man.'

'I don't know about that.'

'He was a good groundskeeper.'

'That's true.'

'I can still smell that smell. Fresh cut grass. Burnt oil.'

'He was a shit mechanic.'

'Hey, Chip.'

'What's that?'

'Still have that Rottweiler? The one that ate eighty million bucks?'

'I loved that dog,' said Chip.

Victor shot me a look. Apparently the lost lottery slip was not a favored topic here.

'What happened?' I said.

Chip downed his drink, flipped his glass on the bar.

'Cut the bitch open. Couldn't find the ticket.'

The phone purred.

'Like I said,' said Victor, clicked off the receiver. 'Driest on record.'

'Say what?' I said.

'That was your father. Don Berlin's Party Garden is on fire.'

I'm sure many of you Catamounts caught the nightly news that night, work shoes kicked off under your coffee tables, ties loosened, bras unsnapped, tattered concert tees slipped into, pistachios, beers in your laps, hands wheedling their way into your sweatpants to adjust a tampon, a testicle. I'm sure most of those watching saw Glen Menninger's younger brother Roger with his Channel Four News Team News microphone standing yards from the blaze, shouting above the sirens while some neighborhood kid held a handmade sign reading 'Dingleberry' above his head.

Black smoke pouring into the blue night.

Roger reported the arson rumors right away. Maybe more than a few in Eastern Valley wondered if Daddy Miner was the firebug. None that knew him, though. Hours later they were leading Don Berlin away in handcuffs. Gasoline stains in his car. Fumes in his suit. Insurance claim in his home office hopper. A real Murnighan scam.

Berlin told the police the whole truth, but it hardly sounded like a confession, more a deposed king's lament. His stateliness never deserted him, even if his buddies at Borough Hall did. His wife, the prettier twin, stuck by, too.

During the perp trot to the cruiser, one of those unnecessary evils we've come to depend on as a viewing public, Roger Menninger poked his Team News microphone at Don Berlin's defiant face.

'Don! Did you do it? Why did you do it?'

'I built it,' said Don. 'It was mine to burn.'

'He means that metaphorically!' screamed a fat man trailing after them.

It was another thrilling Catamount moment, alums, because that fat man was Lee Nygaard, class of '87, Fordham Law graduate and current counsel for Don Berlin.

'A damn good lawyer, too,' said Daddy Miner, when I called him at the Moonbeam.

'He once drank a fifth of crème de menthe before a school assembly and puked on Miss Robinson.'

'I thought that was you,' said my father. 'I tell everybody that was you.'

'I don't think so. Anyway, did you hear what Don said on the news?'

'That man is a tough cookie,' said my father. 'He had me beat all these years. I hate to see him go out like this. He was a warrior. But now the age of the Moonbeam has begun. Your friend already called.'

'What friend?'

'Stacy what's-her-name. The doctor. I don't remember her from your graduation. Did she have big tits? Was she that hippie with the tits going on about some oil spill?'

'I don't know, Dad. What do you mean she called you?'

'The Togethering. It's at the Moonbeam.'

'What about the shamans?'

'Pushed it up. Obviously, you don't have to work the shift, if you don't want to. You might want to spend quality time with your old classmates.'

'Fuck them.'

'Suit yourself.'

'Hey, Dad,' I said. 'I got my license back.'

'Hazel would have been proud. She always said you would drive a car someday.'

'It's her birthday, you know.'

'I know, Lewis.'

'I've been thinking about her today, that's all.'

'You're a good boy, Lewis.'

'Are you proud of me?'

'I didn't say that. I said you were a good boy.'

304

My great-great-grandfather was a horse thief in the Ukraine. So his son could run numbers in the Bronx. So his son could go legit with liquor stores in Queens. So his son could build bars, catering halls, in New Jersey. So his son could be a busboy for his father? Was there supposed to be a glorious continuum to all of this striving? I guess somebody had to break the glorious continuum chain. Even at twelve, thirteen, sitting in my bedroom, imagining myself a man, a man sitting fierce and lonesome at a strip joint at last call, I knew that somebody would be me.

Not to say I never had any plans. I had plans. I could picture myself in various places. But I was never doing anything in these pictures, these places. I was just sort of standing there, being congratulated for something. Sometimes I had a glass of punch in my hand. It was important I finish my punch, not just swish it around in my mouth. The parade was about to begin.

Teabag Day is a big deal around here.

Hollis Wofford was telling us about his narcissism.

'I'm a fucking narcissist,' he said. 'But I'm in serious awareness about it.'

He squeezed his balls, sucked his teeth.

I'd come over to the Retractor Pad to tell Gary about the Togetherness moving to the Moonbeam. Hollis had answered the door, his eyes tracking the slope of my skull.

'Larry's here,' said Hollis.

'I can come back later,' I said.

'Sit down,' he said.

There was something in the air, Catamounts, contrails of evil talk.

'Hollis and I were just discussing secrets,' said Gary.

'We're only as sick as our secrets,' Hollis said. 'Secrets are what destroy us. That and blowcaine. My secrets consume me. Almost as much as my hatred for Larry's cocksucking buddy Fontana.'

'Hey, Hollis,' said Gary. 'I thought we were doing stepwork, here. I think you've gone off message.'

'It's all one message,' said Hollis. 'Many paths leading to one truth.'

'Lewis,' said Gary, 'how's the day treating you?'

I felt funny talking with Hollis in the room, but he seemed to have sunk into his own harm-happy stew. He was huffing on his sunglasses, wiping them down with his shirttails. I told Gary about Don Berlin's Party Garden burning down, which he knew about, and the Togethering now being a Moonbeam affair, which he didn't.

'Will Fontana be there?' said Hollis.

'I doubt it,' I said.

'Well, I can't go anyway. In case you haven't heard, I'm a wanted man. But Fontana better steer clear of me. I've got nothing to lose now. Crimes of passion are where I've drawn the line over the years, but my chalk is getting down to the nub.'

I wondered if Gary was hurt by the word nub. Maybe Gary didn't know he had a nub.

'Listen,' said Hollis. 'You better not tell anyone you saw me. I can trust Gary here because we are bonded by our recovery. But you're an active. You're in denial. People in denial do stupid things. I can assure you our mutual friend Pete will undertake more than eviction procedures on your sorry ass if you speak word one. Is this dug with appropriate depth?'

'I guess so.'

'This is no age for guesswork,' said Hollis, stood, turned back to Gary. 'And as for you, Slippy Slipperton. Renaldo Relapse, Esquire. I know what kind of game you've been running. It's a punk's game. I'm no Mother Teresa. I'm no Venerable Fucking Bede, either, but I've heard your shares in the meetings lately and I just sit there in my folding chair with my little Styrofoam cup and think to myself, "Hollis, that boy is making a damn fool of himself. His stepwork is shit and he's surrendered to nothing. Even now, as he rambles incoherently about his higher power and one-day-at-a-time and easy-does-it, that motherfucking ship is going down." Easy will do you, my friend. And I'll do you, too. I know I'm partly to blame because I keep selling you the stuff, but you're not being cool about it. You're besmirching my reputation in the fellowship. Don't you understand, when you come to me as a buyer I have to sell to you? I'm a dealer, it's who I am. But it breaks my heart every time. It breaks my heart as your sponsor, and as your friend. And to have to sit there and pretend to everybody that you're clean! All those chips and coins and key chains! There are starving kids in Somalia who've been sober their entire lives! They don't get a fucking chip, and you do? Shame, brother. Shame, shame. Keep it up and we'll have it out once and for all, you and me. I'll dance on your teeth in my stiletto heels. My fuck-you pumps. Adios Amigos.'

When Hollis was gone Gary took his bong out from under the sofa, packed a pungent bowl. The weed was nearly iridescent.

'He's right about my stepwork,' he said.

'Maybe it's time for a new sponsor,' I said. 'People grow, change. Don't they?'

'He'd kill me.'

'He'd get over it.'

'After he killed me.'

We smoked up, popped some beers.

I tried to lighten the moment by breaking Gary's heart. I told him about Bob Price and Mira. He seemed grateful for the opportunity to worry a lesser wound.

'That bitch,' he said. 'And that bastard, too. I read that book you gave me. What a load. Well, I liked the softball story. But in the great scheme of things it was still a steaming load. Who are these people? Come to our town, think they can steal our women just because we sit on our asses all day. We should go kick his grin in.'

Seemed like everybody wanted to have it out with everybody, Catamounts. There weren't enough goodies to go around. What is this thing called life that keeps batting our hands away, our hooks, even? Harried grabbers, all of us, even the slack. Feign torpor, you still want the groovy stuff. Torpor itself is a kind of greed.

For time, maybe.

Or that pitiful grail: the absence of pain.

I left Gary to his lesser and greater wounds, went walking in the night. A peel of moon over Cassens Park. Pole lights over it, too, oblong bulbs fitted to the ends of swanning steel. A race of giant grays from Galamere Five. Night watch, cyclopean. Eyes on the nubiles.

This park had a lot of memories, Catamounts, and not just of hot dogs, incontinence.

Witness tiny Lewis, spidering around the monkey bars, or gouging the dirt with a stick.

Later there's Claudine, the dentist's daughter. Her bony hips poke out from beneath her canvas running shorts. She's twelve, has laid her body out like a succulent corpse on the painted slide.

'You can touch around it,' she says.

This is happiness, relief. He wants with all his heart to touch precisely what's around it.

Others gather for games. Smear-the-Queer. Kill-the-Guy-with-Ball. They are the same game, really. The first name is forbidden in Hazel's house. The second makes him tremble with the beginnings of knowledge. Even if you get the ball, especially if you get the ball, they will kill you. Why bother getting the ball?

The Goldschmidtt brothers throw coins at his feet, say, 'Pick it up, Kike.' Gary says they do it because they're called Goldschmidtt. They worry people won't know the difference.

Years on, boys huddle beneath the birches. A place of congress when the Pitch-N-Putt's narcked up. Car trunks full of tallboys, funnels, tubes. Junior scientists on the verge of invention. A major breakthrough in shitfaced. Girls arrive later to gauge the damage. One night Jazz Jasmine holds Lewis' head in her lap while he dribbles Hazel's casserole between her legs. He thinks it could be the start of something but she never really talks to him again.

It's Cassens Park, Catamounts, need I go on? It's the great green field in your hearts!

I called Roni from the payphone near Eastern Valley Video, waited for her headlights to sweep the plaza. She was off tonight. I'd studied the schedule. She pulled up in her dented sedan, a hand-me-down. We sat in cream leather singed with her mother's cigarettes, looked out on the empty parking lot. A dumpster stood nearby with its lid half-loose from its hinges, some kind of troop ship, blasted, beached. I could picture a baby-faced Auggie Tabor rumbling out of it with his rifle, chunks of pavement flying up around him. The great plaza landing. Years in the planning. Now the invasion was over. The bodies had been collected, or paved over, the sidewalks, speed-bumps, scrubbed of blood.

'It gets eerie here,' said Roni.

'You should see it crowded,' I said. 'In sunlight.'

Togethering

That morning I'd risen early for my new fitness regi-
men. Five push-ups, five sit-ups, no excuses. I brewed
some coffee in Hazel's Silex, a bowel-blazer of a pot,
awaited thick exodus from tube town. I had new toilet
reading lined up, too, a dense, glossy bird guide. No
more howls and shrieks from the dark crevices of
experience, no more histories of Barbary pirate slaughter, monographs on Bubonic Plague. Those were the
porcelain comforts of the old Teabag.

Now I'd have the dope on my beaked buddies twit-
tering on the AC.

Tonight's Togethering, though, there was still that
to endure. What the hell had I been thinking,
Catamounts? Bussing flatware for you, my former
classmates, had seemed a gesture of brusque defiance
when I'd demanded the shift on the telephone. This
morning I knew it for what it was: the dumbest idea

I'd ever had in a wretched and ceaseless cavalcade of them.

'Suit yourself,' my father had said.

What I think he meant, Valley Cats, was that we never really suit ourselves. We suit a notion of what we dream we could be in the eyes of others, when in the eyes of others we are at best a blur, at worst a sty, or corneal abrasion.

How do Daddy Miners have so much wisdom? How do they hide it so well?

It was too late to switch my shift, but at least Roni would be working. I was looking forward to some napkin retrieval.

I spent some hours padding my resumé. It's strange to see your life laid out cold on a page. There are all these tricks the resumé people teach you to account for the gaps. I had a good amount of gaps. I figured instead of fudging them I should make the gaps a selling point. I'd tell interviewers to judge my employment history like a piece of music. It's all about the space between the jobs.

For references I listed Penny Bettis, Salvatore Fontana, the undeniable and ever-anarchic beauty of true punk rock and a strangely delectable concoction

Moonbeam Rick had introduced me to: bacon-wrapped prunes. I figured the first two would suffice.

I nearly got derailed cruising for some yarn porn, Catamounts, but I'm delighted to report that though I failed to manage complete abstinence, I did embrace some tantric notions of stricture. My leashed load assumed the properties of a distinct life force as the day progressed. Civilizations rose and fell. City-states emerged. Later, nations. There were holy wars, followed by feverish periods of reason worship. Then more holy wars. So much creation and destruction and partial rebirth, and all because I hadn't blown my wad into a quilted sheet of paper towel.

It would be the first of many revelations that day.

Around noon I walked over to the Bean Counter. Mira was out front on her break, sipping from a can of mango juice, leafing through a leather journal.

'Hey, Tea,' she said.

'What's that, your diary?'

'Maybe.'

'Do you have anything in it about how you screwed over Gary?'

'Why don't you just marry him, Tea?'

'It would ruin our sex life.'

'Look, I'm on break. Donna can get you something if you want.'

'I'm sorry, Mira. It's not your fault. People grow, change.'

'Tell me about it. Bob split. Took off.'

'What do you mean?'

'He said he was done with his research. He was going up to some house he owns in the woods to write the book.'

'Didn't invite, you, huh?'

'Did you know he was married?'

'No.'

'She's an investment banker. He's been trying to keep it under wraps.'

'I'm sorry, Mira.'

'You said that already.'

'So, is that really your diary?'

'I found it in back, under some sacks of Kona. It must be Craig's.'

'The Colette Man? Can I see?'

Mira pushed the journal across the table. The pages were filled with delicate beige ink. I perused a few stray passages, which I'll copy here, as the author was later kind enough to loan me his work:

* * *

In Joe Picarcik's epic fumble there is an exquisiteness, a grace, a nobility no touchdown bomb, delicately threaded upfield strike or even deftly prosecuted hand-off can emulate . . .

There was a time, a better time, when from beneath the helmets of these gladiators flowed the long locks of Apollonian vanity. These boys weren't just faceless football jocks pounding the bejesus out of each other. They were beautiful young men with beautiful hair – blondes, brunettes, redheads, or else members of the Negroid vanguard with Afros efflorescing out the re-enforced plastic edges of their Bike-brand helms. They all possessed the aspect of giant armored schoolgirls, full of spite and power and play. Possibility was in the air. But then came retrenchment, supply side economics, the resuscitation of the buzz saw haircut . . .

'Nutty stuff,' said Mira.
'Nutty how?' I said.

I called Gary from the street. Nobody answered. He'd vowed to avoid the party but I needed a little pep talk. Maybe it was better nobody answered. Gary wasn't much good for pep these days. He wasn't much good for anything, really, save painful pauses and bad coughing fits, not since Doc Felix had hexed him with uncertainty.

Parked outside the Moonbeam was a huge silver bus, *Spacklefinger* painted on the side panel, a U-Haul, unhitched, behind it. Some anemic-looking teen roadies unloaded amplifiers, drums. Another fellow, lanky, his dyed hair falling over a folded bandanna, stood off beneath the eaves of the Moonbeam, smoked a cigarette.

'Glave,' I said.

'Hey, buddy, how are you?'

'Glave Wilkerson,' I said.

'Sorry, man, we're about to set up inside. I can't do the autograph thing right now. Check me later.'

'Still got that sunburst?' I said. 'The Les Paul?'

'Do I know you?'

'No, I just work here.'

'Oh, cool.'

'You guys going to play "Nothing Man" tonight?'

'Our pop song? Yeah, I guess we have to. For the chicks.'

'They're all pop songs, you idiot,' I said, whipped past him into the Moonbeam.

'Envy's a sin!' Glave called after me.

I found Daddy Miner in the banquet hall, stooped down near the buffet table, testing the base of a soup tureen.

'Looks great in here,' I said.

It's my fervent hope most Valley Cats noted the decor that night, those gold balloons and silver service trays, the high-end linen, the fresh roses in cut-glass vases. It's not only the Devil who resides in the details. Quality catering lives there, too.

'Thanks,' said my father. 'I just figured, why not go for broke? These Yups like my style I could have bookings for years to come. No more Rotary dinners. No more third-rate shamans smoking powdered beets, crapping their pants. You missed it last week. They were all on the floor having seizures, visiting ancient civilizations. What a mess. You're early. You'd better not be bailing out. I gave you a chance. I need you now. We're thin tonight. Rick's in a snit, too. I wouldn't let him put his cannibal angel painting in the dining hall.'

'I'm good to go.'

Some roadies lugged a kick drum past us. Glave jogged in after them.

'Be careful with our gear! You know how much debt we're in since our record hit?'

'Rock stars,' said Daddy Miner.

Rick was in the kitchen with some new prep chefs I'd never met, jumpy, pimply kids in hound's-tooth motor caps. One hacked at slabs of uncooked chicken breast. Another slaughtered celery. Their projects were in imminent danger of overlapping as they hopped around with their jumbo knives.

Rick wore a paper chef's hat, carried a clipboard in the crook of his arm.

'No go on the angels, huh?'

'I don't care about that,' said Rick. 'This is a nightmare. I've got these raver clowns prepping and your old man up my ass. Plus some fucking griefer spread syphilis all through my brothel this morning. Tried to blow up my copper mine, too. Then he gets the villagers riled up about independence from the Rick hegemon.'

'I'm sorry, come again?'

'Oh, you don't play Imperium Online? Doesn't matter.'

Roni came in with a stack of blank nametags, winked.

'Has anyone seen my magic marker? Lewis, maybe it's in the stock room. Will you help me look?'

We fell together under the tomato cans, the powder tubs, did as much as we could do in a few minutes, a sort of tasting menu.

'There's more where that came from,' said Roni, guided her breasts back into their gauzy cups.

'How much more?' I said.

'I have no idea. I'm not thinking this one out. Let's just take it one burst of horniness at a time.'

'Why do you like me, Roni?'

'You remind me of this doll I once had, Mr. Gollington. I loved him very much, even after I pulled off his arms and legs. I knew he loved me, too. Then I ripped his eyes off and I wasn't sure if he loved me or not. His head was just this piece of stuffed corduroy with two pale spots where his eyes had been.'

'That didn't really answer my question,' I said.

'I didn't like the question.'

Out in the dining hall I watched Spacklefinger sound-check. Glave kept stopping the song. Not enough Glave in the monitor. The drummer rolled his eyes, twirled his sticks in the manner of a drummer who once worshipped and now disdained drummers who twirled their sticks. The lead guitarist squatted in his tangle of cords. The bassist stood off reading what appeared to be an investment brochure. I'd heard he doubled as their manager. Probably he'd be the one to steal all their money, or what was left of it.

Stardom, I guess, does have a price, with actual numbers. Seeing them here in the Moonbeam softened me. They were old, had taken one last shot, hit big, and it still wouldn't be enough. I guess you reach a certain age and you start rooting for your peers indiscriminately, even sworn foes.

Some of you Catamounts arrived early to tailgate in your sports coats and dresses, guzzle carbonated tequila in the late autumn light. I watched you all from the shade of the gazebo in my short-waisted jacket and bolo tie: Bethany Applebaum filling the parking lot with her false, infectious giggles, Stacy Ryson striking sex pot poses on the hood of Philly's Lexus, Lee Nygaard waddling from one unreconstructed clique to the next, handing out business cards. When that sloop-sized Humvee swerved into the drive, I heard the cheers go up from you twilight toasters.

'Mikey!'

'It's Saladin!'

Mikey stepped out to the macadam, bronzed, absurd, his old varsity number shaved into his head. I shuddered for the Colette Man, who'd made such poetry from the locks of the mighty. Philly Douglas bulled over for a hug and Saladin clasped the forearms of his old buddy with what looked like affectionate dread.

Amidst the hullabaloo you probably didn't notice Fontana's rust-shot Datsun veer past Mikey's Humvee, pull up near the Moonbeam door.

Fontana peeled himself out from behind the wheel, tugged at his wilted tux, crushed velvet. I trotted down from the gazebo to greet him. There was something crushed about his person, too. He'd done a real carve job shaving, stank of bourbon, breath mints.

'Miner,' he said. 'What the fuck are you wearing?'

'My busboy uniform.'

'Are you kidding me?'

'I like your vines, too.'

'I think I got married in this suit once. Fits, too. Bought it when I still ate food.'

'Are you going to be okay tonight?'

'Piece of cake. I've got about ten minutes on my recent colonoscopy. Then another five on how men and women are different. See, for starters, they have completely different sexual organs. Did you know that, Miner?'

'You can still cancel.'

'What are you talking about? I'm going to kill. Where's my dressing room?'

'Follow me,' I said.

I led Fontana across the banquet hall into my

father's office. Daddy Miner was thumbing through some invoices.

'Hey, you remember Sal Fontana. Used to be principal at Eastern Valley?'

'Nice to see you again,' said my father. 'Do you need anything?'

'A blowjob, maybe. I'm not picky. Two lips and wet inside is what I ask. Or how about a gun to blow my brains all over these good people tonight?'

Daddy Miner looked up from his paperwork, his props. Roni did the bills around here, but the way he clicked his ballpoint pen, shuffled slips thick with numbers on his desk, you'd think his only joy was algebra.

'How about some coffee?'

'That'll be fine.'

'What kind of educator are you, anyway? What kind of example do you provide?'

'Well, I'm retired now. But during my career I prided myself on providing the negative example.'

'Get him some coffee.'

'Goddamn phony,' said Fontana, after my father had left.

'Watch it,' I said, 'that's my progenitor.'

'He's still a phony. Ask him how he's doing he'll tell you he's swell.'

'Think for a moment,' I said. 'Where are? When are we?'

'I'll need more than a moment.'

Catamounts, as the hall began to fill it was hard not to notice how gladly you all groped for nametags at the reception table. Maybe some feared mistaken identity, so many slack bellies and hairless heads in the room, faces filigreed with worry, shame, capillary burst. Time had done an odd thing aside from the individual rot. Some alums seemed morphed into startling amalgams, especially the men. Don't be insulted, Catamounts, and I don't exclude yours truly, but only the pistol bulge in Special Agent Brett Meachum's suit, for example, set him apart from his old football linemate Stan Damon. Their identical pug-nosed swaggers were intact from the old days, their hairlines in a match race to oblivion.

Once upon a time, the age of constant measurement, I'd known the ear jut, the nasal flare, of each and every Catamount. I could have sketched the pimple distribution on the chins of boys whose names I barely knew. Now features seemed smeared, indistinct. The joggers looked like other joggers. The boozers looked like other boozers. The rich loosed the same guffaws in coded bursts. The Moonbeam seemed full of types, hugging, kissing, pointing to each other's tagged lapels in disbelief.

All save Mikey Saladin, that is, who stood apart and imperious, odd coif notwithstanding. He served himself spinach-stuffed chicken from the heated trays, retreated to a candlelit corner. Dozens hovered while he ate, poured him Pinot Grigio, whispered in his diamond-stabbed ear. Mikey nodded, grinned, great bright stones for teeth. It was a shame his critics could not see him here tonight, so regal in the Moonbeam. Maybe there were sugarball phenoms with buggy whip arms about to surmount him in dazzle, but for now Saladin's throne seemed safe.

I threaded my way to his table, nodded toward his empty plate.

'May I take that for you, sir?'

'Sure thing,' he said.

Proximate Catamounts may recall how long his look lingered on yours truly.

'Hey,' he said. 'I know you.'

'Damn right you know him!' said Philly Douglas. 'That's fucking Teabag! He's a homo and a loser freak!'

Saladin winced, laid his huge hand on Philly's shoulder, shoved him, tenderly, away.

'It's Lewis,' he said, 'right? Lewis Miner?'

'That's me,' I said.

'I remember you. You wrote that editorial in the school paper about how we shouldn't make racist assumptions about people.'

'I still believe that,' I said.

'It meant a lot to me,' said Saladin. 'Because I'm all different races.'

'I always thought it was a tan.'

'No, I'm like my own race. And I've struggled at times.'

'That's hard to believe.'

'I make it look easy.'

'You're the fucking shit, Mikey!' said Philly.

'Yo, pindick, shut up,' said Saladin. 'I'm talking to Lewis here. Lewis, it's nice to see you. I know what this fool did to you in the locker room. I want you to know that if I'd been there I would have stood up for you, the way you stood up for different races.'

'Mikey,' said Philly. 'You're the one who told me to do it!'

'Shut up, yo,' said Mikey.

'I know you would have,' I said. 'And I also know you're the best shortstop of our era, forget that kid in Detroit.'

'He's good,' said Mikey.

'But you're better. Now, may I take your plate?'

'Let me help,' said Mikey.

We bussed together for a while, as most of you noted with acrid bemusement. A Teabag-Mikey tandem is high comedy, I'm sure. What you may already have suppressed, however, is how much stuff Mikey dropped – platters, decanters, forks – surprising given his five gold gloves, his recent near-error-free season. I chalked it up to the wine, and, really, it wouldn't have mattered much if he hadn't also stopped so often to chat with everyone, pose for photographs, especially after I fetched him my Moonbeam apron to wear over his silk suit. How many pictures of Mikey pushing my bus cart with a dishtowel on his arm did the Catamount community require? A multi-millionaire feigning menial labor! How classic!

Fucking showboat.

That kid in Detroit had a much higher slugging percentage, too.

I stepped out for some air, found Gary in the parking lot kicking an empty champagne bottle against the curb.

'Feeling Togethered?' he said.

Downlit in the sodium lights Gary bore the aspect of a corpse prised newly from the earth, slid into a crisp white shirt.

'Nice shirt,' I said.

'Thanks.'

'So, exactly how high are you?'

'One to ten?'

'Sure.'

'Wait, one to what?'

'You should call Hollis.'

'I thought you hated him.'

'I do. But he's your sponsor.'

'I fired him. Conflict of interest. He's just my dealer now. And anyway, I don't really think he's in the mood to talk to anyone. He's in rant mode. He's been oiling his mace.'

'Is he coming here? You know Brett Meachum's inside.'

'I doubt Hollis will make it up off the sofa.'

'Good. Why don't you come inside? I'll get you some coffee.'

'Coffee's a drug,' said Gary.

'That's why you'll like it.'

'Okay.'

While you Catamounts finished your entrées (and on behalf of Rick, and Martin Miner Enterprises in general, I apologize for the parched fibrosity of the chicken), Fontana took the stage. I'd been keeping tabs on him since his meeting with Daddy Miner, watched him sip club sodas by the kitchen. Sobriety had visited him briefly, departed, like one of his resentful daughters. He was back on the blended malts.

Fontana leapt up there now with the look of the damned, Hell's house comic, doomed to tank for eternity. He bolo'd his microphone in some bizarre approximation of baroque rock stagecraft, paid out inches of the cord with each swing. The mike gunned into the hi-hat cymbal behind him, clattered to the boards in a gale of feedback. Fontana shot a sick-sweet smile, duck-walked towards the shriek like he'd planned it, and somehow it did seem in that moment as though everything – the flopsweat, the flown microphone, the miserable grin, the stunted love, the lost savings, the wasted years, the unfinished manuscript, the hundreds of thousands of Titleists driven deep into the futile, overlit night – was some grim design, the world's most hideous and ingeniously protracted comedy routine.

And this before he'd even spoken.

'Welcome,' said Fontana now.

(As I've mentioned, I realize a good many of you were on hand to witness all of this, but I recreate the moment for those who weren't, absent Catamounts barred from the Moonbeam by those dimensional thugs Time and Space, as well as for the youth of Eastern Valley, potential lifers of these suburban crags and lairs, who, men like Glen Menninger would have us believe, are our future, though I've never fallen prey to that theory myself. The youth are their future, not ours. Still, perhaps this narrative will serve as some kind of measuring stick for tomorrow's disasters. The dead, though, I do not write for the dead. That's Bob Price's deal.)

'Welcome,' said Fontana again. 'Welcome all and sundry to our first official Eastern Valley Togethering, celebrating the ongoing celebration of our lives!'

A cheer went up and I looked about the room, saw Catamounts everywhere bathed in warm Moonbeam gels. There were Curtis Breen and Rhada Gupta, the prom dates who lasted, nuzzling each other's necks. There was Ryan Barwood, gay tech mogul with a private jet, and Devon Leventhal, who'd lived alone our sophomore year, abandoned by his swinger father. There was Jerome Albrecht, science whiz and rare black Catamount, rumored to be perfecting nerve gas for the Pentagon. There was Vinnie Lazlo, hooks agleam, triumphally clenched, and Ms. Tabor, slim-chested once more, wrapped tight in turquoise and gold. There was Gary, listing in cross-chemical tweak. There were Stacy Ryson and Philly Douglas, Glen Menninger, Randy Pittman, Jazzes Jasmine and Brie, and, yes, there in blood-pink shadow, sipping chardonnay, was Jazz Loretta, here to partake with us, to Together with us, Aphrodite alighting from her sea foam chariot to join a beachside wiener roast.

Here we stood, Catamounts, or here most of us stood in glorioles of shifting hue, our scored skin smoothed, our dry throats slaked by Daddy Miner's watery martinis, our bodies asway in the glow of the hall, us quivering and tender again, looking up at Sal Fontana, our ruined leader, who, for all his faults, had only wanted what was best for us, or, if not what was best, at least something with a minimum of degradation that reflected well on the district as a whole.

'Can you hear me, Catamounts?' said Fontana, grunted, wheezed into the microphone.

'For Godsakes,' said Stacy Ryson. 'We hear you. Please don't make that sound again.'

'Shut up, Stacy!' a voice shouted.

'Stuck-up bitch!'

'Fucking Doctor Feelbad!'

'Still-in-the-closet-in-this-day-and-age lesbian!!'

Cruel titters ricocheted through the crowd.

'That's enough, folks,' said Fontana. 'Doctor Ryson has a point. I never could get that cougar sound right.'

'Neither could we!'

'Anyway,' said Fontana, 'what a delight it is to find you all here. A delight and an honor both. I'll be your host tonight, and, as one of my estranged daughters pointed out during a recent, strained telephone conversation, this evening really is a fitting capstone to my career here at Eastern Valley. No, I never did make superintendent, but bureaucracy was never my bag. I'm a hands-on people person. That's what I always loved about being your principal. Back in those days you could touch kids with impunity! Just a joke, folks!'

'We know about you!' someone called.

'Oh, yeah? What do you know?'

'You're the man!'

'That's right, son, I am the man, at least for the next few hours, and this man hereby guarantees you a spectacular Togethering, a night you will never forget! I'm sure I'll have more to say as the evening wears on and the liquor kicks in, but for now, before the music and dancing commence, I'd like to introduce a Catamount who's made us all proud, whose personal warmth and political vision have helped catapult this region out of the cesspit and into the environs of respectable mediocrity. Ladies and gentlemen, the next governor of his own living room, Glen "Double Dip" Menninger!'

The legislator climbed the stage, took the mike from Fontana's hand.

'Thanks, Sal. And I'd just like to say that during my time researching the healthcare sector for a proposed bill I came across several fine rehab clinics which might suit your needs.'

Menninger snickered. Fontana, asquat near the drum riser, swiveled a mammoth, imaginary phallus in the state senator's direction.

'To begin, I just want to convey how much my Eastern Valley days have meant to me as husband, father, public servant, and, perhaps, future congressman from this district who promises to . . . '

'Gracias, El Jefe,' said Fontana, snatched the microphone from Menninger's hand. 'We've got to keep this moving along. And boy do we have a special treat for you now. I remember this kid when he was a whiny little maggot with immaculate hair. He'd come running to my office every time somebody looked at him funny. I'd let him sit there and read his teenybopper magazines, but eventually I got fed up, told him to shut his trap and carry a buck knife. I'm not sure if he ever took my advice, but he returns to us tonight with a calculatingly filthy hairdo and a rather inexplicable run of success with a collection of tired chord progressions and overwrought lyrics he purports to be rock-n-roll. Ladies and gentlemen, I give you Glave Wilkerson and the Spacklers!'

Gary joined me near the kitchen door, a joint reaching roachhood pinched between his lips.

'Fontana's bringing it tonight,' he said. 'Bless him.'

He sparked his lighter and the flame overshot, torched the tip of his nose.

'Shit!'

Spacklefinger took the stage with the stoic, heavy-booted gait of astronauts, men in quiet awe of their imminent triumph. They spent precisely forever strapping on their axes, adjusting their electronics. Space launches, in fact, required fewer systems checks. Finally Glave pushed some loose strands of feral hair away, leaned into the microphone.

'Thanks, Principal Fontana, for that, I guess, introduction. Nonetheless,' Glave paused, 'nonetheless, we intend to rock you full-throttle tonight. I can't say you all believed in me when it counted, or that I couldn't have done it without you, because even the really diehard Spacklefinger fans drifted off a few years ago, but what the fuck, I forgive you. How were you supposed to know how ginormous we'd be? Forgive and let live, that's my motto. He who moves the most units wins, right? But seriously, for all the insults, all the betrayals, all the beatings, all the humiliations in the corridors and around the kegs, all those times you pretended to like me just to get some money off me or fool around with my sister, who, by the way, couldn't be here tonight because her battalion has mobilized for possible action in an undisclosed hotspot, God bless her, I forgive you, every last one of you. And now, in the hardest way that is humanly possible, I, or, rather, we, that is, Spacklefinger, rock you! One-Two-Three-Four!'

It was majestic for a bar or two. They had amps the size of small barns up there for their sonic juggernaut. But it got vague and dreary pretty fast. That was the Spacklefinger way. While the more moronic of us moshed in affirmation of our decay, I fled the din, spotted Bethany Applebaum coming out of the bathroom.

'Lewis?'

She'd wound herself in some fringed and iridescent silk. Her eyeliner looked surgically applied.

'Lewis Miner!'

'Hi, Bethany. You look beautiful.'

'Look at you. Put on some weight, huh?'

'I guess I deserve that.'

'Deserve it for what?'

'For dumping you.'

'Oh my God, are you referring to our high school romance? That's so cute! Now I feel guilty because I've never thought about you once!'

'What about that letter you sent me?'

'What letter?'

'From Cornell.'

'Oh, that. That was a psych project. I got credit for that.'

'You said some really nasty things.'

'I can't remember what I said,' said Bethany, 'but I'm sure you deserved it.'

'You said I was a stupid, insensitive, self-hating, woman-hater who didn't have the looks or personality to pull it off. You said fucking me was like sitting on a wine cork.'

'Well, I hope you haven't been stewing about it for the last fifteen years!'

'No, just stewing.'

'Oh, Lewis, don't take it so hard. I was wrong to

waste that kind of ammunition on you. I just concentrate on helping people now.'

'Yeah, I read about you in *Catamount Notes*. How you work with the advantaged. Must be very fulfilling.'

'That's very funny, Lewis. But as I often tell my clients, you won't find bitter people in the first class cabin. I should really get back to my actual friends now. Have a nice life, if that's what you're calling it.'

Bethany dove back into the crush of the Togethering. I ducked into the bathroom. Philly Douglas, Brett Meachum and Stan Damon were huddled near the stall doors, chugging rum.

'Teabag,' said Philly. 'Come over here.'

'No, thanks.'

'What, you think I'm going to teabag you again?'

'No.'

'Cat got your tongue? You sure had a lot to say to old Mikey. I hope you don't believe his good guy routine. He's the biggest bastard I ever knew. I never wanted to teabag you, Teabag. That was Mikey's idea. He said you and your buddy Gary were giving our school a bad name.'

'I thought it was some kind of initiation.'

'An initiation? Jesus, an initiation into what,

Teabag? Think about it? Into what? There's only one club you could ever be in, and you were born into it. Me, too, though I didn't know that then. I thought you and me were in different clubs, but it's the same club, dude. It's the We're-Not-Mikey-Saladin Club. Come here. I love you, man.'

Philly staggered over with his arms out. Brett Meachum and Stan Damon loomed behind him. Philly draped his arms around my neck, slopped a kiss on my chin.

341

'Sorry,' he whispered.

'Teabag the Freak!' he screamed.

Catamounts, the phrase eternal recurrence comes to mind when I picture how Brett and Stan snatched me by the arms and forced me to the bathroom floor, Philly undoing his suit pants, all of it a blur of beefy white faces and dangling tie silk, me pinned beneath their impossible bulk. Then there was a sliding noise, a skittering.

'Shit!' somebody shouted, and I felt a great weight roll off me with a thud.

'Brett?' Philly said.

Brett Meachum lay still beside me on the tiles. Blood ribboned from a raised lump on his head. There was a dent in the stall door above him.

'He's out cold,' said Stan Damon. 'Don't touch him.'

'Never had good footwork,' said Philly, tucked himself into his pants. 'Always slipping on the line.'

'We should call an ambulance.'

'Teabag,' said Philly. 'Call an ambulance.'

Philly and Stan Damon stumbled out of the bathroom. Near the door Philly bent down behind the garbage pail.

'Look at that shit,' he said, came up with Brett's pistol, slipped it in his suit pocket. 'I'll make sure the cops get this.'

I checked to see that Meachum was still breathing, went out to the parking lot payphone to make the call. I figured I'd leave Daddy Miner out of this. He had enough to worry about.

Spacklefinger had reached some crescendo of roaring derivation when the paramedics arrived, so most Catamounts probably didn't notice Brett Meachum being wheeled away. Spacklefinger, in fact, were evincing a genius I hadn't understood before, ripping off bands half their age, bands that stole from music Spacklefinger had ostensibly lived through, but which they, Spacklefinger, had actually missed the first time around. By jumping on the retro bandwagon, Glave and company were discovering the music of their youth.

After the paramedics left I slipped into the kitchen, found Rick and Roni on milk crates near the meat-locker, sipping beer.

'How's it going?' said Roni. 'Having flashbacks?'

'It's all been one big horrible flashback,' I said. 'Until you.'

'Cue lame power ballad,' said Rick. 'Oh, sorry, too late.'

'Hey, man,' I said, 'I'm taking a whack at sincerity here. Go chop a cherub. Roll in his fluffy blood.'

Rick kicked his crate away, retreated to the stove.

Roni rose, took me in her arms, spun us on the rubber floor.

'My mom dropped by!' she shouted.

'That's why we're dancing?'

'Damn right,' said Roni, held an official-looking letter up to the light.

'Law school?'

'Call me counselor.'

'California?'

'Thank God. I can't share a coast with my mother anymore.'

'I'll follow you,' I said. 'I've got a mobile profession.'

'You mean out-of-work? You'll just be in my hair.'

'I'll hang out at the twenty-four-hour store. I'll be the older guy there.'

'Sounds wonderful.'

'I'll help you study at night. You can practice suing me.'

'We'll see.'

Now Daddy Miner burst through the doors, his hands on his ears.

'Christ, this is crap,' he said. 'I remember when men played rock-n-roll.'

Catamounts, I never figured so many of you for heavy juicers, but after witnessing the way you charged the bar the moment Glave Wilkerson started in with his amplified harmonica, it occurred to me that guys like me and Gary and Chip Gallagher shouldn't feel such shame for our ceaseless stoking of the neural furnace. The rave kids, doubling as bartenders now, flipped fifths of spirits in the air, much like an old movie their parents had maybe forced them to watch in jest. Valley Cats hooted as bottles of whisky and gin smashed to the parquet.

Chip Gallagher caught one in mid-air, tipped it into his mouth. The metal spout hooked his teeth. Bourbon dribbled down his shirt.

'Holding up?' I said.

'Bleak shit, this, here,' he said. 'Open bar. Open casket.'

'Well put.'

'Fuck your well put. Put this in your fuck.'

'Nice talking,' I said.

'No, wait,' said Chip. 'I'm sorry, man. You're okay. It's just that I came here tonight . . .'

'Yeah?'

'I came here tonight to find out if it was them I hated all these years, or if, really, like, in the end, it was me.'

'Did you figure it out?'

'Tie goes to the runner.'

'Who's the runner?'

'I don't know, dude. It's complicated. My old man was the fucking janitor.'

'Groundskeeper.'

'That's an outdoor janitor, man. That's just a dude mops the grass.'

I felt a hard grip on my forearm. It was Stacy Ryson, with pansies in her hair.

'Lewis, can I have a word?'

'I've got to go, Chip.'

'Get this,' said Chip. 'What if it was my wife who ate

the ticket and she just said it was the dog? And me cutting my poor baby open?'

'Later, Chip.'

'More, later, yeah. For to be revealed.'

I followed Stacy to an alcove near the coat check.

'What's up, Stacy?'

'What do you think is up?'

'Have you been crying?'

'What? Oh, my eyes. It's Philly. Sometimes he makes me so . . . oh, it doesn't matter.'

'I don't get it, Stacy,' I said. 'You're this smart, wonderful woman. He's a money-grubbing cretin. What do you see in him?'

'What do you mean, what do I see in him? He's my fiancé, that's what I see in him! And don't give me that. I'm smart, but I'm not wonderful. This isn't what I wanted to talk to you about. It's Fontana. We've got to do something. He's out of control.'

'I think he's doing a great job.'

'He's drunk and who knows what else.'

'Honest, maybe?'

'It's not funny, Lewis. Don't defend him. He's ruining the Togethering! This is your father's place. Do something!'

Stacy marched off, blew past Gary. Goony pulled a

pansy from her hair, sniffed it, tucked it in his pants.

'Pigfuck!' said Stacy Ryson.

Goony shrugged.

Now it was time to dance, Catamounts, strobe lights, air raid sirens cranked to hell-of-the-senses levels, warnings of an imminent disco catastrophe no city could withstand. DJ Randy Pittman bobbed behind the turntables to some inner trank-powered beat, his shirt open, his bare chest popping fluorescent green. He'd affixed glowing stickers to all his old buckshot scars.

The floor filled up with Valley Kitties. I'd like to think we flailed with just enough humor to forgive ourselves the soullessness of our every move. I'd like to think that. There were exceptions to the mediocrity, of course, Ryan Barwood's urbane and seemingly sincere sodomite thrusts and Devon Leventhal's head spins chief among them, but even these displays seemed borrowed from more authentic precincts, and on the whole, Catamounts, nothing was evinced on the dance floor to reverse my suspicion we were no more than some lamentable congress of half-ass herkers, clods and clownish shimmiers, and even, by dint of unpiloted knuckles, knees, and elbows, bonafide, if inadvertent, threats. Nor, again, do I exclude yours truly. For those of you who missed my Robot, or, more precisely, Teabot, which I had the misfortune of viewing on videotape, simply close your eyes and picture a fattish man with severe groin strain reaching for his shoe tips.

Our slaggardly paroxysms were, thankfully, short-lived. Randy Pittman, effecting interminable and fawning shout-outs to former torturers, was unprepared when Fontana bumrushed the DJ booth, snatched the microphone, shoved Randy away. Fontana pumped his fist to the foment, the throb, Moses on Mount Sinai, his comeback special, two tablets, one night, standing room only.

'Lordy lord, Catamounts, are we ready to get it on! We've got something that will blow your mindwad forthwith! We're going to reach new, soul-shattering heights of Togethering in just a few minutes. We're going to revisit the source-text of all Eastern Valley belief and desire. You know of what I speak, kids. And let me tell you, it will not disappoint. I've seen the rehearsals and it's a wonder I still walk among you. But first, can we cut the sirens for a second? Can we kill the kliegs? What is this, a fucking stalag? A fucking gulag? This ain't no totalitarian hoosegow, folks! That's it, nice and quiet, okay, a little dimmer please, which reminds me – Mrs. Strobe where are you? Ah, there you are. You all remember Mrs. Strobe. What an educator. And did you know that she was only one long-buried college pot bust away from being the first science teacher to blow up on the Space Shuttle Challenger? That's right. We're just glad you didn't go, Gladys. That's it, bring the lights down, thank you, yes, intimacy, that's what I'm after here, an intimate moment of quiet intimacy with my former charges. In Loco Parentis. Do you know what that means? It's Latin for mom and dad are fucking fruitsacks! Look at all you people. I see Catamounts of every stripe: fat ones, dumb ones, lazy ones, sure, but the brave and the beautiful, too. All of us together here at the Togethering. I bet we've got near perfect attendance here tonight. Can you pipe down in back? Yes, kids, I do mean to take attendance. I've asked Ms. Tabor here to keep tabs, too. We'll compare our lists, just like in the old days. Take a bow, Judy!'

There were claps from the crowd and somewhere above it a slender hand fluttered, dipped.

'That's it, Judy. Judy Tabor, ladies and gentlemen. A brilliant woman and gifted teacher who gave it all up for several million dollars and a new pair of tits! I'm just kidding, Judy! Love is love. It's just that we loved you, too, honey, and not just because of your commitment to academic excellence, but also because you were, and remain, an astonishing piece of grade A ass. That combination is a serious fucking rarity in the public school system, trust me.'

There were boos from the crowd. Hisses, too. Some of the hisses had begun as boos.

'What, you don't think she's hot?' said Fontana, bugged his eyes in mock incredulity. Or maybe it was genuine incredulity. The man this hammered, it was splitting hairs.

'Wrap it up, Fontana!' somebody said.

'You're a has-been!'

A Lazlovian hook veered through the lights.

'I'll wrap it up when I'm good and ready,' said Fontana.

Maybe he would have, Catamounts, but we'll never know because at that moment Fontana finally lost his cage match with the hootch, crumpled to the floor. Daddy Miner shot me a wild stare and I jogged over to retrieve the microphone, tamp its screech.

Fontana was having a peaceful snooze at my feet.

'Teabag!' somebody shouted.

'Hey,' I said into the microphone.

'Miner smokes poles!'

'Not like I do!' Ryan Barwood called. The more enlightened louts in the crowd started clapping. Ryan flashed me a thumbs up.

'Are there any MCs in the house?' I said weakly, held the microphone out.

'You!'

'Come on, man!'

The room had hushed down. Somebody crushed a plastic cup. I was about to set the microphone on the stage, slink away, when I spotted Gary shoving his way over. He reached up, grabbed my collar, yanked me close. His grip was weak, his eyes watery. A few flakes of coke had caked in his nose.

'Step up,' he whispered. 'Be a fucking hero.'

Gary careened off into the darkness of the hall and I was alone up there again. I looked off to the edge of the stage, saw Loretta and the other Jazz Lovelies. Loretta smiled.

'Ladies and gentlemen,' I said. 'My name is Lewis Miner. It seems it's fallen to me to introduce the next and final act. But before I do –'

'Tell it, Teabag!'

'Pardon?'

'Tell it like it motherfucking is, motherfucker!'

'I'm telling it,' I said. 'I've been trying to tell it all

along. If they'd only let me have my say in the . . . I mean, does anyone even read *Catamount Notes*? I didn't think so. Look, here's the deal. Here's my update. I didn't pan out. Okay? I did not pan out. But what the hell does that mean, anyway? What's success? What's achievement? What's wealth? What's power? Is it anything besides climbing over the corpses of your fellow human fucking beings? And when you get there, then what? Everybody's gunning for you. Look at Glen Menninger. Look at Mikey Saladin. Look at Stacy Ryson, Glave Wilkerson. They've got it all. But for how long? At what cost? Is it worth it?'

'Yes, it's worth it!' somebody called.

'Okay,' I said. 'Maybe it's worth it. I don't know. I'll never know. Look, I like to beat off. A lot. I eat shitty food. I'm a fat fuck. I used to tell myself it was because I couldn't afford non-shitty food but it's probably laziness. I mean how much is a head of lettuce? Or some asparagus? I drink too much, Catamounts. I lost my bride-to-be. I'm falling in love with another woman and I'll probably lose her, too. I used to be bright for my age, but then I got older. These days when I read a book I can't remember a word of it. But a bad line from a stupid movie sticks with me for weeks. Did I mention how much I beat off? My mom died.

Everybody's mom dies. Can you believe that shit? But that's not even the worst of it. You know what the worst of it is, Catamounts. We all know what the worst of it is. But you know what? I'll tell you what. I'm going to live my life, not die of it. Or, rather, I'll live it until I die of it. I'll always be Teabag. I know who I am. I was Teabag long before those bastards threw me down on the locker-room floor. I don't blame them. It couldn't be helped. Even Will Paulsen, beautiful, beautiful Will, even he couldn't help it in the end. We live our lives wanting to love, to be loved. We are not loved. We sense the darkness just beyond. It's a scary fucking darkness. Where is the light? There is no light. We lash out in the darkness.'

'What should we do, Teabag?'

'How the hell should I know?'

'You've got the microphone. Tell us what to do! Tell us what to be!'

'What to do?' I said. 'You want to know what to do? What to be?'

'Yizza!'

'Huzza!'

'Booyah!'

'Well,' I said, 'let's start with what not to be. Don't be an evil-doer! Don't even be an evil can-doer!

Conversely, don't sit on your ass all day wondering why "cleave" means two completely opposite things! I spent a month on this, and to no avail. Avoid fried or fatty narcotics. Make an effort. Maintain eye contact with the mutated. Volunteer in your community. Bathe the children. Keep a dream journal. Send it to your congressman. Flood the legislature with dream journals. The government will have to respond to our unconscious desires. Keep it simple, simpleton. Buy your best friend flowers. Buy your lover a beer. Covet thy father. Covet thy neighbor's father. Honor thy lover's beer. Covet thy neighbor's father's wife's sister. Take her to bingo night. But mostly it's about the don'ts, Catamounts. Don't lie with beasts of the field, at least not without their consent. Don't be a borrower nor a lenderbee. Don't sweat the sweaty stuff. Don't touch turtles without washing your hands afterwards. Don't confuse the issue. Don't let anybody pack your luggage. Don't downplay the importance of air superiority. Don't walk. Don't walk under ladders. Don't live near power lines. Don't be born into difficult circumstances. Don't get all "Third-World" on me. Don't struggle with depression. Don't expect a goddamn handout from the very people who have worked so hard to hijack your opportunities. Give a man a fish, he eats for a day. Teach him to corner the market on fish and be thankful for the small acts of philanthropy he may perform while depriving most of the world of fish. Don't be with us. Don't be against us. We are not of us. Don't play the bounce. Don't steer into the skid. Don't let them see you shit your pants. Don't fuck a gift horse in the mouth. If you can't do the crime, do the time..We're at a critical juncture in the history of our homeland, Valley Kitties. We must choose now: police state or police state!'

'Yeah!'

'Whoo-hoo!'

'Wowza!'

'Bowza!'

'Alright already!' somebody called. 'Bring on the dancers!'

'The dancers!' I said. 'Yes, the dancers. What the hell am I doing, not bringing on the dancers? I will now bring on the dancers! You asked for the best you got the best. Ladies and gentlemen, alumni of Eastern Valley High School, I present to you the astonishing and inimitable Loretta Moran and the Catamount Jazz Dancing Club, featuring Jasmine Herman and Brie Nachumi!'

Now the sirens started up again. An organ note, deep, sustained, filled the hall like some sonorous gas.

Out from shadows floated the Jazz Lovelies, Loretta first, Brie and Jasmine hovering close behind. They assembled themselves with asymmetrical grandeur in a stark oval of light. Brie and Jasmine wore canary yellow body suits, feathered belts. Loretta stood between them in a purple leotard, her hair pulled back in a burnished bun severe enough it seemed a coat of lustrous paint.

The other Lovelies commenced a swift methodic rocking, tilted sideways from their hips. They seemed the matched functions of some multi-form machine. Each time their torsos, shoulders, swung together, as though to pinion their leader in the vise of their pates, Loretta would plunge forward, down between her knees, clasp her wool-slung heels, her fingers bunching yarn for purchase.

Some cheered, bland and lewd, made high animal sounds, but seeing Loretta there in her limber majesty, the rhinestones in her legwarmers catching sweeps of light, put me in a holy state of mind. Loretta was our high priestess, almost sexless in her beauty, fulcrum of desires born not of scrotal ache. The other Lovelies looked a bit undone by their canary sheaths. They had humanity, wore winces. They were just trying to get through this. Perhaps somebody, a therapist, a therapeutic sister-in-law, had said this was something to be gotten through.

Not Loretta.

She seemed seized with dreamy perfection, a beloved ballerina making her adieu.

She would accept just enough love for the next farewell plié.

I thought I would puke from all the love I had left over.

'Go, Brie!' some doofus shouted.

I caught sight of Fontana waking, sitting up. He wore the look of a man in sudden awe of the everyday, the sunset out his kitchen window, the lush slope of his yard, the fawn shitting pellets at the edge of it.

The organ paused, the deep note died. The hall fell silent and the dancers froze. Lit smoke billowed up from their feet. We were all of us frozen now, waiting, waiting. Here it came, Catamounts! Synths, saxophones, a heaving beat. Our awful ancient music! The Jazz Lovelies detonated themselves to it. A roar rose up and the dancers flew into their schemed deliriums, their steps loosely synchronized, so that for each pivot which flung a Lovely away from the thick, another reeled one back. They were a whirling panorama, a Moebius snarl. Now they were snakes, now eels, now flowers, soldiers, dolphins, cities, engines, curls of ocean, ribbons of steam, stalks of waving wheat. Whatever they were, Loretta was their lodestar, their queen, her light-flecked legwarmers slipping down her calves with the force of her slides, her splits, her dips, her huge antelope leaps.

They danced, and danced, and of a sudden came a shudder, a rip, an invisible wave concussing the crowd. I figured it for some natural buckling, us pitched by the power of our witness. Then I saw him, bushwhacking through the Togethering, carving a path with low sweeps of his mace. Catamounts parted, pressed in behind the barricades the buffet tables made. Brie and Jasmine were the last to flee, bared stricken, courage-sapped looks to their fellow Lovely, peeled off for the safety of the throng.

Loretta and Hollis stood alone. Or Hollis stood, mace up easy on his shoulder, Evil's yeoman, a farmer of skulls. Loretta, she kept dancing, the music killed now, Valley Kitties shouting, shoving. Yes, Loretta kept dancing, or kept herself in some version of motion, as though her life depended on her continuing to undulate, sway, enact some artful swoon, refuse the monster's tinted gaze. Hollis watched until the room got quiet. He'd waited all night for his scene.

'You dumb fucking hag,' he said. 'Look at you.'

Loretta did look, studied the curve of her arm, the arch of her foot, calm with craft.

'Go away,' said Loretta.

'You stupid fucking bitch,' said Hollis.

'Leave.'

'Let's go then.'

'No. Just you, Hollis.'

'Just me? Okay. But first I'm going to kill you right here in front of all these people.'

'No, you won't,' said Loretta, long fingers up like tongs, spread now for some luminous butterfly pose.

'Fucking A I won't!' said Hollis. 'Keep still and hear what I'm saying! I'll crack your bitch skull you don't come with me right now! You want that? You want our son should want that?'

'My son,' said Loretta.

'That's not even funny.'

Loretta fell still, gathered up a stare.

'It's not supposed to be funny.'

'You saggy stinkhole, I swear to God, I'm going to do you right here.'

'Do me, babycakes,' came a voice, liquid, silken, through the speakers. 'Do me first, you big phony.'

Fontana strode out from the darkness, woozy, the microphone in his hand.

'What did you say?' said Hollis.

'You heard me,' said Fontana. 'Everybody heard me. Everybody's heard me all night. What do you think I'm saying?'

'You active,' said Hollis. 'Get out of my face. I'll do you, too.'

'Exactly, babylove. Except you're missing the big picture. I'm saying do me first. You want to, quote unquote, do this kind, talented, beautiful lady because she won't bend to your vile whims? I say unto you: do me the fuck first.'

'You better watch it, sport.'

'Okay,' said Fontana. 'I take it back. I'm sorry. I don't know what got into me. I need help. I'm ready to surrender to a higher power. A higher power I call hairy sky pie. Will you help me?'

'Hell, no.'

'Then fucking do me, nihil-humper!'

I'm not sure how many Catamounts witnessed the blow. All I saw was Hollis rear back with his mace as though fixing to hammer a tent stake. Chip Gallagher was falling on top of me, the bottom of his clenched bourbon bottle mashing my nose, when I heard the muted crunch, Loretta's scream. I wormed up out of the swarm, saw Fontana folded over, blood running out his stove head, its seep lit by bulbs in the dance floor. Hollis paced around his fallen prey, mace up, as though expecting reprisal.

He was wise to expect it. Catamounts edged in from all sides. Hollis kept them at bay with big swings of his mace. Philly stepped forward with Brett Meachum's pistol.

'Put the club down!' he shouted, maybe imagining that along with Brett Meachum's pistol came Brett Meachum's training.

'Fuck off,' said Hollis, stepped in, banged the flanged iron mace head down on Philly's arm. Philly shrieked and the pistol dropped to the floor. Hollis snatched it up, waved it at the room.

'I'm walking out of here!' he said.

Hollis hauled Philly up by the collar, pressed the pistol at the back of Philly's head, made for the fire exit.

'You're the worst fucking sponsor in the world!' came a shout, and here came Gary, flying out the shadows.

He crashed into Hollis and Philly and the three of them went down in a writhing heap. We heard a shot. Gary rolled off the pile holding his shin.

Now Hollis was up on top of Philly, choking him, working the pistol into Philly's mouth. I took a running start, dove at Hollis' ribs, knocked him over, pinned his arms under my knees. It was stupid, Catamounts, I know, but I was lucky, lucky I'd watched so many goddamn cop shows. I guess you get one move like that in your lifetime. The pistol skidded clear of both of us. Bethany Applebaum picked it up.

'Oh my God, is it on?' I heard her say.

Hollis squirmed beneath my knees. Philly winced up at me, clutched his crushed arm.

'Teabag him, Teabag,' said Philly.

'Shut up, Philly.'

'Kill me, Larry,' said Hollis.

'For real?' I said.

Now Philly stood, stomped on Hollis' gut.

'You're fucked!' he said.

Hollis wheezed for air.

'Pile on!' Mikey Saladin called. Catamounts poured in for the gang pounce. I could hear the crunches and moans and ecstatic sighs behind me as I scooted over to where Fontana lay.

Loretta cradled his broken head in her lap. Stacy Ryson had slipped off one of Loretta's legwarmers to stanch the wound. Bits of brain clung to the wool. I knelt, took Fontana's damp hand, laid my knuckles on his brow. His eyes swiveled in faraway milk. I figured he was falling through folds of time.

'Miner,' he said.

'I'm here,' I said.

'Tell Loretta I love her.'

'I'm here, Sal,' said Loretta. 'I love you, too, baby.'

'Oh, baby,' said Fontana.

'It's okay,' said Loretta.

'Oh, fuck,' said Fontana. 'It's not fair. I don't want to wake up. No wakey, no wakey.'

'It's okay, baby.'

'Miner?' said Fontana.

'I'm here,' I said.

'Wakey, wakey, eggs and bakey.'

'No wakey,' I said.

'My sweet baby,' said Loretta. 'My poor horsy.'

'No eggs,' I said. 'No bakey.'

'No bakey,' I said again, but I don't think he heard me. Fontana was pretty much dead by then.

The Erasing Angel

Catamounts, once more I stuff my heart into the firing tube of language, loft it into the void.

See the wet meat soar?

I swore an oath off updates after the death of Fontana, but I've been checking the bulletin board on occasion, shocked anew each time at the dearth of soul-searching there. It's as though that night at the Moonbeam never occurred, our lives one unruptured procession of promotions and breeding success, summer cottages, marathons. Who called for the moratorium on feeling? Who pulled the plug on the true? Or was it always just me, feeble Tea, who believed in the power of updates, who thought that by sharing with my brethren of the valley the story of my days and nights, my fears and joys, or even just the febrile murmurings of my mind, our forts of ruinous solitude might be breached?

Okay, maybe it was just me.

Saith the man: Wakey, wakey.

I'll keep it short, Catamounts. I know you are all busy with your lives, your amnesia. It's been seasons since the Togethering, seasons since we gathered at the Nearmont cemetery, too, recited homilies, prayers, sank our principal into the loam. (I think it was loam – kind of clay-ey?) Autumn was cold, winter colder, the snow like white dirt. Now it's spring and I'm giving it one last go at telling you what's happened.

I don't think you'll be hearing from old Teabag again.

Hollis Wofford, as you're probably aware, was convicted of two counts of murder in the second degree. He awaits sentencing in a special wing of the county jail.

I attended the trial, had the pleasure of hearing Hollis' testimony regarding the night of the Togethering.

'Fontana got up in my face,' explained Hollis. 'I happened to have my war mace with me. I figured, what the fuck, I'm already wanted for that punk's OD. This tragedy, Your Honor, is the direct result of our society's dragony drug laws.'

Hollis' mace, as it happened, had been missing from a traveling exhibition of tribal Germanic artifacts. Hollis had some urns adorned with Wotan's visage, too, fakes from the 1950s. He'd filled these with cocaine.

Rumor had it Hollis had shared a cell for a few weeks with Georgie Mays, who was being held on an assault charge. Georgie had exposed himself to the maiden aunt of a noted but recently disgraced historian whose latest bestseller included this index entry:

'It's been brought to my attention that one of the historians responsible for the ensmearment of my family name has been accused of plagiarism,' Georgie later wrote in an open letter to the *Eastern Valley Gazette*. 'If this proves true, I apologize to this man and his old bag of an aunt. As for the originator of these so-called historical facts about my forebear, please understand I intend to track you down and inflict hurt of notable severity on your person. I will not tire until the Mays name is cleared or I am dead. And even if I'm dead, I won't really be tired. Just dead.'

Let's see, what else? Mikey Saladin caused an uproar after coming clean about his steroid use on a prime-time magazine show. He rolled up his sleeve to show the interviewer, a kindly woman in lavender, his needle marks.

'What's the big deal?' he said. 'There are five guys in the world who can do what I do, with or without the juice. Do you hate me because I'm multi-racial, or because I'm trying to help kids stay off the streets? Make up your minds, America. One day human clones will play baseball on the moon. They won't care what you think.'

Who's to say he's wrong, Catamounts?

Mikey signed with St. Louis and, if you haven't been watching the highlight reels, he's been putting up monstrous numbers. The league has ruled any records he breaks will be tainted by his confession. The taint will be designated with an asterisk, a likeness of which Mikey had tattoo'd on his forehead.

Many of you Catamounts attended the wedding of Doctor Stacy Ryson and Philly Douglas of Willoughby and Stern. I was not present, of course, but according to the 'Hitchings' section of the *Notes* bulletin board, the sunset ceremony at the recently refurbished boat basin was quite a stunner. The bride wore cream, the groom a sporty sling for his mangled arm. Newly elected Congressman Glen Menninger made a rousing speech about the sanctity of marriage. He also condemned those who would attempt to regulate the ingenuity and shininess of the American dreamscape.

'The roads of our great nation were built by men and women,' he added, somewhat cryptically.

Pete the Landlord came by a few weeks after the Togethering to disavow his hoodlum stint. He'd stowed away his knuckle-dusters, his cologne.

'Sorry about all that,' he said. 'I don't know what came over me. I've stopped watching those Mafia shows. They're an affront to my heritage anyhow.'

'I thought you were Greek,' I said.

'I am. How come we don't get a show? Tell your Jewish friends in the media to do a Greek mob show.'

'I'll get on that,' I said.

Pete seemed a bit sad and I invited him in for a beer. His troubles had nothing to do with his heritage, though, or even Hollis Wofford. A dust-up at our alma mater had him worked up. The Eastern Valley school board had sent down a memo banning obstacle courses, even use of the phrase. Challenge Trail was the preferred nomenclature, but whatever the term, a single pliant traffic cone would now replace those old assemblages of ropes and radials and two-by-fours. Every child would charge the cone unimpeded, touch it with self-empowering triumph, no exceptions.

'Fucking fools,' said Pete. 'It's like they *want* the empire to crumble.'

The Challenge Trail sounded like an improvement on the old Catamount style of physical education, which, as you may recall, was predicated mostly on pummeling people with hard rubber balls or else enacting their humiliation via hanging rings, but I nodded along with Pete enough to buy a few more weeks in the apartment. I'd have his rent money soon. Penny Bettis had already risen like some Lady of the Artificial Lake to hand me the sword of temporary employment. A major athletic wear company wanted to promote its child workers in Malaysia as master craftspeople. Consumers would be able to choose which set of malnourished fingers stitched their cross-trainers and Penny had somehow convinced the project managers I was the man for the job, which was, and still is, to fabricate kiddie-cobbler biographies on the company's website.

Teabag is back in the saddle, Valley Cats!

Daddy Miner, sad to say, has not been riding so high. Business at the Moonbeam has fallen off since the Togethering, and the opening of Don Berlin Jr.'s Orchard of Bliss, erected on the site of Don Berlin's Party Garden in an ambiguous swirl of filial redemption and Oedipal zoning, hasn't helped matters. Still, at least my old man isn't doing okay.

I wouldn't have the nerve to honor his wish.

I still see a good deal of Captain Thorazine. I'm happy to report he's up and about with only the barest of limps. His shin wound was painful but shallow, healed in a few weeks. He's living at home in Ben and Clara's den, deals weed out of a reasonable facsimile of the Retractor Pad, which he had to abandon when he gave his money away.

No terrace, but a patio.

He smokes bales of his own supply but at least he's been going to meetings again. I know it's supposed to be anonymous and so forth, but Stacy Ryson's sister Tiffany is not only born-again but an ex-crackhead, too. Maybe I'm revealing too many secrets but, according to Gary, Tiffany hates her sister's guts for good reason. You should hear the sick manipulations Stacy pulled when they were tots, like convincing Tiff the only way their father would ever love her as much as he loved Stacy was to eat worms and defecate on the sidewalk.

Kids do the darnedest things, detest each other forevermore.

Gary still won't talk to Mira, but I visit her sometimes at the Bean Counter. She's dating Dean Longo's brother Darren, studying pharmacology at night. Darren Longo is an inspector for Taco King, drives up and down the state ensuring the guacamole is fresh and feces-free. This gives Mira extra time to brush up on biochemistry, which I believe is her euphemism for popping fistfuls of Percoset. Sometimes when I drop by the Bean Counter I talk to the Colette Man, whose real name is Craig Sperlman. Turns out he used to be a well-regarded college sports affinity marketer before he had a breakdown at the Fiesta Bowl, ran out on the field in a flowing robe, waved a scythe. Craig's a little crazy from a stint in the bughouse, but at least he has his convictions, heads up the local chapter of the National Anti-Circumcision Coalition.

'The cut stops here,' he told me, pointed to his crotch.

He doesn't read Colette anymore.

'Burned out on the bitch,' he said. 'I'm heavily into feminists from the Seventies now. Hairy first-wave hags with a seriously valid point about patriarchy.'

He loaned me some of his books and it turned out I remembered a few of them from my mother's bedside table. I used to page through them whenever Hazel was out of the house, skip past the manifestos to the fucking, the sun-soaked orgies in a manless paradise. This time, though, I read the books for their arguments, and when I'd finished I wanted to call every woman I'd ever known, make amends, the way Gary does whenever he goes a few weeks without getting loaded. Maybe I'd call Bethany Applebaum, or even Sarah Chin. No, Tea, I finally told myself, that's too easy. You're not Gary. Just try to be a good guy for a while.

Besides, the only person I wanted to talk to was Gwendolyn, and I didn't even know where to find her anymore, except on Tuesday evenings at eight-thirty PM. That's when her sitcom is on TV. It's about a girl with big dreams living in a boring suburban town with her nowhere boyfriend, Grinder. It's called 'North Hills' and, as a veteran of those aforementioned twenty-five thousand hours of commercial television, I predict without hesitation this tripe won't last the month.

Days I don't visit the faux-Retractor Pad, or work on my sneakersmith bios, I drive all over town. That's right, Catamounts, Teabag is now a mobile bundle of anxiety and remorse. Fontana wasn't kidding that day at the diner. He really did leave me his old Datsun. It was in his will, notarized the morning of the Togethering. I've tried not to think about that part too much. Let's just conclude the man had a peek at the cosmic calendar, saw his name penciled in.

It was Loretta who called to say the car was mine. She'd finally gone over to Fontana's house. The place was mostly shut down, the water turned off, the furniture covered with sheets. He'd left a strange assortment of objects behind. There was a leaf blower in the bathroom, a trash bag full of golf balls in the refrigerator. He'd Scotch-taped Bat Masterson to the TV screen.

'He died typing,' I told Loretta.

'Lucky him.'

We were boxing up Fontana's books when I flipped open a steamer trunk heaped with yokes, straps, bits. Loretta wept at the sight of their old love gear.

'Goddamn it,' she said. 'He just wanted to open up the earth for me.'

We sat and I held her for a while. It was nice to hold

her, it was beginning to be more than nice, the smooth warmth of her shoulders beneath her blouse, the blackberry scent in her hair.

'He really admired you, Lewis,' said Loretta, tugged herself away.

'I admired him.'

'He said you were a guy who did the best you could with what you'd been given.'

'What the hell does that mean?'

This comment didn't sit well with me, Catamounts. I guess secretly I'd been operating under the assumption the opposite was the case, that I'd been paralyzed by my enormous gifts, but what the hell did Fontana know? He was dead, for one thing.

'Don't take it the wrong way,' said Loretta.

'I've got to go,' I said.

I drove out to the cliffs, parked at a scenic overlook. Barges loaded with garbage chugged down the river. Sick-looking gulls swooped, cawed. Factories on the far bank blew black smoke into the sky. A perfect May day.

Fontana had left me a note with the car keys:

Dear Lewis,
    Like I said, nothing never happens. Keep an eye on Loretta.

Don't put any moves on her, though. If she finds true love again encourage her to trust in it.

> Cheers,
>
> Dead Fontana

P.S. Best get the brakes aligned or we'll be having a putrefaction contest, and I have a head start, though the booze may finally hamper me in this, too.

I slipped the letter into a plastic sleeve with the Datsun's papers, drove to Fontana's grave.

I hadn't been there since the funeral, which a few of you, to your everlasting Catamount credit, attended. I've forgiven Mikey Saladin his absence. He was playing a crucial doubleheader in Atlanta (two for four, three for five, one error). Why our illustrious representative Glen Menninger couldn't make it is less clear, but even sending his minion Lazlo would have been gesture enough.

You never had my vote, Congressman, but Gary was always on the fence concerning your legislative gifts. Yes, he's just one man, but all you need do is alienate a single undecided a day and your next election could be your last. It's such political miscalculations which confirm my belief you will never be more than a junior drone on Ways and Means.

Glave, your rendition of 'People Get Ready' was a travesty, but we were all touched by your presence, and I won't soon forget the lone tear coursing down your meth-carved cheek as you, Gary, Chip and I lowered our troubled but beloved mentor into the earth.

That day I drove back to the Nearmont cemetery in Fontana's car I made a funny discovery. Walking up to the plot I noticed the lawn all around it dotted with bright white orbs, hailstones from heaven. Just beyond the treeline, I realized, was the Nearmont Driving Range. I picked up one of the golf balls, made to balance it on the flat edge of the gravestone. I'd seen grievers do it with pebbles in movies about my people, the Jews, but the ball just kept rolling off, plopping into the grass.

I laid down in it myself, boots up on Fontana's tomb. I guess I was waiting for something, some kind of inner montage, but aside from a few stray images, Fontana on parade in the corridors of Eastern Valley High, or brooding on life's purpose behind his cluttered desk, or harnessed to his Hoover in the buff, no suitable reel unspooled. I did recall that book on his office windowsill: *What the Aztecs Knew*. What did the Aztecs know? How to carve a beating heart from some poor bastard's chest? Actually, according to Craig

Sperlman, who'd been on a pre-Columbian kick before Colette, the Aztecs knew a good deal. They knew the stars, the jungle, the vagaries of lake travel, the secret to spicy cuisine. They knew crowd control and how to exact tribute from client tribes. Obviously they knew show business. But most of all, I think, they knew, as Will Paulsen may or may not have known, that they were fucked.

380　　　It had been foretold.

The longer I stayed there at Fontana's grave, the less I could remember him, the more I dwelled on other things: how I'd better get some car insurance and what a hassle that would be, how Penny Bettis was lowballing me on the Malaysian biographies and there was nothing I could do except pick up more work at the Moonbeam, or, God forbid, Don Berlin Jr.'s Orchard of Bliss.

Roni was on my mind, too. We'd hit the apex of our passions a few months after Fontana's funeral. Winter had been a steep, achesome slide to uncertainty: jittery phone calls, canceled dates. Roni started picking fights for sport, wore a Spacklefinger hat to goad me. She'd disagree with everything I said, even, 'Good burger,' talked incessantly about anal sex in the manner of her favorite radio jocks, which I took to be the symptom of some greater cultural malaise, but when I finally said 'I'm sticking it in your ass' and stuck it in her ass, she screamed, swiveled, punched me in the nuts.

'Pigfuck!' she said.

I told her that was Stacy Ryson's word, and besides, a pigfuck wouldn't have warned her first.

'I'm trying to be a good guy,' I said. 'You can stick something in my ass, too, if you want. I hear that's the happening thing now, anyway.'

'Fuckpig,' said Roni.

'That's more like it,' I said.

Roni calmed down and we made some popcorn, watched an old movie on Old Boring Movie Channel, the kind with men in suits and women in veils and nobody trusting each other much.

It was no submarine flick, but it was one of Roni's favorites and I pretended to be engrossed.

'This is so great,' I said.

'Lying sack of shit.'

I let it go because I loved her, Catamounts, but most of me knew it was over. She'd refused to wear the leg-warmers I'd bought for her birthday. She was going to California and I guess she wanted to be certain she'd ruined everything so she wouldn't come back. Or maybe she was just sort of done with me, looking past my shoulder into the blur of better days.

Another Hazel in the making.

Driving out from the Nearmont Cemetery I thought about the Erasing Angel, that memory cleanser I'd once pictured myself becoming, roving from town to town, burying all the badness, leaching out the poison history. The Kid could have ridden shotgun, his spent, dribbly member flapping in his lap as we rattled over the roads of this great nation, highways and byways cut by men and women through our shiny, ingenious land. We'd be weary fellows, far from our dreamer, the sun burning through the windshield, the trees and cities and deserts and fields unfurling before our tremulous advance. We'd drive on with the truth in our hearts: the mission was pure folly.

There's nothing for the pain, as Doc Felix knew.

'Love it or leave it,' he'd said.

This Catamount wasn't going anywhere, Catamounts.

I took a shortcut down Mavis to Gary's house. We sat out on his patio, passed the bong between us. The view here isn't much, no mayonnaise factory, just bushes, birds. I knew the names of them now.

'What are you, a fucking ornithologist?' said Gary.

'A bird guy?' I said.

'Yes,' said Gary, 'that would be a bird guy, moron.'

It was good to be here with Guano again. It's not so bad at the Palace of Satan, either. Gary's father, maybe out of guilt, lets us do as we please, serves us trays of hoagies and beer. The patio thick with our smoke, he'll sniff it up, say, 'Good harvest this year.'

Sometimes he'll take a hit, too, tell us how everything going down in the world these days is a joke, that Alexander the Great, Jesus Christ and Leon Trotsky, his Big Three from history, are sitting around busting their guts at how bad we've botched it. Then he'll go back inside, bid for antique candy on the internet. It's his hobby. He has lollipops from the Wilson administration.

'Son-fondler,' Gary will hiss when he leaves.

This time Ben and Clara were gone to visit Todd in the city and we had the house to ourselves. We stayed out on the patio anyway. Gary had that week's *Gazette* and he pointed to a picture of Judy Tabor, the same wind-swept beach shot I'd seen at Auggie's house, the rich husband cropped out. 'Popular Teacher Returns to Heal Catamount Community,' read the headline. She'd been appointed the new principal of Eastern Valley High.

'Maybe she'll publish your updates,' said Gary. 'You still writing those?'

'Not really,' I said. 'Time to move on.'

'You've said your piece?'

'I'm up to date.'

'Maybe you should send them to Bob Price.'

'Fuck Bob Price.'

'Amen, brother.'

'"Good Hands" is good, though,' I said.

'It's okay. If you like sentimental bullshit. I'm happy he screwed over Mira, though. The whore deserved it.'

'Gary, you're pathetic.'

'Yeah, right, me, I'm pathetic.'

'She didn't like you as much as she liked Bob. Can't you just accept that? Why does that make her a whore?'

'Are you hanging out with that Sperlman guy, going all feminist on me? You know he goes to sex addict meetings? Crackhead Jesus freak Tiffany, who's also a nympho, she sees him there.'

'It's none of my business, Gary. People do what they have to do to get well.'

'Oh, do they? You should be on a fucking talk show with wisdom like that. The fucking Teabag show. The nation is going nuts for Teabag. He just wants us all to get well. We'll do what we have to do.'

I stood.

'Where you going?'

'I don't know,' I said.

'Sit down,' said Gary. 'I was just kidding. It's this weed. Must be the pesticides or something. They make you all bitter about life. I bought this stuff from Loretta.'

'Loretta's dealing?'

'Just to me. It's Hollis' leftover stash. Loretta wanted to unload it. You know, pay for their kid. It's going to be a bitch moving it, though. Guess I'll have to smoke it myself.'

'Her kid,' I said. 'The kid is Will Paulsen's kid.'

'Will Paulsen? Really?'

'Yeah.'

'That guy was a headcase. But a good bike rider.'

'He stood up for me in the locker room,' I said.

'Good for him.'

'You weren't there, Gary. He was.'

'I was in study hall.'

'Still, it was Will Paulsen. Don't pop shit about him.'

'Copy that,' said Gary.

We sat there, listened to the birds for a while. Maybe Gary was a bit pissed about my Will Paulsen worship, but I didn't care. Will was on my mind and

I could see him now, thirteen, fourteen, cruising around on his puny bike, flipping curbs, popping wheelies, riding the wide circuit of the neighborhoods, nodding kindly and pedaling onward, maybe back to the fields behind the power plant. He'd sit there and dream of his escape, maybe never quite able to picture it, not the philosophy, not the squash, not the ocean life, not knowing he'd be home again, either, with a son who called another man, a bad man, 'Dad.'

Maybe he'd be dreaming of nothing at all, just sitting in the high grass with a breeze on his face. I guess it didn't matter because he was somebody else's dream now, mine, in fact, had been since that hit-and-run on the County Road. Will was dead like Hazel and Fontana were dead, like all of us would be dead.

It was a dumb thought, Catamounts, I know, a pretty fucking obvious thought, but it was that kind of weed, maybe, the kind that if you smoked enough of it even the dog turds on the curb would glisten with meaning. The pesticides, if there were pesticides on the weed, they definitely gave the world a bitter taste, too, or at least made the world fall away from you somehow, like you could be strapped to some satellite spinning off through space, a satellite beaming sea stars and factory fights and unjust wars and second-rate sitcoms all across the earth, a satellite in deep orbit shooting out rays of entertainment, its hazard lights winking red in the void. Yes, there must have been some seriously bad spray on Gary's weed that could make you think you were truly harnessed to this device, able to breathe in cold airless space, plus blessed with supersonic vision like one of those floating telescopes, so you could look down on the earth and see all the ant-people running around like crazy as though it all meant something, and you not wanting to mock them like Jesus or Trotsky but wanting to comfort them, to fly down on your satellite ship and land softly before the ant-people like some kind of entertainment-beaming space priest, caress their antennae, their carapaces, their pincered mouths, only to discover that as you do, the ant shells fall away, all the ant-people you touch, the antness of them falls away and there beneath the carapaces are fluffy little cougar cubs, that's right, alums, tiny baby catamounts, scared but playful mountain kitties lost down here in Eastern Valley. You must take them up in your arms, my brothers, my sisters, if you are such a satellite flyer, an ant-person toucher, you must take these soft and weepy needballs up in your arms, tug at the fur on their necks (they like that), hush them, kiss them, cuddle them, tell them it's going to be okay, everything will be okay, even though, of course, it won't, it can't, but still, there they are in your arms, so sad, so fuzzy, so confused, what else should you say? What else should anyone ever say, ever?

'What the fuck are you mumbling about?' said Gary.

'Me? Nothing.'

Gary hacked some lung chunks into his hand, started to smear them into his army pants. He picked up the *Gazette* instead, laid the biggest loogie under the photo of Judy Tabor.

'I'm glad they hired her,' I said. 'It's what Fontana would have wanted.'

'Would have wanted?' said Gary. 'Why do people say shit like that? You can say that about anything. Maybe Fontana would have wanted me to dig up your dead mother and bang my dick on her brittle, powdery skull until it crumbled.'

I've never punched someone smack in the jaw before, Catamounts. It was a strange combination of sickening satisfaction and searing pain that shot through my wrist like something electrical. Dirtfuck teetered on his iron-wrought chair, pitched over to the patio stones. He looked up from where he lay, rubbed his teeth, shook off the daze.

'What the fuck was that?' said Dirtfuck.

'That would be love,' I said.

P.S.

Ideas,
interviews
& features …

Sam Lipsyte talks to Travis Elborough

IT TAKES ABOUT TWENTY minutes or so but finally, inevitably, the topic of semen-encrusted legwarmers comes up; to have mentioned them any earlier, I think, would have been rude, really; any later and I might have appeared prudish or, worse, grossly uninquisitive. 'Yeah, it is sort of strange,' Sam Lipsyte muses, on the phone from Queens. In the late sixties, it's worth recalling, Philip Roth fled to Yaddo, the upstate artists' colony, after his masturbatory opus *Portnoy's Complaint* made living in New York untenable. Lipsyte is considerably more sanguine about being labelled a sexual freak in today's post-*Sex in the City* city. 'You see, I never get recognized at parties but this one time, this woman came up to me and said, "Oh my Gawwwd! You're the legwarmer guy." In that instant I felt the whole ordeal of this novel had been worth it.' Just for the record, Lewis's peccadillo is not one shared by his creator, though Lipsyte did play in a hardcore noise band called Dungbeetle. 'What I always say about the autobiographical question when people bring it up, and people tend to, is you can't make up your feelings, those are autobiographical, the felt actuality is autobiographical; everything else is changed and tweaked to create a fictional universe but it starts with a certain kind of emotional truth. I didn't make up the Jazz dancing club, my high school had one. It must,' he adds, barely stifling a laugh, 'have had a big effect on me.'

When Lipsyte refers to the novel as an 'ordeal' though, he's not indulging in hyperbole. At the time of this interview, July 2004, *Home Land* has yet to appear in the States. After being rejected by 24 American publishers, it's finally going to hit the stores in January 2005. 'It was a kind of hardship but along the way I found people who were really behind the book and I've been publishing bits of it here and there. And it got passed around and I talked to a lot of people who read it in manuscript. Almost,' he concedes, evidently amused by the bitter irony of it all, 'a Teabag situation.'

Writing about his experiences of September 11, the novelist Jay McInerney recalled visiting Bret Easton Ellis's apartment and, spotting a book party invite, remarked that at least he didn't have a book coming out that month. (To his relief, Easton Ellis confessed he'd had exactly the same thought.) Sam Lipsyte did. His brilliant and critically acclaimed debut novel, *The Subject Steve*, was not only published on September 11, but it was also, for those who haven't read it yet, a coruscating and ribald satire about mortality. (Oh, and a mother has to fellate her own son at one point. *The Corrections* it was not.) With equally inopportune timing, *Home Land* began, Lipsyte informs me, 'making the rounds at publishers just as the US was about to invade Iraq'. Paraphrasing Roth, he adds, 'It's difficult to write about the present and not feel outstripped by it. I find a lot of people in full retreat, burying ▶

> 6 Lipsyte is considerably more sanguine about being labelled a sexual freak in today's post-*Sex in the City* city. 9

3

Sam Lipsyte talks to Travis Elborough
(continued)

◄ themselves in historical fiction, picking a time and mining that.'

Home Land, in its gleeful subversion of the familiar high school genre, is Lipsyte's riposte to that prevalent yearning for simpler times and the folksy homespun rhetoric coming from Bush's White House – 'Nostalgia is fear smeared with Vaseline', as his good book says. 'It's sort of a critique; there *is* a lot of remembering in it, not a lot of warm nostalgia. I do think the way we currently choose to remember our high school days and the way we remember recent history, the way we talk about the people we were, the country we were, all of these things are interconnected. But also I wanted to get away from the extremes. I didn't want it to be this idyllic thing nor did I want it to be that high school and youth are all darkness – the Columbine thing.'

One of the novel's finest comic set pieces – Lewis's speech at the Togethering – was, Lipsyte tells me, deliberately contrived both 'to create a moment true to the form – the bit where the geek speaks – and to echo certain things that have been said in the last few years in public discourse. To get to the sheer inanity of all of that.' The notion of actually including a full-blown high school reunion, he claims, didn't really occur to him until he was nearly halfway through writing the book; nor, incidentally, has he attended his own school's reunions. 'I guess the next one is due in a couple of years but no, I kind of like leaving it in the realm of fiction, so this is not based on a true story or inspired by true events, as they say with TV movies. I was

6 It's difficult to write about the present and not feel outstripped by it. I find a lot of people in full retreat, burying themselves in historical fiction. 9

really just playing with the form of alumni news bulletins. My own high school bulletin wasn't that advanced, but I'd been online and seen lots of others from schools in New Jersey, the area where I grew up. So I had the sense that people did write in and ask questions about each other, and I found this voice, the voice of Lewis Miner. And then the world and events began to form round it. At a certain point, I realized I was revisiting a certain kind of territory that I'd been writing about in *Venus Drive*. [Lipsyte's debut, a collection of short stories.] I was starting to write in the voice of Lewis Miner about a friend, and that friend, naturally, became Gary [a recurring figure in *Venus Drive*]. So I thought why not let him be Gary, there's always a sort of Gary figure around.'

And a Lewis, arguably – a character cut from the same cloth as such ugly/beautiful losers as Dostoevsky's nameless underground man, Holden Caulfield or Harvey Pekar, *American Splendor*'s moribund creator. 'Well, I've known a lot of people who were really brilliant, with witty mordant views of the world. They are self-destructive not in a grand way; the daily self-sabotage is a grind.'

Like Joseph Heller, Lipsyte's métier is word play and, specifically, the double negative – Steve of *The Subject Steve* is not called Steve, his doctors may or may not be doctors and in *Home Land*, of course, Gary retracts his retraction. 'I just like playing with the negatives, the dualities we live with. The given world,' he opines, 'is what comes through the television and the swirl of ▶

❛ The notion of actually including a full-blown high school reunion didn't really occur to him until he was nearly halfway through writing the book. ❜

Sam Lipsyte talks to Travis Elborough
(continued)

◄ ignorance and optimism, at least in this country, can get crazy. So again [with *Home Land*] I was just playing around with the idea of success, that very American idea that if you are not a success there's a moral failure implicit in that.' Lewis, he contends, 'is not the biggest failure in the school'; success, however, in the traditional sense, is nonetheless antithetical to him.

'The whole idea of the underground man is that because he is on the margins, he can see in and have a clearer view, and I think I did see Lewis in that tradition. It's part of the self-defeating mechanism that you don't want to be at the centre of the action because you lose perspective and you hold that perspective so dear even if it's the thing that's crucifying you. I think, at times, he mimics that therapeutic idea of getting things off his chest but other times he's offering his cock-eyed philosophy or he's admonishing people and laying in with judgements of other people or just trying – and this is really the heart of the book – to say what happened. Trying to find a narrative thread for life, which doesn't really offer one, it's an artificial idea.' Now about those legwarmers . . . ∎

Q & A

What's your favourite high school movie?
I guess when all is said and done it would have to be *Fast Times at Ridgemont High*, with the *Scared Straight* TV series a close second. Do you remember *Scared Straight*? It was a show where they'd bring high school age petty criminals to prison to have hardened convicts scream in their faces and 'scare' them 'straight'.

What is your idea of perfect happiness?
A state of fearless ecstasy.

What is your greatest fear?
Perfect happiness.

What objects do you always carry with you?
A bowie knife, flint, beef jerky and an ATM card.

Where do you go for inspiration?
To my desk.

Which living person do you most admire?
It's hard to admire the living. That's what the dead are for.

LIFE AT A GLANCE

BORN

I was born in 1968 in New York City.

CAREER

What career?

A Critical Eye

In the UK, *Home Land* surpassed the expectations of many reviewers whose appetites had been whetted by *The Subject Steve* and *Venus Drive*. Matt Thorne, writing in **Zembla**, pronounced it 'much better than *The Subject Steve*'. 'The dialogue,' he said, 'is excellent, the comic situations beautifully constructed.' **Arena**'s reviewer found 'every page dripping with scabrous wit'. Lipsyte was 'as ever . . . the stellar stylist' but the 'narrative arc' and 'satirical edge' of *Home Land* made it 'an affecting and hilarious encounter'. Satire was also on Chris Roberts at **Uncut**'s mind. 'They say satire is dead, that reality has outdone it, but,' he argued, 'this awesome writer takes on contemporary reality and gives it one hell of a fight.' The book was, he maintained, 'playful, serious as a death mask, inventive, filthy . . . a despairing riot of laughs'. Thomas Fleming in the **Literary Review** was similarly impressed. 'It's all,' he observed, 'executed with an ear for the deadpan cadence of absurdism, which reminds one of the best contemporary American satire.' He noted that Lipsyte took 'the same delight in bathos as the early written work of Woody Allen'. Lorna Russell in the **Big Issue** described it as 'fat with ideas and dialogue . . . incredibly funny', while Tina Jackson in **Metro** London felt it turned 'the clichés of Middle America on their head with coruscating originality'. But an honorary lifetime subscription to *Catamount Notes* must go to David Belcher of the **Glasgow Herald**, who concluded that: 'No pocket can possibly be complete without a copy.' ∎

No More Pencils
by Travis Elborough

'There's No Going Back,' wailed vegetarian rockers Midtown on their jejune grunge theme tune to the American 'reality' TV show *High School Reunion*. Their wise words were, of course, blithely ignored by the seventeen former students of Round Rock High, Class of '93, who by appearing on the programme were trying to do just that. Having, seemingly, eschewed the usual humdrum hour or two swapping anecdotes about invariably fantastic real-estate deals in a Texan country club, they'd volunteered instead to spend two weeks on a Hawaiian island with a camera crew and former teen sweethearts and tormentors they hadn't seen for a decade. Why put themselves through this? As their participation and the series' subtitle – *it's time to settle the score* – implied, these were people with 'issues' who wanted some 'closure' on their past. Helpfully nicknamed (presumably by the show's producers) The Jock, The Gossip, The Pipsqueak, The Geek, The Sophomore Vixen etc, it was difficult not to get the feeling that this gang's 'past' owed as much to their collective memories of John Hughes's movies as to actual lived experience. For Heather C, 'the Ugly Duckling', who admitted that at Round Rock she 'often felt like Molly Ringwald in *Sixteen Candles*' the distinction had clearly ceased to be that important. (Like Molly, I guess, she was on TV now, warbling on about stuff she'd done years ago too.)

America, as is frequently stated, is not a country with deep-rooted myths; it manufactures its own, largely propagated ▶

> ❝ America is not a country with deep-rooted myths; it manufactures its own, largely propagated through films and television. ❞

No More Pencils *(continued)*

◄ through films and television. Newish nations have a tendency to idealize youth; in a society of immigrants, school *can* serve as a shared collective experience, one reinforced in the national psyche, officially since 1942, by the daily ritual of the pledge of allegiance to the flag. The words 'my flag' in the original pledge, which dated from the 1890s, were, in fact, changed to 'the flag of the United States of America' because it was feared that the children of immigrants might confuse 'my flag' with the flag of their homeland. (Eisenhower added the 'under God' bit in 1954.) The high school, therefore, occupies a quite unique place in the cultural landscape. One that despite *Tom Brown's Schooldays, Molesworth, If . . . , Grange Hill, Gregory's Girl* and the phenomenal successes of Friends Reunited, Harry Potter and Skool Disco really lacks a convincing equivalent in Britain. The widespread introduction of 'proms nights' in 'bog standard comprehensives' shows only that British educationalists will stop at nothing to inflict emotional traumas on the vulnerable.

Interestingly, Lipsyte's own preferred high school flick – *Fast Times at Ridgemont High* – grew out of Cameron Crowe's desire to create an authentic portrait of adolescent life; to do this Crowe, then a 22-year-old writer for *Rolling Stone*, quite literally went back to school. In 1979, as teenage punks were flocking to the cinema to see The Ramones teaching the students of Vince Lombardi High the 'Blitzkrieg Bop' in *Rock 'n' Roll High School*, Crowe, passing himself off as a 17-year-old, was taking classes at San

6 School can serve as a shared collective experience, one reinforced in the national psyche by the daily ritual of the pledge of allegiance to the flag. 9

Diego's Clairemont High. His experiences formed the basis of a best-selling book, *Fast Times at Ridgemont High: A True Story* (1981) and a screenplay. The film, released the following year, was directed by Amy Heckerling (later responsible for *Clueless*, the Valley Girl version of Jane Austen's *Emma*) and, as well as introducing the phrase 'Hey, dude, let's party' into the lexicon, featured youthful performances from Sean Penn, Forest Whitaker and Jennifer Jason Leigh, and the screen debuts of Nicolas Cage and Eric Stolz. The sight of a long-haired Sean Penn, starring as school stoner Jeff Spicoli, cracking himself about the head with a plimsoll whilst announcing 'That's my skull! I am soooo wasted', remains one of American cinema's gems.

The film spawned a TV series and continues to enjoy a cult status, and, winningly, Mr Lipsyte's endorsement. On the tenth anniversary of Crowe's stint at Clairemont, *Premiere* magazine tracked down and interviewed the real pupils who had inspired Jeff, Stacy and chums, on the brink of their official high school reunion. Crowe was sent an invitation but told *Premiere* he wouldn't be going, as a few people were 'still upset about the movie'. Among the 'upset' possibly was class geek, Andrew 'A. Rat' Rathbone, thinly transformed into Mark 'Rat' Ratner in the film, who'd threatened to sue Crowe for defamation of character. The issue was eventually settled out of court. (In a bizarre *Revenge of the Nerds* turn of fate, Rathbone went on to become the bestselling author ▶

❝ The high school occupies a quite unique place in the cultural landscape. ❞

11

No More Pencils *(continued)*

◄ of the *For Dummies* computer manuals.)

Given the circumstances, Crowe's nervousness about attending what, after all, wasn't even his *own* reunion is understandable, but fear is a perfectly rational response to the prospect of *any* kind of school reunion. And yet in a study of the phenomenon by the sociologist Vinitzky-Seroussi (who describes reunions as 'autobiographical occasions') attendance rates were close to 40 per cent in the American schools she examined. Sixty-nine per cent of those she interviewed confessed to dieting before the reunion, and 'most returnees', she writes, 'made efforts, often at great psychic costs'. *Romy and Michele's High School Reunion* (1997), the cutesy ironic outing in which Lisa Kudrow and Mira Sorvino play a couple of airhead party girls who hit on the scheme of pretending to be the fabulously wealthy inventors of the Post-it note to impress their old school buddies, becomes just that little bit more believable.

So long a stock device in movies and in romance and crime fiction – consult, if you must, 'New Jersey's Mystery Queen' Mary Higgins Clark's *Nighttime Is My Time* and *Terror Stalks the Class Reunion* for serial-killing times '*to settle the score*' – this collision of past and present selves, as *Home Land*'s satirical take on the form attests, has, in recent times, been firmly embraced by America's literary practitioners. Joyce Carol Oates (*Broke Back Blues*), Tim O'Brien (*July, July*) and Philip Roth (*American Pastoral*) have all claimed the reunion as their own. Memorably, Roth's alter ego/narrator

❝ Fear is a perfectly rational response to the prospect of any kind of school reunion. ❞

Nathan Zuckerman gorges himself on *rugelach* after his shindig in emulation of Proust. In Search of Lost Time in a Locker-room, if you will. Now there's an idea ... Marcel, The Pipsqueak; Odette, The Sophomore Vixen; Charlus, The Gossip ... ◼

❛ Sixty-nine per cent confessed to dieting before the reunion, and most returnees made efforts, often at great psychic costs. ❜

Have You Read?
Other fiction by Sam Lipsyte

The Subject Steve
The eponymous Steve (who claims his name is not Steve) is a mild-mannered 37-year-old ad man who pens slogans celebrating the 'ongoing orgasm of the information lifestyle'. Unfortunately, he's dying, but 'he's dying of something nobody has ever died of before: he's actually going to die of boredom'.

'Smart deliveries and cracking ideas ... reminiscent of Douglas Coupland or *A Heartbreaking Work of Staggering Genius*' *Observer*

'Brilliant ... sentence after sentence merits blowing up and sticking in a frame' *Time Out*

'I laughed out loud – and I never laugh out loud' Chuck Palahniuk

Venus Drive
Peopled by a cast of America's walking wounded – dope fiends, had-it hardcore rock heroes, telemarketers and summer camp sadists – this collection of 13 short stories crackles with wickedly funny dialogue.

'Pitch perfect. *Venus Drive* explores the complexity of despair with poignancy and sly wit' *New York Times*

'Stories that bring Raymond Carver's low-life minimalism to mind ... It's fascinating to read a writer who can bring you so efficiently to such an uncomfortable place' *Village Voice*

If You Loved This,
You'll Like ...

The Age of Wire and String
by Ben Marcus
Dogs, birds, horses, Ohio, strange foods, cars
and the weather come under the microscope
in this audacious collection of
interconnected tales.

The Verificationist
by Donald Antrim
Pancakes and psychotherapy collide in
Antrim's wonderfully surreal novel about 20
therapists meeting for an informal supper in
a diner.

An Underachiever's Diary
by Benjamin Anastas
A kind of *Notes from the Underground* for
Generation X, Anastas's novel presents the
life, thoughts and philosophy of William –
a dedicated underachiever.

Forty Stories
by Donald Barthelme
This volume of pithy, ironic short stories
captures the late, great godfather of
American post-modern fiction at his best.

White Noise
by Don DeLillo
An airborne toxic event and a head of Hitler
studies at a Middle American college who
doesn't speak German feature in DeLillo's
classic satire of contemporary life.

Hey Nostradamus!
by Douglas Coupland
Fizzing with his usual pop culture references, Coupland's fictional take on a tragic high school shooting offers some rather profound reflections on life and death, faith and forgiveness.

The Web Detective

www.samlipsyte.com
Read extracts, articles and reviews at Lipsyte's own website – no legwarmers were harmed, worn or molested in any way during the construction of this site, apparently.

www.taintmagazine.com
Read extracts from Lipsyte's debut novel *The Subject Steve* at this lively online culture zine which publishes stories, poems and reviews from a variety of young literary wags.

http://www.thememoryhole.org/
Lipsyte is an admirer of this freedom of information website.

http://www.eightyeightynine.com/culture/legwarmers.html
This website dedicated to the devil's own decade – the 1980s – includes a homage to the legwarmer. Be warned – this site contains stills from *Footloose*.